Sailing
Home

PRESS

Box 115, Superior, WI 54880 (715) 394-9513

First Edition

Copyright 2004, Lori J. Glad

Cover design: Debbie Zime

Cover photo: Jason Branz

ISBN Number 1-886028-67-2

Library of Congress Catalog Card Number: 20041012345

Published by:

    Savage Press
    P.O. Box 115
    Superior, WI 54880

Phone: 715-394-9513

E-mail: mail@savpress.com

Web Site: www.savpress.com

Printed in the USA

Sailing Home

by
Lori J. Glad

To Carol,

Your support is so wonderful and appreciated. Thanks so much. Let me know what you think about Ajai.

Sincerely
Lori Glad
11-04

To

My Daughters and Sister

1

Deana Michaels steered her battered Ford Escort up and down the long narrow parking lot in front of the white pole building looking for a parking spot. The little red car bounced across the rough field that was jammed with big trucks and trailers. At the very end, she braked and turned into a space that was nearly too small for even a compact car. She turned off the engine and cautiously opened the door. A drainage ditch filled with slimy water made her recoil and slam the door shut. She shimmied across the bucket seat to the passenger door. Opening it she could see a shiny new truck parked too close. Sighing with frustration, Deana climbed over the back seat and threw open the back door. It too was blocked. Sweaty and out of breath she muttered, "Geeze, this can't be worth it." Stretching back across the front seat, she pulled the rear hatch lever and scrambled out the rear of the car.

The parking lot was empty of life, but the voice of the auctioneer echoed clearly in the still air. For a moment, Deana stood with the spring sun beating down on her shoulders. She closed her eyes and took a deep breath. The smell of sun-warmed grass, the road dust in the air, and the chant of the auctioneer sparked memories of springs past. In its full splendid force, spring had arrived.

Nothing made the coming of summer more real than a Saturday afternoon spent among the local cowboys and farmers of the Northland. The spring auction enticed prospective buyers from all over the county who were interested in the line-up of prime stock that was paraded for the public. The line-up of horses for sale was Deana's main interest.

The oversized pole barn was known unofficially as the Lakewood Auction Barn. After the winter days that seemed unending, people wanted to be out of doors. And they wanted to fill their empty barns and fields with new life. Not Deana Michaels, she only came to window shop. Deana already had one horse and had no use for any others, but it was fun to look.

"Sold!" Squealed the speaker inside the building.

She ran the last few steps across the gravel through the open double-wide doors.

A layer of dust floated in the dim interior. Several spotlights hanging from the ceiling sent shafts of light to the center ring. The acrid smell of cow manure, sweat, and dust overpowered her for a moment, but Deana ignored it. She peered around a group of broad-shouldered men and said to the closest stranger, "Excuse me, have they started the horses yet?"

The big man turned around. He was wearing a thick winter beard and a heavy frown. He looked down at the slim girl next to him.

"What's that, honey?"

Deana raised her voice to a shout, "What's being auctioned now?"

"A driving team of ponies is out there right now. Haven't seen the likes of them in years. If you hurry, the bidding's just started."

Deana gave a quick smile of thanks before she ducked her head and slipped under his arm.

"Hey," The man yelled in surprise.

Deana moved quickly past the crowd, past the wooden bleacher seats above the show ring, and followed the cement walkway to the powdery sawdust that the animals walked on. Deana picked her way past the seats to the front rail. The people there shuffled aside, clearing a small area for Deana to stand.

She leaned against the wood of the top rail. A team of matching blood red bay Shetland ponies with cream colored flowing manes and tales were trotting in tandem around the ring. They were quite a charming sight. The auctioneer began his rapid chant. The auctioneer's crew heralded each higher bid with a yip of excitement. At the sound of "Sold," the boy showing the team led the Shetlands out of the ring.

The boy looked about ten-years old. The memory of when was ten and bought her paint gelding, Journey, in this same auction barn flooded into her mind. Later that spring Deana found out her mother, Colleen, had cancer. The news shattered her life. During the next three years they could barely afford the medical bills. Her father, Frank, refused to let Colleen go to a nursing home. For the entire length of her mother's illness, Deana lived in fear; fear that her mother would die, fear that they would have to sell Journey to make ends meet. Deana felt terribly torn. She loved her mother and wanted her to get well, but Journey was her best friend and the only thing that was keeping her sane.

2

The auctioneer's voice announcing the next horse for sale snapped her back from the memories of those terrible days gone by. Deana watched with pleasure as the attendant, wearing a bold red and white striped shirt, rode a mare into the ring. She knew from experience that this horse was just what the parents sitting in the stands came to the spring auction to find, a gentle, well-broken, nice-looking horse.

"Lookee here folks," The auctioneer barked into the microphone. "Idn't she a beaut! Steady for that young rider just starting out and only nine-years old. She's still got years ahead of her. She's been trained for Western or English Pleasure and already has some points in gaming. She's a real winner folks. Let's get the biddin' started!"

The price of the mare went up as the bids flew around the barn. Deana settled against the rail watching the excitement build.

"Sold."

The mare went fast and so did the next ten horses, all of them the breed many parents present wanted their children to learn to ride on.

During a lull in the action, Deana smiled as she listened to the excited chatter going on around her. Many people were rushing out of the stands. Deana stayed glued to the rail, but turned her attention to the crowd. Scanning the faces, her gaze stopped on Chip Davies, a familiar sight at the spring auction, his sun-darkened face was highlighted by the salt and pepper hair peeking around the corners of his Jacoubi Stables baseball cap. He sat in his usual seat three rows up, directly in front of the show ring. Deana smiled and waved at him. Chip lifted his baseball cap in return.

While in college, Deana worked for Chip who was the General Manager of Jacoubi Farms and Head Trainer at Jacoubi Stables. He ran their horse farm and trained their polo ponies for the summer circuit polo teams. He also trained and sold his own prize-winning ponies at private sale.

The Jacoubi's were the illustrious royal family of Duluth and the wealthiest family in town, excluding the pizza roll king, Jeno Paulucci. The Jacoubi's owned the largest business in downtown Duluth, Jacoubi Enterprises. It employed more of Duluth's population than the government. When Deana graduated with a degree in accounting and computer science, she got a job with Jacoubi Enterprises.

Next to Chip sat a man that Deana did not recognize. Deana stared. For some reason he looked familiar, but why? She nudged the man beside her and asked, "Who is that sitting next to Chip?"

The man glanced up and said, "That young guy? That's Ajai Jacoubi."

The young man turned and when Deana saw him full faced, her mouth fell open. Her breath died in her throat. She exclaimed, "Ajai!"

Her surprise was drowned by the auctioneer's voice over the loudspeaker, though the man next to her did a brief double-take and flashed a little grin at Deana.

The only son of the owner of Jacoubi Stables and Jacoubi Enterprises, the heir to the riches of the royal family of Duluth, she thought, what's he doing back in Duluth?

Ajai, as if he heard her say his name, lifted his head to stare across the ring directly at her. His expression remained blank until he turned, finally, to Chip. She could see his lips form the words, "Who is that?" And Chip looked her way.

Suddenly a shrill whinny bounced around the metal building catching everyone's attention. Silence fell over the crowd while excited shouts were heard from the interior of the barn.

"Loose horse in the barn... stand clear."

"Watch out."

A hasty warning over the loudspeaker, "Clear the gate! Outta the way boys!"

A gray cloud of dust rolled out of the open door into the auction house causing a collective cough amongst those closest to the tempest. Through the cloud, the figure of a horse burst into the show ring and raced around the tight circle. He stood on his back legs pawing the air and whinnying in fright. The lead rope whipped against his front legs. The panicked animal began another frenzied race around the enclosed circle. There was nowhere for him to go. At the heavy rail fence, he slid to a stop and tossed his fine head. With nostrils fully dilated and flaring pink, he swung around kicking up dirt at the closest people. As the dust began to settle, the bright spotlights flooded the ring and illuminated the animal. The horse had long legs and a muscled chest. Patches of winter hair hung in matted clumps from his unkempt chestnut coat. Knots of burrs snarled his mane and tail. Dried mud covered his fetlocks and hooves. He danced nervously as the hush fell more deeply over the crowd. Men holding ropes moved silently into the ring and began to circle the animal. The horse saw them and reeled his big body back and forth banging against the fence. White foam slicked along his withers as he turned and leaped toward the gate. Simultaneously, the two men threw ropes that snaked around the big animal's neck. Once roped, the chestnut didn't fight, but continued to paw the ground and nervously dance around the ropers who stayed clear of the animal's powerful hooves. The two men snubbed the ropes taut through the iron restraining post in the center of the ring and then dodged out of harm's way.

Deana looked at the powerful horse with his fine tapered head and intelligent eyes. After these wild antics, she thought, the only market for him was the meat man. Deana doubted any person in the building was going to take a chance and buy a full-grown wild horse.

When the auctioneer called for the first bid, an uncomfortable hush was the only reply. Even the chestnut seemed to quiet down. After the auctioneer lowered the bid by several hundred dollars, the bidder's silence broke. The call of a single bid sounded in the dense air. The people who attended the auction regularly knew instantly who made it. It was the dreaded number eleven. Eleven, the meat man's number. The meat man, of course, had a purpose for animals too old, too bold, or too broken down by life. It was the spirited Chestnut's end.

Not this horse, Deana thought bitterly. She wanted to make a bid and save the horse from the terrible fate the meat man had in store. But she was helpless to do anything. Deana found it impossible to even look away from the animal, silently praying under her breath that someone, anyone, would make an opposing bid. Inside she knew it wasn't going to happen. Nobody wanted to put their life in jeopardy because of an unpredictable, wild horse. A thousand pounds of dangerous gelding was definitely a threat, even to an experienced rider. Watching the entire show with Deana were experienced men who were better judges of horse flesh. If none of them countered the low bid, they knew the magnificent animal's life would end tragically.

Just when she thought the animal was lost, the auctioneer yelped and accepted another bid. Only seconds later the single word echoed in the stunned silence, "Sold."

The new owner's auction number was called off, and Deana was not the only person in the arena craning her neck to see who it was that bought the chestnut.

The bidder became obvious when Deana saw Chip laughing. Ajai, sitting next to him, looked smug as he shrugged his shoulders and shook his head at what Chip was saying.

Deana turned away. She stared at the chestnut and felt a strange mixture of jealousy and admiration. Ajai bought the chestnut. He saved him from the meat man! Chip was going to train the horse, but Ajai owned him. How ironic, she thought, things hadn't changed much. What Ajai wants Ajai always gets. He's got the money, the ego and the means to gentle the gelding.

The two ring men led the gelding out. The end of the procession of horses brought many people out of their seats. Some hurried to crowd around Ajai and Chip. Others left the barn. Deana decided after the excitement of the morning, it was the right time for her to leave, before Chip sought her out.

Hurrying toward the exit, she thought, "What a spring auction this has turned out to be; the saga of the fiery gelding and seeing Ajai so suddenly after all these years. I feel exhilarated and drained."

3

The bright sunlight greeted her as she walked outside of the building. She paused in the doorway to slide her sunglasses down onto her nose. Inhaling the clean air, she could breathe freely again.

The mild pandemonium of loading animals had turned the parking lot into a tangle of horse trailers and pick-ups. Deana moved cautiously around the jam of vehicles to avoid being run over by either a four-legged or a four-wheeled beast. As she walked around a beat up two-stall horse trailer, she saw that it completely blocked her from leaving.

"What?" she cried out loud. She walked to the front of the trailer to look inside the equally beat up truck it was attached to. The cab was empty. The trailer was empty and there wasn't a soul nearby.

Deana muttered, "I can't believe how rude people can be."

She left the truck and walked over to her car. She unlocked the rear hatch and tossed her purse inside. With a frustrated sigh, she stood in the grass watching the few people who walked in her direction. None of them belonged to the rig blocking her car. After fifteen minutes of watching, with not one person going near the truck, she decided there was nothing to do but get comfortable while she was stuck. She thought, "I can't wait to meet the owner of this heap. I'm going to give him a clear picture of what good manners are."

A half hour later, the spring sun which only a few hours before she felt overjoyed at seeing, now beat mercilessly down on her. She climbed onto the hood settling her shoulders against the windshield. Her mouth had long ago dried out, and she wished for a cold bottle of Coke. The vending machine inside the auction barn was tempting, but too far away.

Deana lifted her arm to glance at her watch. "I'm already

sunburned," she said, pressing her finger into the pink skin. "I've been sitting here so long I'm actually sunburned." That made the wait not a total waste of time. She turned so she could close her eyes and lift her face directly to the sun.

As soon as she closed her eyes to rest, a young girl's voice came to her. "Daddy, be careful. You're going to hurt her."

Deana slowly lifted her head off the windshield to see who was talking. The back end of the horse trailer blocking her car was now open and a small bay horse was shying away from it. The animal stepped sideways, easily avoiding the tug of the lead rope.

Deana saw a bright pink lead rope pulled taut into the ratty old trailer. Finally, when the mare wouldn't move, a man's head appeared. He stepped out of the trailer. A shock of untidy fair hair fell into his face. He just stood and stared at the horse with a mystified expression. Then he led the horse in a circle before stepping up into the trailer and pulling the shortened lead hard for the horse to follow.

Deana watched the mare do exactly what she had done before and almost laughed. The expression of painful frustration on the man's face stopped her. He placed his hands on his hips to stare at the mare. Deana wondered how he planned to handle the stubborn animal. "Daddy, what's wrong?" the little girl's voice echoed from inside the trailer.

With a shake of his head, he walked to the mare's head and rubbed the stripe of white that trickled down her forehead. His mouth was moving as he began to scratch around the horse's flickering ears. Deana watched and forgot her anger at being delayed. Suddenly, a girl appeared next to him. Her pale blond, almost white, hair was done in tight pigtails that reached to her thin shoulders. Her farmer jeans were patched at the knees.

"What's wrong with her, daddy?" she asked with a despairing look from her father to the horse and back to her father again.

"Nothing, honey," he said softly. "She just idn't used to us yet. I'm just telling her she'll be fine in the back of this trailer 'til we get her home."

"Will we have to stay here all night if she won't go in?" the soft-voiced child asked.

Deana had heard enough. She swung her legs off the car and stood in a fluid movement, brushing the road dust off her clothes. As Deana walked toward the trailer, she called out a cheerful, "Hi there."

Surprised at the interruption, the man looked over at her, "Hi." he mumbled.

"Is the mare giving you some trouble?"

He nodded, "I don't know what's wrong, but she won't git into the trailer."

Deana walked across the gravel to where the mare stood with her head down and her back leg relaxed. "She isn't afraid," Deana said with a laugh. "She looks ready to take a nap. Don't you think so?" she said, turning to the girl.

The little blond girl stared without blinking. The look in her eyes remained cautious, but she nodded.

"Is this your first horse?" Deana asked running her hand down the mare's shoulder as she spoke to the girl.

The girl nodded again.

"I think your Dad picked a good horse for you to start on. She seems really sweet. What's her name?"

"I don't know yet."

"How about for now we call her Sweets? At least until your Dad and I get her into the trailer," Deana suggested, glancing at the girl's father.

He remained silent.

"I'll give you a hand loading Sweets, if you like."

Deana saw him eye the stocky mare and then her slight stature. Without any confidence in his voice, he asked, "What do you think we can do?"

Deana laughed, "Try to get her in the trailer so you can go

17

home. Do you have any grain with you?"

The man shook his head.

Deana frowned. "Do you have an extra lead rope?"

Again he shook his head no.

"Hi," a deep voice interrupted. A tall figure appeared from behind the horse, "Can't get the mare loaded? Maybe she's used to a ramp. If that's the case we'll have to convince her that one time without it won't cause any harm."

Deana admitted to herself before she turned around that what was said made sense. She turned and was about to explain they had no grain or extra rope until she saw who it was that was giving advice so freely.

Ajai Jacoubi.

Instant resentment filled her heart. If it isn't Mr. Perfect, Ajai the Wonder Boy, she thought. In flesh and blood, not just some bad Associated Press photograph in the newspaper.

He looked good, older looking than when he left three years ago, but more relaxed.

He was looking at her looking at him. Suddenly he grinned and, Deana, embarrassed, spun away, moving closer to the mare.

The little girl's father saved the awkward moment by asking, "How do we git her to do that?"

"Well this young lady had the right idea," Ajai said, nodding to Deana, "but I don't think we need anything but the lead rope. If she would be so kind as to get up into the trailer then you and I can brace our arms behind the mare and she should jump right in."

"In a perfect world," Deana muttered.

Ajai gave her a puzzled look, "What did you say?"

"Nothing," she said as she hurried to step up into the trailer.

The father handed the pink lead-rope to her. Deana wrapped it once around the middle post of the trailer. If it came down to her strength against the mare's, there was no doubt who the winner would be, and getting a broken finger was not something Deana wanted to take a chance with.

"Ready, on three," Ajai said when the two men stood in position. "One, two, three, pull."

Deana pulled the rope tight and hung on. The mare reared, fighting the pressure of the rope for a moment, until the two men with their shoulders digging together into the back of her haunches gave a hard shove. They half lifted her off the ground. Startled into motion the mare gave one leap forward and shot straight into the trailer. Deana deftly whipped the rope off the post and, keeping the rein taut, ducked under the bar separating the two sides, and ran to the front of the trailer to tie it securely.

"Yippee," Deana heard the child's joyful yell outside.

Deana hopped out of the trailer to see the man and his daughter excitedly crowd around Ajai. The three laughed together looking like old friends.

Deana smiled ruefully as she walked to her car and climbed inside. She pulled the hatch down and clambered over the seats again. With an irritated sigh at how hot it was inside, she rolled the window down and turned the key. As the truck and trailer pulled away, she backed up and heard, "Hey, that was really nice of you to help them out," Ajai said standing outside her open window, "They asked me to say thanks."

Deana looked up and nodded, "It was obvious I wasn't going anyplace until they loaded the mare. Why did you help them?"

He pointed at the four-wheel drive truck towering over her Escort, "I was in the same predicament as you."

"Oh," Deana said shifting into drive.

"By the way, I don't think we've met before. My name's Ajai."

Deana rigidly stared straight out the front windshield. "I know," she said abruptly, and, without looking at him drove away. She controlled the urge to watch his reaction in the rear view mirror. Her heart was pounding like a drum in her chest. For the first time in her life, she had actually spoken to Ajai Jacoubi.

She laughed out loud and spoke to the windshield as she sped down Jean Duluth Road, "I actually talked to him without tripping over my tongue or saying something really stupid. This is a great day, Ajai's back in town."

4

The old house felt cool after the heat outside. Deana carried a bag of groceries in one arm as she pushed open the screen door with her elbow.

"I'm home," she yelled into the silence. "Hey Dad, I could use some help." Deana set the groceries on the counter and went back for the rest.

With a sigh, Deana looked over the numerous bags of groceries, the dry cleaning bags, and the bags from the hardware store. She did not look forward to putting all of this stuff away by her self. This is completely unfair, she thought. Our agreement was whoever shopped did not have to put stuff away. Deana, dusty and hot, walked across the scarred linoleum floor into the front hallway. From here she didn't have to yell as loud. The sound of her voice traveled up the stairs and into her father's office at the back of the house. "Dad, I could use some help in here. Where in the heck are you?" She yelled again when there was still no reply.

Deana returned to the kitchen, began looking through bags and pulling out items for the refrigerator. One of them was ice cream. "Oh no," she cried. As she lifted the soggy container, thick chocolate liquid oozed out from under the lid. "Darn, darn, what a waste."

The sunburn on her arms began to tingle with pain. Deana opened the top of the rocky road to see if any had survived. The muck in the middle looked solid so it could be saved. Unable to resist the temptation of melted chocolate, she reached her finger inside and took a deep swipe of the ice cream. She licked the chocolate from her fingers and then put it in the freezer. "If he thinks I'm going to do all the work without him, he's wrong. Not this time." Without bothering to wash the sticky sweet from her hands, she left the kitchen.

"Dad," she shouted with renewed force from the bottom of the staircase.

"Out here," came a faint response through the screen on the front porch door. Deana walked through the foyer. "What are you doing out here?" she asked opening the door to peek outside.

"Visiting with the neighbor," Frank Michaels said.

"Visiting with the neighbor? We don't have neighbors."

Frank laughed, "Of course we have neighbors."

"Well not any that we sit and visit with," Deana said to herself. Feeling curious, she pushed the door open even more.

Frank was sitting on the rickety porch swing. Ever since Deana could remember, the ancient wooden swing had hung from the rotted ceiling beams of the porch by deeply rusted chains.

Sitting on the porch rail facing Frank sat a large, impressive figure of a man. With the glare of the sun to the side of him, Deana had to take another step outside to get a better look at the visitor. Suddenly, she stopped. The handsome tawny-haired man she had seen at the auction was now sitting on the rail of her front porch. Worse, he looked like he had done the same thing a hundred times before. How can this be happening? she thought. Ajai had not been in Duluth for years and now all of a sudden she ran into him twice in the same afternoon. When he lived next door for fifteen years she had not seen him more than five times at best.

Amazed, Deana allowed herself the pleasure of actually looking at him. At the auction, it had been such a shock to see him, she had been too nervous then, and too shy to stare. What if he caught her staring? Now, she saw that even age did not work against Ajai. It only made him more attractive in a disturbing way. Gone was the mischievous boy she had a childish crush on; but the man he had grown into demanded a second look. Too bad, he was not a nice person.

Deana realized she was staring and dropped her gaze to

the floor, "Sorry, I didn't...."

"Ajai Jacoubi, I am pleased to introduce you to my daughter, Deana."

Ajai stood and moved toward her. A forced smile curved his mouth. "I believe I met your daughter once already today." Ajai said, "Though we didn't have the chance to exchange names."

As she lifted her head to meet his eyes, Deana's heart pounded in panic. At the auction she had deliberately been rude to him. Why? I'm not a rude person, she thought. Was it possible he meant to point out her lack of manners to her father? Frank would be mortified to think of her treating anyone rudely. But, in the long run, it didn't matter. Deana was not a little girl any longer.

Ajai simply stared at her. Deana squirmed, debating whether an apology was necessary. She stepped closer and opened her mouth to explain. Only then did she notice the strange color of his eyes. They were such an odd color, light brown with what looked like gold flecks. It must be the lighting. Nobody had gold colored eyes. It wasn't possible except for the golden boy of Duluth. Deana stared, dumbstruck, into his eyes.

Frank chuckled as he watched the two of them, "You already know her?"

Ajai slowly looked over each feature of her face and in a low voice said, "I didn't realize how much time had passed since I'd last seen her."

Frank laughed, "And what were you doing in a grocery store, Ajai?"

"It was at the spring auction," Deana hastily added quickly turning away.

Ajai grinned at her, "You remember, Frank. I told you about the auction and about the girl that was helping that man and his daughter..." He paused, his grin widening as he turned to look at Frank, "It seems that very same girl has turned out to be your daughter and I didn't know it."

Deana shot Ajai a suspicious look. She had the distinct feeling that she was the brunt of some joke between the two men and the thought annoyed her.

Frank said from the swing, "Deana, what's that all over your shirtfront?"

Deana frowned and looked down. The tell-tale signs of chocolate in thick drippings smeared across the white material.

Frank laughed, "It looks like you were cleaning or something."

Deana flushed, "Chocolate ice cream." She explained. "I was cleaning up the stuff that melted in the sun on my way home from the store. I really better get back to the kitchen. I have to take care of the groceries."

With the men's laughter in her ears, she beat a hasty retreat. Once safely in the kitchen she exclaimed out loud, "What a mess I am. Why couldn't I have just left the darn ice cream alone? Ohhh, the only time I'll ever speak to Ajai face to face and I ruin it."

5

Using the maid's staircase, Deana hurried upstairs to change. Remembering the endless days of high school, Deana felt eternally grateful Ajai had never taken notice of her. Ajai was a couple of years older than Deana and two grades ahead, so in reality he was, and always had been, just a foolish school girl's romantic crush. Puppy love that never should have been noticed. When she was a freshman at East, Ajai was a junior. Ajai also happened to be rich, handsome and popular. Deana was none of those things. Ajai ranked as a talented sports star in both football and basketball. His adoring friends and fans constantly surrounded him, including the cheerleaders, especially the cheerleaders. Deana remembered he also dated the president of the senior class. Who, also by chance, was the head cheerleader of the football squad. When he turned sixteen, Ajai drove a sports car to school. He had everything money could buy. His title in the Birchlog yearbook had been Golden Boy and not because of the color of his eyes. Deana believed he was still the golden boy, his every wish coming true.

She hid behind corners just to watch him at his locker. Deana did not like sports of any kind unless it had to do with horses, but she went to every game Ajai played in. She constantly collected bits of Ajai memorabilia, like the game number that decorated his locker before tournaments. When she waited for the school bus, she did a very daring thing. She took a parking ticket off the windshield of his car. Deana wondered what the fine on that ticket would be today. The ticket was still hidden in the bottom of her hope chest.

Many times over the years, Deana contemplated looking through the Ajai junk she collected, to toss out the useless trinkets from high school, but always decided it was not the time to start throwing things away.

Where Ajai Jacoubi had been concerned, Deana had no pride. She remembered how obvious her infatuation must have been to everyone. Now her past did not matter. None of the people from high school were a part of her life any longer. Her life had become filled with new faces from her job. Ajai had not been a part of her life for a long time. Of course, now that he had returned, and she had actually met him face to face, things might be different. Ajai was not acting when he looked at her like she was a complete stranger. "How strange that, to him, I am a complete stranger," she exclaimed staring into the full-length mirror that hung on the back of her closet door.

Deana studied her face. There was not much she could do to change it or Ajai's first impression. The mirror revealed that she had chocolate not only on her shirt, but also on her face, and hands. She looked a mess. What difference would it make for her to worry about it now?

In spite of her brave intention to not primp or worry, she did take extra time brushing her hair and debated for a moment whether make-up might help.

A meeting with Ajai Jacoubi was something that had occupied many of Deana's sleepless nights. In one dream, she'd won the gold in the Equestrian Division of the Olympics, and Ajai was playing Olympic polo.

How different the real meeting was, with chocolate ice cream all over her face and shirt, and in an ancient pair of blue jeans with her thick midnight black hair pulled back in a ponytail. She didn't see that her skin was clear and smooth, with a light sprinkling of freckles across her nose, that her large gray eyes, tilted at the corner, were surrounded by dark black lashes, and that her mouth was generous. When she smiled, the point of her chin softened, and her eyes glowed with light.

Deana saw none of this, busy as she was critiquing herself. This is definitely not a meeting I've ever envisioned.

No, this is reality. she thought, making a face at herself.

No use in crying over what never would have been. Ajai Jacoubi and a little nobody like me. That's laughable. He still wouldn't know I existed except he's in my house. Hey! What is Ajai doing at my house acting all chummy with Dad?

Deana left her bedroom and soft-footed down the stairs to the front hall. The door to the porch stood open. They must still be outside, she thought. She paused at the screen door to listen. Along with the mutter of voices, Deana heard bursts of laughter from not only Ajai but also her father. Her father's laughter was not something Deana heard often. What had Ajai said that made her father laugh? Deana reached for the door handle when the door was flung open from the other side.

Deana jumped back. Once again she stood face to face with Ajai, his expression almost comedic.

He looked from her to the door handle, "it's sticky," he said, wiping his hand on his pants.

Deana smiled faintly, "That must be my fault. It's probably ice cream. I'll get a cloth from the kitchen to wipe it off."

"Ice cream, oh." Carelessly he swiped his hand across his jeans again.

They both remained in the doorway staring at each other. Deana, before she completely lost her composure asked, "Did you need something?"

"Huh, oh yeah, your dad sent me to get some iced tea."

Deana frowned, "So you'll be staying?"

A slow grin softened his features as he looked at her, "If that's okay with you."

Deana shrugged, "It's not up to me." She turned on her heel and hurried away.

The kitchen counter was littered with half emptied grocery bags. She glanced at the clock and thought with a sigh, I have to get moving. There's so much left to do and soon it'll be time to start dinner.

She filled a pitcher with ice cubes and stirred in instant tea. Her thoughts raced, "What is my father thinking? Ajai Jacoubi never had anything to do with us while he lived in Duluth. Now suddenly, Frank was inviting him to stay for tea? None of this made sense.

She carried the tray with tea and glasses and a plate of banana bread she'd baked that morning. As soon as she appeared in the doorway, Ajai jumped up to help her. He took the tray from her hands and carried it to the table. "There's only two glasses, aren't you joining us?"

Deana debated for a second. She wanted to find out what they were talking about, but shook her head no.

"I'm so far behind already."

"Behind what?" Ajai prompted her.

"My Saturday chores," she said, her tone suddenly sharp. He acted like he was genuinely interested in what she had to do, and it unnerved her.

Frank asked in his soft-spoken way, "Deana, are the demands of the housework too much?"

Deana felt embarrassed. She shook her head, "Of course not, Dad. I'm sorry." She apologized, but she didn't know whether it was to Frank or Ajai. "If you'll excuse me, it was… nice to meet you."

She turned to leave. Ajai reached the door handle before she did.

"I don't need any apology," he said softly.

His quiet consideration made her feel worse. Deana glanced up at him, "Please, I have to go."

"Can I help you with anything?"

Deana's eyes widened in surprise as she studied his face. He looked sincere. She had no idea if he was just acting like some kind of Victorian gentleman in front of her father, or if this was what Ajai was truly like. If so, the tabloids, for years, had portrayed a very different Ajai.

In the articles Deana read, Ajai was described as a

rude, selfish, daredevil, thrill-crazy, womanizing playboy.

"No I don't need any help from you." She said backing inside the open door.

Ajai looked puzzled, "Okay," he said with a shrug. Without a second glance, he returned to where Frank was drinking tea.

Deana returned to the kitchen. Standing in front of the sink, staring out the window she thought, maybe this entire day is really just a bad dream. Going to the auction was crazy. Then Ajai was there. And then he saved that gelding from the meat man. Then he helped that man and his daughter load their new pony and just now he acted like such … such a… normal person.

6

The black hands on the small wall clock above Deana's desk pointed at ten o'clock. It was Monday morning, Deana flexed her tense back muscles and turned away from the computer screen for the first time since she had arrived at her office.

A loud voice from the hallway called out, "Hey you workaholic, it's time for a coffee break. Get away from that computer. It doesn't own you."

Deana smiled, watching the door expectantly, already on her feet. Genie Caldwell, the only other woman in the basement department of accounting and bookkeeping at Jacoubi Enterprises, breezed through the open door.

"I'm ready for a break," Deana said with a yawn.

Genie held out a shapely hand with fashionably long fingernails painted bright crimson, "Great. Then hand over the cup and I'll be back in a flash." Deana handed her the official Jac. E. coffee mug with the logo printed across it.

When Genie left the room, Deana straightened the numerous printouts strewn across her desk. Mondays always kept her extra busy after the weekend, but this one started off especially hectic

Genie walked into the office whistling off key, balancing full coffee mugs while walking in ridiculously high heels.

"I will never understand why you don't wipe out in those things. The wax on the floors out there is at least an inch thick and dangerous." Deana exclaimed.

"Not for me. I never have a problem."

Deana laughed, "If anybody should, it's you. That strut of yours is enough to give any man a seizure."

Genie sat on the edge of Deana's desk ignoring the extra chair right next to her. She crossed her shapely and bare to mid-thigh legs. "So tell me, how was your weekend? Did you spend it with that smelly beast you like so much?"

Mondays had taken on a familiar routine now that Genie had settled into her position in the accounting department. At first the younger woman had caused quite a stir in the basement. Genie was another computer whiz kid straight out of college, but while Deana had worked hard to fit into the antiseptic atmosphere of the accounting department, Genie had done her best to throw everything into an uproar. She refused to give in to the quiet, studious men who had been the backbone of Edward Jacoubi's award-winning department for many years. The bright yellow hair was bad enough. The outlandish outfits she chose to wear were definitely not proper office attire. She had five earrings in one ear and each one was different. She mixed and matched clothes without regard for colors. Once the men in the department found Genie planned to ignore their demands for propriety, they deliberately stayed out of her way. Genie did not care. A natural extrovert, she directed all of her boisterous nature onto Deana.

Deana at first only tolerated the attention from the newcomer. She definitely did not approve of Genie's flamboyant nature. Until she discovered that, under all that glitz, Genie really was a genuine down-to-earth person. Genie merely wanted all the attention all the time.

Deana shook her head, "As a matter of record, no I never did get to ride this weekend." She sipped the steaming brew in her cup, watching Genie's face brighten with interest.

"Finally, you found a man worthy of taking you away from that horse. Go on! I want to hear all the details."

"I went to an auction instead of riding. Beginning and end of story."

"An auction. What kind of auction? Antiques, masterpieces of the art world?

"A horse auction," Deana said.

"Not an animal auction! Deana, your life is so boring!

When are you going to start living? When are going to look for a man?"

"Why should I? I get to hear all about your escapades with men. I'll tell you one thing, I'm afraid to go on a date after listening to what happens on yours."

"That's not fair, Deana. You aren't going to attract the same kind of men I do and you know it. You'll attract the intellectual sensitive type while I attract any guy within twenty miles who owns a Harley."

"Don't be too upset about that. A lot of doctors and lawyers ride Harleys."

Genie looked thoughtful for a second. "Really? I didn't know that. Maybe there's hope for me in this town. Though, I wasn't so lucky this weekend. I was at C.W. Chips and …

Deana smiled, though her mind was already tuning out Genie's weekend date story. She toyed with the idea of mentioning that Ajai Jacoubi had returned to Duluth and about his abrupt appearance in her life. Just the mention of Ajai's name would shock her. Genie made it quite clear she was after a man, but she'd said that only a man with money would be the crème on the cake.

"What are you smiling about?" Genie's sharp voice cut into her thoughts. She snapped her fingers under Deana's nose. "Why are you smiling about Edward Jacoubi being admitted to the hospital this weekend? Do you know something I don't?"

Deana stared at her dumbfounded. "What?"

"Hello!?! Did you listen to a single word I said? The announcement was all over the front page of today's paper."

"I didn't have any time to look at the paper this morning. What did it say? Is he all right?"

"The paper doesn't have any idea what's wrong with him. Everything is very hush, hush and no one's talking."

Deana bit her lip, and muttered, "So that's why Ajai's home."

"Isn't Edward Jacoubi the president of this company?" Genie asked inspecting the polish on her nails. "I think that's what I read in the paper. I wonder what'll happen around here if he croaks?"

Deana shook her head, horrified at both the language and the thought. The note of callousness in Genie's questions sparked Deana's anger, "How can you speak about his death so, so casually? Don't you realize how terrible this must be for his...family?"

"I don't know anything about the family. Do you?" Genie asked.

"No, I don't... but this is so sudden."

"Whew, that's a relief I thought you might be one of those sappy types who loudly cries about every person who is suffering, whether or not they know them."

Genie hauled herself off the desktop, "I'm sure the afternoon news will say something about it. If we sneak into the lounge we can watch it."

"We don't have to sneak. We have as much right in there as they do."

"Not at that time. I'm not sure what they might do, tar and feather us probably."

"They wouldn't dare do anything, but I don't want to watch it on television," Deana said.

"The television is the only reliable news we get in this town," Genie answered. She stopped and stared at Deana.

Deana looked up and saw her expression, "What?"

"Your face is all red. I've never seen you this flustered before. What is it about this Mr. Jacoubi that's got you so concerned?"

Deana gave a dismissive wave of her hand, "Don't be so ridiculous. Maybe I am just one of those professional mourners, like you said."

Genie walked around the desk to stand in front of her, "Uh uh, I ain't buying it, Deana. Fess up. The rumors are true then. You do know the son, don't you? His name is Hadji or something like that."

"It's A-Jay," Deana said. And she instantly regretted it.

"It's true then! I've heard stories about why you were the only woman considered for this position, but I never believed any of them."

Deana held her tongue.

Genie said, "I read in the paper that Ajai is back in town and spending twenty-four hours at his dad's bedside in the hospital."

Deana kept her coffee cup in front of her face and carefully inspected the small drop that remained in the bottom.

Genie eyed Deana for a second and exclaimed, "You already knew! Okay what is this? Are you two secret lovers or something?"

Silence fell like a wave over the room. With narrowed eyes, Deana lowered the coffee cup and gave Genie an icy glare.

Genie's face fell until she forced a careless laugh and blurted, "You have to know the stories. It's all because you're the Jacoubi's neighbor and you and their son went to the same schools. The one I like the best is that Ajai ditched town because of you and his father felt so guilty he hired you for a position down here where he wouldn't have to see you. It's not true, Deana, anyone who knows you has to know it could never be true."

Deana silently watched her face and worked hard to keep her composure. "I have no idea what you're talking about."

Genie looked shocked "I... I... I should go. Me and my big mouth. When will I ever shut up? I'm sorry, Deana." She glanced at the clock and gulped, "Coffee break was over ten minutes ago." Genie darted from behind the desk and flew out the door, leaving her coffee cup behind.

7

Alone in the office with white walls, white linoleum flooring, and white file cabinets; Deana rubbed her arms hard. The cold room, the emotionless white computer screen, and Genie's thoughtless words brought to mind the rumors Deana had thought were dead. A chill of anger inflamed her. "How foolish can I be?" She thought, rising to pace the floor. "No matter what I do at this place, no matter how hard I work, those rumors will continue to haunt me."

She walked over to her office door. She rarely found the need to keep it closed. Right now, she fought an overwhelming desire to slam it as hard as she could. The real desire was that she wanted to shut out Genie, the accounting men, and the rumors. With enormous willpower, gently she pushed against the wood. The only sound in the silent room was a soft click as the door swung closed. The noise did nothing to appease her anger.

The mirror on the back of the door showed the reflection of a stranger. Deana stared at the woman. Medium height, dressed in a straight-line dark blue suit with a crisp white button-down shirt underneath the matching coat. Her shiny black hair was pulled back perfectly into a metal clip at the base of her neck. Her make-up covered the healthy glow her skin maintained all year from being outdoors. The woman in the mirror who worked at Jacoubi Enterprises was nothing but a shell of Deana. The accounting department at Jacoubi Enterprises wanted an accountant who resembled a piece of office furniture. Dependable, durable and invisible, Deana wanted the job so she became just that.

From the first computer class she took in college, Deana discovered she really liked working with computers. For the most part, computers were neat and orderly, just like work-ing with numbers. Accounting had always been an easy sub-ject for her to master. It turned out that working with comput-ers was just as easy. She liked her work, but it wasn't who she was. The real Deana was the girl who rode a paint geld-ing bareback at a dead run across Jacoubi Ridge. She liked antiques; she liked to paint houses. She loved her father and enjoyed taking care of him and their family home. Secretly, in the deep recesses of her soul that she didn't even admit existed, Deana Michaels still loved Ajai Jacoubi. Nobody at Jacoubi Enterprises knew the other Deana Michaels existed.

The rumors started the first year Deana was hired. Deana's family happened to live on the very northern edge of the Jacoubi estate. At one time the house had been a part of the farm, the estate's manager lived there until he died. For some reason never revealed to the Michaels family, Edward Jacoubi had decided to sell the house and two acres of land with it. Frank Michaels bought the house when Deana was a child.

8

Walking to the stable behind her house, Deana looked at the clouds drifting past the blazing orange sun setting in the sky just above the tree line. Deana paused to stare at the sight. Spring was here and soon summer. Now was the time she began her trail rides before supper. But not tonight. She wanted to talk to her dad about Edward Jacoubi. Deana hurried into the house and slammed the door. The kitchen was empty and she stopped to search the table and chairs for the newspaper before walking into the hallway. On the entry table sat today's mail, but not the paper. She walked around the corner into the living room and began flipping through the pile of newspapers on the coffee table.

"Looking for this," Frank said from his study door. He held the newspaper in his hand. "Pretty awful news about Edward, isn't it?"

Deana moved toward him, "Did Ajai say anything to you?"

"Not directly, but I could tell something serious was going on."

Deana kissed her father's warm, stubbled cheek. "You didn't shave today."

Frank shrugged, "I didn't have anywhere to go. What was the word at work? Anyone say if Edward was doing all right or not?"

"Nobody I talked to knew anything more than what the news reported. I was hoping you might know more because of Ajai coming over here yesterday. Why did he come over, Dad? I didn't even know you knew the Jacoubi's."

Frank laughed. He walked into the living room. Tall, lanky with steel gray hair that always looked like it needed to be trimmed, he moved with the grace of an athlete, but was a total bookworm and always had been as far as Deana could remember. "Of course I know the Jacoubi's. We've been neighbors for almost twenty years."

"I've never seen them around here and you've never mentioned that you'd ever been to their house."

Frank shrugged. "I suppose that's true. We've been friends but when your mother was alive we played cards together and visited at holidays. You were young and probably don't remember. When Ajai was kicked off the basketball team because of bad grades, I tutored him for a while. Edward asked me to help. He was always really bright but he had a terrible attitude. I'm glad he's grown up and turned out to be quite a good man."

"So, why was he here yesterday?"

"Just to say hello. He always stops over when he comes into town."

Deana laughed giving her father a disbelieving look, "Since when?"

Frank shot her a puzzled look, "As far back as I can remember—ever since he left."

Deana stared at her father, "You're kidding. He's been coming here all along and you never told me. How could you, Dad?"

"I never thought you'd care."

Deana stopped. Of course, Frank was right. Why would she care that Ajai came to the house? With a flustered laugh she said, "The only thing I've ever heard about Ajai Jacoubi is what a selfish man he is and how he neglects not only his family but every one of his responsibilities."

Frank chuckled, "That sounds like the garbage straight out of the tabloids. You can't believe the newspaper, honey. It's nothing but a rag sheet now. I believe it's called yellow journalism. Ajai's gotten a bad reputation that follows him." Frank picked up the remote control for the television and turned it on. "The six o'clock news might give us more information. Otherwise I'll call the house to find out what's going on."

In unison, the two sank onto the broken down couch, leaning forward to listen. The news flashed onto the screen and showed the entrance of the medical center on Fourth Street. The cameraman panned to a close-up of the female reporter holding a large microphone in front a medical person's mouth.

"Mr. Jacoubi is in stable condition." The man said. Writing crawled across the bottom of the screen: *Dr. Milt Peterson, Edward Jacoubi's physician.* "He has been moved from the Intensive Care Unit into a private room. There will be no visitors allowed except immediate family."

Suddenly, the reporter snatched the microphone away from the doctor. She said quickly, with excitement into the camera, "Follow me. Ajai...Ajai Jacoubi, wait. Do you have any information to tell us?"

The camera bounced as the cameraman shifted his position and then re-focused on the back of a tall man in a long raincoat. Then the man, without a backward, glance hurried through the hospital doors.

Without losing a beat the reporter jumped in front of the camera, she said quickly, "That was the son, the only son of Edward Jacoubi. He has been in South America playing polo for Team U.S.A. It is unconfirmed, but I believe he arrived from Minneapolis this morning in a helicopter."

Frank turned the television off with an angry grunt. "They act like it's a sports arena."

"What exactly happened when Ajai was here?"

Frank laughed and turned toward the kitchen, "Nothing. We talked about the past. The changes in Duluth." He stopped to give her a searching look with his serious brown eyes. "After your mother died, a teenage daughter was a challenge I wasn't prepared for. I'm sure I made many mistakes during those first years. You dealt with so much on your own. I wish I'd pushed and made you talk about things more, but I didn't know. Men deal with things differently. I prefer silence until I've had a chance to sort things out."

Deana saw the regret in his face. His predicament was both a teenage daughter and the loss of his spouse, plus dealing with his own grief.

"You were a serious child, but not overly melancholy. I never saw anything wrong with you thinking you were in love with Ajai. It seemed pretty natural with the Jacoubi's so close, and you spending all that time with Chip at the stable. Ajai was a go-getter, even back then, and basically he was a good kid. Although in college he got pretty wild. He was no threat to you."

"Not a threat to me," Deana repeated softly. "So you knew all along that I had a crush on him and never said anything?" She jumped to her feet, "I can't believe I was such a fool. I was so busy chasing Ajai around the high school I missed out on my high school years." Her irritation softened to humor as she pictured herself then. "Did you deliberately keep the tutoring and your friendship with the Jacoubi's a secret to protect me?"

Frank sniffed. The smell of the casserole in the oven reached them in the living room, "Smells like dinner's ready."

Deana followed close behind him, "Well?"

Frank sighed as he opened the oven door to remove the casserole dish. He set it on the table, "Will you set the table, please? I could have possibly avoided mentioning Ajai. I did not deliberately keep any secrets from you, and I don't believe I ever thought you needed to be protected from the Jacoubi's. Ajai's been spoiled most of his life, but he was taught right from wrong. The Jacoubi's are good people. Edward worked hard to accomplish what he did. The only strike against him is that he accomplished the American dream and now everybody resents it."

As Deana quickly set the table, he said, "I didn't hide Ajai's tutoring from you, but he might have."

Deana stared at him in surprise, "Ajai knew about me?"

Frank gave an exasperated snort, "Of course, you weren't completely invisible honey, though at times I know you would have liked to be. Of course Ajai knew about you. You are my only daughter."

"I don't believe it. He never acknowledged me once... not ever. I knew he was a jerk, but not as bad as that."

Deana slammed the plates on the tabletop feeling terribly disappointed. He never acted like he knew her. She took the silverware and finished setting the table. Frank kept silent as he dished out the familiar casserole and sat down.

Deana muttered under her breath as she placed the forks and knives in their proper places, "The nerve of him. He always hung around with the popular group, but I was so certain he wasn't like them. He had to be different and the... the only reason he didn't notice me..."

"If he had, would he have fallen in love with you?"

Deana froze, the bottle of milk she held was suspended above her glass. A laugh escaped her, "Are you crazy? No. But at least then I wouldn't have wasted my time mooning over him like a love-sick puppy." A voice inside of Deana argued, "Are you sure? Ajai was the boy dreams were made of. Good-looking, athletic, lots of money, and charm. He had oodles of charm." A chill of excitement caused Deana to smile.

Later that night after Frank had eaten and then left to work in his study, she piled the supper dishes into the sink and filled it with hot, soapy water. Yes, some of her high school memories filled her with regret because she always harbored thoughts that she had missed out on so much. Deana's thoughts raced. She held the cloth rag, wringing it into a tight coil. I just can't believe Ajai knew. He probably figured me out just like my father did. He was probably laughing at me the entire time I followed him around.

A groan escaped her as a picture filled her thoughts. The popular group standing together in the narrow halls during the break between classes, Deana could see herself walking by. Ajai leaning against the locker with the entire group and all of them snickering and laughing as soon as she walked past. How embarrassing.

Deana scrubbed the worn countertop viciously. She finished by wiping down the appliances before she drained the sink. Her mortification from the past quieted into irritation. Ajai had done her a huge favor by ignoring her. To be rejected by him then would have been the bitterest of pills.

9

"What is going on with you, Deana?" Genie said from the doorway.

Her voice startled Deana out of her daydreaming.

"You've been moping around for days." Genie sauntered across the floor to lean a hip against Deana's desk. "I've never seen you like this and if you tell me one more time, 'nothing,' I'm going to scream. With the way this tomb echoes, just think of what the sound will be like. Is it a guy? Please tell me it's some exciting story about a guy."

Deana laughed, "What?" She said quickly moving her hands to re-arrange the pages of data from her printer.

Genie reached over and grabbed the papers out of her hands. "First piece of evidence is right here in front of your nose. Is this all the work you've done today?"

Deana demanded, trying to keep her humor, "Hand those over, Genie. What's the amount of paperwork got to do with anything?"

"Look at this," Genie rattled the papers. "This is the amount of paperwork I've done today. By this time, you usually have a pile twice this size."

Deana snatched the papers out of Genie's waving hands. "I can't believe you keep track of how much paperwork we do. You call me competitive? And keep your voice down. You're practically yelling and my door is open."

"Your door is always open," Genie said unconcerned. "I'll chill only if you start talking. I've never seen you act like this before and I've been dying to give you the third degree all week. Unfortunately, this is the first time I've caught you red-handed sleeping on the job."

Deana stood. Shaking her head, she said, "I wasn't sleeping and just forget it Genie. There's nothing to tell. Except maybe I have spring fever. The weather is staying so warm, I can start riding Journey after work now."

Genie's face fell, "Oh big whoop, the horse again. I'm beginning to think you're a hopeless case, Deana. Doesn't any guy in this town interest you?"

Deana laughed. It sounded louder than normal to her, she said, "Really, Genie, there's more to life than men. I've never been the type to believe true love was going to crash into my life and rescue me. For one thing, I don't need rescuing. My life is way too busy. I've already got my entire summer planned. Do you want to hear what it is?"

Genie shrugged, "Oh sure, I guess so. I still have ten minutes until I have to go back to my office and clean up. Remember, it's the first of the month. You know, pay day, my favorite time."

Deana glanced at her watch and sighed, "Oh my gosh, you're right, our obligatory visit with the boss. So much for getting out of here fast."

"Well, aren't you going to tell me your great plans for the summer? Maybe you can afford a cruise or some kind of vacation... I certainly can't."

"If you'd lay off your credit cards, you could clean up your debt."

"Don't get that accountant tone with me. I haven't hired you. Anyway, if I was using my plastic, then I could afford a cruise. For your information, I've frozen my credit cards in ice trays so there. Now tell me in eight minutes what your big plans are. I'm on the edge of my seat." She faked a yawn, patting her brightly painted scarlet lips.

Ignoring her sarcasm, Deana said, "I just got done figuring out our finances and I'm so excited. We're going to have some extra money so I can afford to buy the paint and paint the outside of the house... finally."

Genie's blank expression made Deana giggle, "I guess that's not your idea of exciting, but I love to paint houses and fences and barns. Everything looks so neat and clean with fresh paint on it."

"That is the most pathetic excuse for making plans that I've ever heard." Genie complained. "I can't believe I expected to hear that for once you planned a vacation out of Duluth. Why couldn't you use that extra money to travel? I mean why does painting the house even matter? One more year, how much difference can it make?"

"It matters if the exposed wood underneath rots. Think of the expense. I've never replaced boards on a house before. I'd have to hire somebody to do it."

Genie held her hands up in surrender, "Okay, okay I take it back. I just wish I could afford to take a trip anywhere out of here."

"But why? When there's so much to do around here. Just think. Pretty soon we'll be able to watch the sailboat races from the executive parking lot again."

A spark of interest showed in Genie's face. "I've got a better idea. Why don't we sneak down to the racer's private dock and meet some of the single members. I heard they have cocktail parties after the races with a band and food. Think of how romantic it would be at the lake at night with the lights on the bridge..."

A voice in the hallway startled the girls. "Ahem, ladies, excuse us."

Genie gave a squeal of surprise as the two whirled around. When Deana saw Ajai standing with Mr. Bascomb, the floor supervisor, in her doorway, her mouth fell open. "Ajai," fell from her lips.

Genie glanced over at her and said softly, "So, you do know each other."

Deana hid her annoyance. She said in a more formal tone, "Please come in."

10

At the sight of Ajai standing in the doorway, Deana's heart thumped wildly. Caught, cornered, were her first frantic thoughts when she met his level gaze. He didn't look surprised. He looked like he expected to see her.

Her head cleared and her panic caused her to smile. The top of Mr. Bascomb's head barely reached Ajai's shoulders. This was the Ajai she recognized. An Ajai, devastatingly handsome, wearing a charcoal gray suit jacket with the smooth look of suede, dress pants and, underneath, an unusually casual dark gray tee shirt. His gold streaked hair curled along the collar. A tee shirt, Deana thought, ever indifferent to propriety, even in the temporary position as his father's replacement.

Ajai seemed unaware of the tension in the room. Genie was nervous because she always felt guilty even though she had done nothing wrong. Deana was nervous because she felt guilty and deserved it. Never had she mentioned to Ajai that she worked at his father's business. First the snub at the parking lot, and now this deception. She waited anxiously for his reaction.

Ajai's eyes moved briefly over her face and then he turned to Genie. "Hello, I take it your office is the empty one down the hall?"

Genie swallowed and nodded opening her mouth to explain. Ajai cut her off with a congenial, "Your name is Genie Caldwell?"

Genie nodded again.

Ajai stepped further into the office and held out his hand, "I'm Ajai. It's nice to meet you."

"Th-thank you, Mr. Jacoubi."

He gave her a faint smile before he asked, "Just call me Ajai. How long have you worked here, Miss Caldwell?"

Genie visibly relaxed and smiled, "Please call me Genie. You pronounce your name A-Jay? It looks so foreign on paper. I've worked here for nine months."

"Really? I thought I read it was three years." He turned to Deana who had remained motionless, unable to think. "Hello Deana, so you must be the accountant hired three years ago? I didn't realize you had already graduated from DBU and have been working here for three years." He raised an expressive eyebrow that showed Deana he was well aware she deliberately kept the information from him.

Deana raised her chin a notch to look him directly in the eye. "I don't believe it has actually been a full three years. Not until next fall."

His lips twitched at her correction. Though his eyes lingered on her face, his voice remained cool, "I see. The other day you looked younger. It must've been the chocolate all over your face. I'm amazed how much I'm learning today and not everything pertains to business."

His gaze lingered on Deana's face for just a second too long, he extended his hand, "Genie, it's been a pleasure. I'll be helping out around here until my father returns. You'll probably be seeing me in the halls." He turned to Julius Bascomb, "Perhaps we should move on to the rest of the accounting staff. I'm sure they will be as full of surprises as these two ladies have been."

Genie took a hurried step forward and said quickly, "Mr. Jac... Ajai, we, Deana and I would like to wish your father a full and quick recovery. We've been very concerned since we heard about him."

Deana glared at the back of Genie's head. She had been concerned for the Jacoubi family, not Genie. Genie had been indifferent about his father.

Ajai smiled, "Thank you. That's very kind. I'll pass along

your best wishes."

Deana silently cursed her own awkwardness. Why hadn't she thought to ask about his father?

Without another word to Deana, Ajai turned his back and said, "Bascomb? Are you ready?"

Julius gave a nervous snort. He glanced at the two women before replying, "Of course, right this way," he said quickly. He turned to follow Ajai to the door, but stopped, turning back to Deana. "I almost forgot. Here, Deana," he shoved two envelopes into her hand before he hurried out the door ,moving fast to catch up with Ajai's long-legged gait.

Deana and Genie gaped at each other.

Deana blurted, "That's the first time he's ever called me by my first name."

Genie crossed her arms and gave her a reproachful look, "Okay girl, you have some explaining to do. Ajai Jacoubi called you Deana and from what he said, it's obvious you two know each other."

Deana shuffled through the paycheck envelopes and handed Genie's over to her. She shrugged, moving behind her desk. "We're neighbors, Genie. I'm sure you already knew that. You've heard the rumors about me and Ajai." Deana spoke softly, keeping her voice indifferent. "Look at the man. Do you really believe there was ever a romantic fling between us?" Deana laughed hoping to convey how absurd it was, though her gray eyes remained dark and serious. She reached in her desk drawer for a letter opener, "Besides, last weekend was the first time we ever met face to face. My father had to do the introductions. It's plain to see Ajai's not at all impressed with his female neighbor slash accountant."

Genie frowned. She brushed her bright blond curls behind one ear, "Now why do you have to go and do that. You can successfully bomb even the juiciest bits of gossip. I'm glad there's nothing between you two. That man is hot," She gave an exaggerated sigh, "Sizzlin' hot."

Deana gave a disgusted sigh, "So now you decide to believe me. Deana stared at the empty doorway and frowned.

Genie studied Deana's face, "You're right about the grapevine. It's usually pretty lame, but in my experience most rumors have a small grain of truth. Are you sure there's nothing between you two?" She laughed at Deana's icy glare, "Don't blame me for wanting to give you a tainted past, Deana. Your lifestyle is way too puritan to be real. I just want you to have vices like the rest of us."

Deana gave her head an emphatic shake no. Then retorted, "Let me remember a few of your other comments about me. I believe the words were pathetic and boring. And now you add Puritan. I'm beginning to think you're jealous. Maybe you've become bored with chasing men."

A hysterical peal of laughter burst from Genie's lips. "I don't think so. If I ever prefer the company of a mangy horse to that of a warm blooded American male, especially one that looks like Ajai Jacoubi, please just put me out of my misery."

Deana leaned forward and said insistently, "If you don't scram and let me finish my work so I can get out of here, I may do it now."

Genie stepped back in mock fear. "Right, you're so tough. Well anyway I'll wish you a nice weekend even though you're wasting it with that horse and your house painting. See you on Monday."

"Bye, Genie, and Journey's not a mangy horse," Deana called after her as Genie disappeared around the corner.

Finally alone, Deana sank into the chair. Her legs felt like jelly. Ajai is going to be working at Jacoubi? How can this be happening? The only part of my life that man has not thrown into complete confusion with his overpowering presence is here in this office. Now he's going to be working here. What am I going to do? She ran her hand along her aching temple. With a silent laugh she brushed away her concern. What am I so worried about? It's unlikely Ajai has changed enough to actually buckle down and take up his responsibilities. Soon he'll run off for another one of his wild adventures and Jac. E. and I will return to normal. Voices in the hallway caught her attention. With the sound came a feeling of panic. Ajai and Julius! She had to get out of here. The voices faded away, but Deana continued to hurry. She shoved the unfinished paperwork on her desk into the top drawer. She turned the key and locked it, then picked up her briefcase and jacket and headed for the door with key in hand. At least for a blessed two days, she did not have to worry about Ajai Jacoubi disturbing her life.

11

The lights glowed in Edward Jacoubi's office on the top floor of the Jac. E. building. Ajai stood alone looking out at the glittering pinpoints of starlight in the darkness. From this height, the panoramic view of the Aerial Lift Bridge, the bay and the lake still amazed him. Just beyond the ship canal, the white deck-lights of a huge ore boat reflected off the black water.

Years had passed since Ajai had stood here looking at this view. Years he filled nurturing resentment for his father. Years he wasted in the pursuit of an empty lifestyle that left him feeling nothing but dissatisfied. His life seemed destined to continue on the same destructive path until he met an amazing man. While playing a last minute polo match in a small town in South America, his path crossed with a Spanish polo player named Alberto Casilda. By example, Alberto taught Ajai how to live life gallantly not wastefully. Soon Ajai began to make lifestyle changes. He retired from polo. He walked away from it all, the excitement, the fans, and the party life. Then he returned to Minnesota and, without his family's knowledge, applied for entrance into a business school in Minneapolis. He then applied for a job at the office building of Jacoubi Enterprises-Minneapolis. As soon as the Human Resources Department read his application they contacted Edward. Ajai hoped his father appreciated how he applied for any job, even one at the bottom of the corporate ladder. He was back and he wanted to learn the business starting at the ground level. Edward did nothing to help speed Ajai's passage through the halls of Jacoubi. He worked his way past the junior positions at Jacoubi while taking night classes. He graduated from business school the following spring and was ready to begin working full time for Jacoubi Enterprises. Ajai would have preferred to return to the Duluth office but he had to be patient and wait for his father to ask him to come home. His life fell into a routine that kept him busy, until the emergency phone call.

In quiet hysteria, Ajai's mother relayed the events of his father's heart attack that caused the car crash. Every thing from scrambling to secure the corporate helicopter, to the bumpy flight to Duluth was a blur for Ajai. Cocooning himself in numbness seemed to be his only defense.

When he arrived at the intensive care unit, Ajai found his mother standing outside the glassed-in room. Her emotion-strained face was pressed against the plate glass window. He stood next to her, not speaking a word, as she slipped her arm around his waist. She pressed her cheek against his arm, never taking her eyes from the scene playing out inside of the room. Observing the medical staff frantically working over Edward's body was like watching an episode of a television medical drama.

When Ajai saw his father, his throat tightened. This man was not the father he remembered. Ajai remembered him as a man who seemed ageless, six feet tall, a trim build, and closely cropped white hair. Edward did not spend time in a health club to stay physically fit. He jogged the stairs to his office on the tenth floor two or three times a day. He swam, he rode horseback. His father was active and relatively young.

The small part of Edward's face that was visible through the tubes and tape was a pasty white color. A cap covered his hair and it was obvious his hairline was receding. For the first time, the fact that his father was aging, struck Ajai.

He watched the medical personnel work quickly and efficiently. Their movements were precise as they worked in complete silence, anticipating each other's moves. Suddenly, they packed up and vacated the room pushing their equipment carts.

The doctor had explained that the preliminary tests showed Edward had a heart attack that caused the car accident. Running into a tree at fifty miles an hour had left its own damage. What worried the doctors most was Edward had not regained consciousness. The doctors were concerned about internal damage and brain trauma.

The bang on his head had put Edward in a coma that lasted for twelve hours. During that time, Ajai spent most of it thinking about his father. He might never have the chance to tell him how much he owed him.

For the first time in his life, Ajai took care of his mother. He offered her food and drink, anything he could think of. The stuffiness of the waiting room added to his frustration at not being able to assuage his mother's fear. For the first time in his life, Ajai worried about his mother. It was a lonely twosome that remained those long hours in the hospital, silently praying.

The scare for Edward's life ended as abruptly as it happened. He woke up and demanded something to eat. His mother instantly bloomed back into her old self, and Ajai hoped for the chance to clear away all the misunderstandings he had caused with his father and perhaps start anew.

Ever since his father woke up, the doctors had only good news. There was no permanent damage from the heart attack, but combined with the car crash and the fact that Edward had not had a complete physical for many years, the doctors insisted he remain for testing.

Ajai knew he had to make amends and ask for his father's forgiveness. The years of his exile, as Ajai liked to remember them, had been wild years filled with racy living, self-indulgence, and taking full advantage of Edward's generous allowance. Ajai's exploits were well documented. ESPN played a lot of footage from the polo tournaments. The post-game activities that followed the game of kings and princes were just as newsworthy as the actual event. Ajai's name, usually coupled with a high profile female's name, was often mentioned. Over the years, he knew his parents had become continually upset by his scandalous behavior. Ajai never found the nerve to return home to ask for forgiveness. Ajai feared his lifestyle was unforgivable to his highly principled father.

While Edward was in the hospital, Ajai had finally summoned the courage to approach him. His father's response astounded him. Edward's generosity extended far beyond his bank account. It included complete forgiveness to his son. Edward wholeheartedly accepted Ajai's apology. He asked when and if Ajai had thought of putting in a transfer to the Duluth office. When Ajai admitted that's what he was working toward, Edward began laying out plans for Ajai to begin work in the Duluth office while he was out on sick leave. That is how Ajai ended up standing in Edward's office right now and why he felt like a complete fraud. He didn't know how to run the business, and it was obvious.

Ajai turned away from the window and walked across the room to where a portable bar was fitted against the wall next to a bookshelf. A small refrigerator held several bottles of beer and pop. Ajai selected a beer and twisted the top. The brew hissed to the surface. He had spent only five days working in the halls of Jac. E.

Ajai took a swallow of beer. The reaction from the employees to his presence was magnified by Deana Michaels' expressive face. For a split second, when she first looked at him, he glimpsed the same stark suspicion and mistrust he'd felt when meeting the rest of the employees. Oh, she was quick to hide it, but the feeling remained hidden just beneath the surface.

He hadn't expected to be welcomed, but the distrust baffled him. He was beginning to have serious doubts about his father's rapid introduction plan. It might end up doing more harm than good. Ajai rubbed the back of his neck. He drained the beer and tossed the bottle into the garbage before he crossed the room to his father's desk. Personnel files of the employees he'd met today and those he planned on being introduced to on Monday were strewn across the polished mahogany surface. Sitting on top of the pile was a file marked Michaels, D.

When he first read the file, he wasn't aware of who the file referred to. There were no pictures included. He didn't recognize the name Deana Michaels and he had no idea she was his neighbor. He never dreamed that Frank's daughter was old enough to be working here. When he'd met her at the house on Saturday, he could have sworn the girl was a gangly seventeen year old, not the woman of twenty-six he'd seen in the basement office. Ajai reached down to flip the file open. He had read it earlier before he'd known it was Deana. The file contained the familiar Jacoubi job application. There was a letter of recommendation from her professor at Duluth Business University, who recommended her to be hired before she graduated. The folder also contained a write up of an I.Q. test the company had stopped issuing because it was obsolete, and last, a standard sized envelope that contained the specifics about her degree. It told him nothing about the black-haired woman whose gray eyes shot daggers at him this afternoon. He stared at the papers, puzzled about Deana and her reaction to him, and he wondered why Frank hadn't told him she was an accountant at Jac. E.

With a sigh, he shut the file and stretched. It was late. Time to go home and forget about Deana Michaels. He straightened the files into one pile and left them on the corner of the desk before he checked his watch. His dad had plenty of time to rest after his release from the hospital. Ajai wanted to tell him about today and ask him some of the hundred questions he had about the business. Ajai locked his father's desk, pocketed the small brass key, and left the room.

12

Deana and Frank Michaels lived in the old caretaker's cottage on the northern edge of the Jacoubi estate. The Jacoubi home did not compete with the true castles of America where such notable millionaires as the Vanderbilts or the DuPonts lived. Captain Joshua Stanfield, a Michigan lumberman who followed the trail of white pine to Duluth, built this estate, surrounded by a thick grove of pine, oak and birch trees, in 1920. He built the estate as a retirement home but did not live to see the completion of the house. Captain Stanfield's wife sold it without moving in.

The Jacoubi brothers bought the mansion. They were businessmen from the East Coast who moved their families to the Great Lakes looking for adventure and business opportunities. They arrived on the Great Lakes in time for the explosion of industry, shipping, lumber, iron ore, and architecture.

The architecture of the mansion was classic Georgian in mellow gold brick. Along the north side of the compound stood the stable with 60 stalls, and a number of paddocks surrounding it. In the stable, Chip Davies supervised a string of thoroughbreds, racing quarter horses and a donkey named Elvis. There was an outdoor pool, only used in the summer months of late July, August and sometimes September; Tennis courts and a genuine Finnish outdoor stand-alone sauna resided on one side of the impressive estate. A full-sized polo field had been installed at the back of the property, but nine years ago Edward had it dismantled. It was now a part of the expansive, well-tailored garden and lawn. The entire property portrayed a charming simplistic elegance.

"Beautiful," Deana said with a sigh. From her vantage point on Jacoubi ridge, the entire estate spread out before her, looking like a nugget of gold in the Kelly green background. Journey, impatient to be off across the rolling hills in front of him, snorted, pulled at the bit and tossed his head, "Alright, alright," Deana laughed and took one last look at the scene as it sprawled across the valley. Purple, pink and orange from the sunrise colored the clouds. She never tired of the sunrise over the Jacoubi house.

She touched the reins to Journey's neck and sent him at a run down the sloping hill. The sharp early morning air cleared her mind and set her blood racing. She leaned into the warmth of the horse's neck and urged him on. They raced the length of the ridge at the back of the Jacoubi estate. The bank of the small creek appeared in front of them. Deana felt Journey tense as they sailed over the obstacle and continued at the same headlong pace on the other side. Until they reached the end of the clearing, the pace did not slow. Deana pulled back on the reins firmly. The horse obeyed and lowered his head to eat a meal of sweet grass. For years they had been riding this same route, always stopping to take a breather and one last look at the house

Against the dark trunks of the pine trees surrounding Jacoubi's property, there was a flash of red. Deana stared, trying to discern what it could be when the sound of pounding hooves drifted across the field. She watched a horse and rider gallop up the rocky flank of Jacoubi ridge where she never dared to ride. The loose gravel and jutting boulders made it too dangerous. This rider did not seem to care about the danger. Suddenly, when the horse and rider were hidden from view by the trees, Deana realized who the rider was. Ajai. He's an idiot! She thought, even though she had to admire his guts and skill.

Journey's head lifted when the wind brought scent of the approaching horse.

"Some Indian horse you turned out to be," Deana said crossly when Ajai came into view. Oh great, here I am, a sitting duck trespassing on his property, she thought, chastising herself for her poor judgment. After the last meeting they had, she was sure Ajai would either be coy about her trespassing or demand she leave. Either way she didn't like the idea of being caught again by the man. It was too late for her to try and high-tail it back home across the trampled fence that led to her house. Ajai already knew she was here. He was heading directly toward her.

"Good morning." His voice carried across the remaining empty space between them.

Deana lifted her hand in greeting.

Ajai rode the chestnut gelding within a few feet of where Journey stood. "That's quite a climb," he said, out of breath.

"I'm surprised you rode it."

"Why? There's a trail. It's steep but climbable."

Deana did not answer. She was looking over the horse. "Is that the gelding from the auction?"

Ajai nodded. He reached down to slap the hard shoulder of the big animal. "Chip was right about him. He was so full of worms, the poor thing was miserable. Once we flushed him out with de-worming medicine and gave him some decent feed, he settled right down. He's strong. That hill didn't even make him breathe heavy."

Deana was impressed, "Chip told you to buy him?"

Ajai laughed, the sound echoing off the valley below them. "No, Chip said I was still a crazy fool. He wasn't going to break his back trying to settle him down. But he sure knew what was wrong with him."

Deana smiled, "I'm so glad you bought him." She tried to keep her tone composed. She did not want to start gushing. He was probably neck deep in gushing females who were after his attention. "All the gelding needed was a second chance and you've given it to him when nobody else would."

Ajai looked toward the mansion. He murmured to himself, "A lot of people would give their right arm to get a second chance with no strings attached, like what my father did for me." He looked at his mount, then added, "I never thought of this horse like that. Maybe I should call him Chance."

"You don't have a name for him yet?"

Ajai shrugged, "I don't usually name the horses I use playing polo. With switching mounts after each checker, it's too hard to keep track."

Deana's eyes flew to his face, "I've never heard of anyone not naming their horses. Do you name any other animals you keep as pets?"

Ajai chuckled, "I don't have any pets. My horses work for me, they're like employees. Of course, this horse won't be."

"Won't what?"

"Worry about working. He's not a polo horse. I doubt I'll use him for anything except pleasure riding."

A sharp note crept into Deana's voice, "Oh, so it's okay to give him another name, I mean, besides just horse."

"Actually, I usually call every horse I ride, boy,"

"You have a fifty-fifty chance of getting that right, and I know for a fact that Chip has names for all the horses in the stables." Deana's angry comment drew his full attention.

He grinned at her, his face alight with amusement. "You sound angry with me."

Deana tore her eyes away from his handsome face and said with a touch of haughtiness, "Don't be ridiculous. I hardly believe the few sentences we've said to each other give me the right to be angry with you."

Ajai laughed. He moved the horse closer to her, "You're angry with me anyway. Why?"

Bristling at his tone, Deana blurted out, "Okay you're right. I am. It's the way you talk. You have everything, but you don't take any joy in it. You buy a horse on a whim. Did you even realize you saved him from the meat man? Look at this place you live in. It's paradise. I've ridden this area all my life. I've never grown tired of looking at it for just pure enjoyment. Did you even bother to take a look at that sunrise?"

Ajai stared at her.

Deana lowered her eyes, feeling her face flame with embarrassment. She had obviously once again blurted out thoughts that made no sense. Why couldn't she learn to keep her mouth shut?

"How do you do it?"

She jerked her head to look at him, "Do what?"

"How do you feel such emotion about a sunrise when you've seen the exact same thing so many times before?"

Deana forgot her irritation with him and looked across the field at the ball of glowing yellow and a pale blue sky stretching across the horizon. Her voice softened, "I don't know what you mean. I've never seen the exact same sunrise, ever. How could there be? I've always believed that nothing in God's world can be duplicated. You know, like snowflakes are never exactly the same."

"I guess I never thought about it."

Deana laughed, "Of course you've thought about it. You just forgot. What kid doesn't lie on his back and watch the clouds, trying to figure out the different shapes? Never do you see the same cloud formation twice. I've tried."

"If I ever did, you're right, I don't remember. What are you doing out here riding at sunrise on a Saturday? Isn't this the only day for a working stiff to sleep in?"

Was this a subtle hint on his part to remind Deana that she was trespassing? She shifted her seat in the saddle and lifted the reins to pull Journey's nose out of the grass. She glanced at him and then away, "I guess it depends on how important sleep is to a person. I must be going. I've been trespassing long enough." Deana turned Journey toward the path leading home and trotted away.

Ajai watched her, holding a tight rein on his horse to keep him at a stand still. "Why does she keep taking off like that?" He muttered out loud, "Like a cowboy in a movie she rides off into the sunrise."

13

Deana walked through the heavy steel security doors into the hallway with its gleaming tile floor. There wasn't a sound except for her own footsteps to greet her. This morning she was running late and was irritated with herself. For some silly reason, she spent twice as long getting her hair and make-up ready before leaving the house. The only possible explanation was because Ajai was going to be a permanent fixture at Jacoubi Enterprises.

While in front of the bathroom mirror, she worked on applying her eye shadow, arguing with her self, "What I look like makes no difference," She said to her reflection. "I won't see Ajai at work. It was different to meet him at home or in his own back yard, a surprise, but understandable. I'm sure it won't happen again."

Deana walked swiftly past the offices with closed doors and then Genie's office.

"Hey!" Genie yelled at her, "Where are you going in such a hurry?"

Deana did not stop for Genie, whose disembodied head and neck appeared around the frame of the door. Deana called, "Sorry, I'm running late. Talk to you at break."

Genie yelled back, "See yah then."

Deana unlocked her office door and hurried inside reaching for the light switch and then hurrying over to her computer. She reprimanded herself, "Pull your self together, girl. Ajai is not lurking around every corner in this building."

The hours of the morning flew by. When the hand of the clock showed eleven, Genie walked into Deana's office. "Good morning," she said standing in the doorway. "I'm sick of sitting in your office every day. Let's head upstairs for coffee today."

Deana stood and reached inside her desk drawer for her purse. She gave Genie a suspicious look, "Why, some new guy ask you out?"

"No, but if one wants to, I'd hate to deprive him of the opportunity."

The two girls walked down the empty hallway toward the elevator. Genie's voice had the amazing capacity to carry in the hollow basement corridor. "You know, if I'd known how isolated my office was when I took the job in accounting, I'd have thought twice about accepting the offer. I'm sure if I'd have applied to other places, I'd have an office with a view and at least there would be other people walking around. This place is a tomb."

"And it has been for the past nine months, so why whine about it now?"

Genie did not answer as they stood in front of the elevator waiting. "See how long we're expected to wait for an elevator? Lucky the coffee shop isn't in the cafeteria on the ninth floor. Our break will have ended before we even get there."

"Okay Genie what's up? We decided a long time ago to have coffee down here because it took too long for the elevator. Of course, we can walk up the four flights of stairs if you like. As a matter of fact I could use the exercise." Deana said with a move for the stairwell door.

Genie sniffed indignantly at her. She stuck her foot out, "In these shoes I'm lucky I can walk from my car to my office."

Deana nodded, "I thought so. When are you going to tell me who the latest would-be conquest is?"

Genie waited for the elevator doors to clamp shut before she said, "Did you see our new boss on television last night?"

Deana shook her head no.

"Well, he announced that his father is leaving the hospital to finish his recovery at home."

A look of relief spread across Deana's face, "I did hear that on TV Saturday morning. What a relief for the family."

"I guess you were right. Ajai won't be working here very long, so if I want to get to know him, I'll have to move fast."

Deana gave her a sharp look, "Ajai? He's the new conquest?"

Genie nodded. "Why not, it was obvious we connected the other day."

Deana's gray eyes widened.

"Well, he did know my name. What have I got to lose?"

The light on the panel flashed the number three in orange. Deana said with a sigh, "This is why we're going to the coffee shop today. You're hoping to see Ajai?"

Genie tossed her tightly curled hair as she declared brightly, "Of course."

The doors slid open to reveal the Patio Coffee Shop, an open room filled with sunlight flooding in through the tinted glass atrium ceiling. Trees of different types from palms to orange trees that sprouted small oranges all year round, were set in strategic positions to give the effect of being outdoors. Despite the coffee shop's large dimensions to house the three hundred plus employees of Jacoubi Enterprises, the Patio was a charming restaurant. Deana enjoyed eating in here, especially on sunny days in the winter. The plants gave off a rich smell of moist dirt.

They were dismayed to see that most of the tables and chairs were already taken. People stood around chatting and drinking everything from latte to Gatorade.

Genie cried out suddenly and grabbed Deana's arm, "Over there I see a couple of open seats, come on."

Deana followed Genie's weaving path through the café style chairs until they reached a table with two women already seated. There were two empty chairs. They looked up at Deana and Genie expectantly.

Deana smiled, "Excuse us. Are these taken?"

The redhead smiled back. Deana recognized her. They had been hired here at about the same time and both attended the same school, though they had only met occasionally since then. "I guess our friends are a no-show so help your selves."

Genie sank into the seat, "Thanks, that sprint over here just about did me in."

Deana remained standing and shot Genie an indignant look, "I'll get the coffee then."

When Deana returned, Genie was busy talking and the other two women were leaning across the table to listen. The conversation obviously intrigued them and Deana did not have to search her mind to figure out what it centered on—the new boss.

The redhead confirmed Deana's suspicions by blurting out as soon as Deana sat down, "The new Jacoubi came to your office?"

Deana gave Genie a sharp glance and a short nod, "I guess from what he said, he plans on visiting each floor and talking to as many of the employees as he can."

The brunette wearing fashionable wire-framed glasses said with a snicker, "Wow, that could take years."

The redhead agreed giving a quick bird-like nod, "Maybe that's what he wants."

Genie stared at her then turned to Deana, "What do you think? Is Ajai trying to worm his way into Jac E?"

Deana, thinking fast, frowned. If she denied any knowledge about Ajai then Genie might argue and take this moment to point out how Deana knew the boss. No matter, the gossips were going to say whatever they wanted anyway. "I have no idea." Deana said with a negligent shrug and deliberately picked up her cup.

The brunette leaned forward and said in a conspiratorial tone "Well, I think he wants to get a foot in the business now that he has the chance. You know, with his dad sick and out of the picture. That way when Mr. Jacoubi Senior does come back, the son is already settled into the business. Then I bet he refuses to leave. Makes sense doesn't it? Why else would he want to be seen by all the employees? He's hoping to win our loyalty away from his dad. It's called a hostile take-over."

Deana almost choked.

Genie piped up excitedly, "You know, I heard the Senior Jacoubi disowned Ajai for all that trouble he got into when he was younger. Maybe the only way he can get his inheritance is to take over."

The redhead spoke up with a confident voice, "I for one, will follow the son. He's young and he's going to be here for a lot longer than Senior."

Genie said with a giggle, "Besides being drop dead gorgeous."

The three burst out laughing while Deana watched them in total disbelief.

"This is absolutely the most absurd conversation I have ever heard!" Deana said, "You guys are making up a Hollywood murder mystery and believing every word. His father never disowned Ajai. Edward Jacoubi is as strong as a horse and basically a young man at sixty four, and you think because he had an accident and ended up in the hospital for awhile Ajai's going to steal his business out from under him? I cannot believe you are that..." A word that would not completely offend refused to come to mind so Deana snapped her mouth shut and pushed her chair back to jump to her feet. She added with a glare at all three of the young women, "I can't sit here and listen to such blatant lies. I certainly hope all of you forget what you were just spouting because those are pretty nasty things to say about anybody, especially about people you don't even know." Deana turned away in disgust and hurried for the door.

14

The solid door slammed behind her, echoing up the empty stairwell. The instant the sound faded, Deana realized she had forgotten her purse at the table. With a frustrated groan, she muttered, "No way am I going back in there." Deana hesitated and wondered what the chances were that Genie might see the bag hanging on the back of her chair and bring it to her. "With that girl, who knows?"

Nervously, Deana paced the stairwell. She did not want to go in there and face that group now. She had no idea what Genie was telling her captive audience.

"Hello? Talking to yourself?"

Deana glanced up the stairs to see Ajai looking down over the railing. "Why, no… I mean yes, I was just rehearsing something,"

Ajai quickly walked down the rest of the steps until he was in front of her. "Rehearsing what?"

Deana was not a convincing liar, and she did not like to mislead people. With reluctance she admitted, "I forgot my purse in there and now I have to go and get it."

Ajai nodded with an exaggerated expression of wisdom on his face. He said solemnly, "I see."

Deana snapped, "You do not. That sounded utterly ridiculous, even to me."

Ajai looked surprised, "Not really. There are people in there you don't want to see and they are sitting in the exact spot where the forgotten purse is and you don't want to talk to them again when you retrieve your purse. The problem is the purse is too important. Someone may not return it if you chicken out and don't go back in there."

Deana was shocked at his perception. She added to it, "Besides, my office is locked and the keys are in it."

Ajai grinned, "That makes it all the more of a dilemma. I suggest you wait out here for a few more moments and the coffee shop will pretty much have cleared out. The unwanted group might have too."

Deana frowned. "And how do you know that?"

"Elementary, my dear. Coffee break is over." He stepped over to the door and opened it and he was right. They watched as the room slowly emptied. A few people walked past them to use the stairs and the others were lined up at the elevators waiting.

Deana glanced at Ajai and could not help laughing, "You are a prophet."

Ajai held the door open for her to pass through. Deana gave a quick look in the direction of the table where she had been sitting and was relieved to see none of the women were still there. She was not in the mood to explain Ajai's presence to anyone, especially not to Genie, "Thank you." She said as she hurried away from him hoping he would go away.

Ajai kept in step with her. At her inquiring look he shrugged, "What if your purse is missing? Maybe I can help find the criminals."

"I don't think there are any criminals here," Deana said as she edged through the chairs. "See? There it is, right where I left it. Is that something someone could do in Minneapolis? I think not." Deana grabbed the strap of her purse and slipped it over her shoulder.

Ajai, with his hands in his pockets, watched the elevators as a group of dark-suited men carrying briefcases emerged. He glanced at Deana, "I'm glad you found it. Are you taking the elevator or walking downstairs?'

Deana thought Ajai looked nervous when he saw the six men. They remained in front of the elevator in a cluster talking. She wondered who they were. "Um, I'm walking down the stairs. Thanks again." She said, ready to move away.

Ajai abruptly turned to her. He grabbed the back of the

chair in front of her that was blocking the aisle and set it into place at the table, "I'll walk you back to the stairs."

"Really, you don't have to bother. I'm sure you must be busy."

He said, "Nothing I can't gladly put off."

Deana searched her mind for something to say that did not sound idiotic like the rest of her conversations. She blurted out, "I was so glad to hear your father returned home. You must be so pleased."

Ajai gave a heavy sigh, "I wish he was here with me right now, more than you can know."

Deana thought she must be imagining the husky tone of regret she heard in his voice. Before she could say anything more, he opened the door to the stairs and said with his usual carefree grin, "See you."

As the door swung shut, Deana remembered to say a hasty, "Thanks."

She whirled around and almost fell off the top step. Grabbing the rail, she cried, "Oh, why do I have to sound like such a ninny whenever I see him?" Then she remembered that her conversation earlier had been overheard and did not want it to happen again. Without stopping, she ran down the four flights of stairs. When she reached the bottom, she was out of breath, so she waited before stepping brisklydown the hall past Genie's office until she reached her own. As no commentary came from Genie's office, Deana figured Genie must want to remain silent and hidden. Deana quickly unlocked her door and shut it behind her.

What am I doing? First I defend Ajai in front of the biggest gossips in the building and then I run into him on the stairs. If Genie had seen us together it would have blown her away. Deana still did not know whether to laugh or scream. Suddenly, her world was beginning to resemble a circus. She leaned back against the door and began to laugh. He's funny, she thought. For some reason I never knew he was funny...

and he's… charming. Of course he's charming.

She crossed to her desk, recalling the charismatic Ajai of her youth. What am I thinking? He's renowned for his devastating charm. He has women falling all over him whenever he wants. What a dope I am. The first time the guy smiles at me, I'm falling a part. Well, if Ajai thinks I'm going to be another one of his casual flirtations, he's wrong. I'm determined to completely avoid him. That man is way more trouble than I can handle.

15

Deana watched the rebroadcast of Edward Jacoubi's hospital release on the six o'clock news. Ajai was there with Edward and his mother. Deana watched the little family on the screen and thought they looked like a fine example of a functional family, at least from this news clip. What really went on in the Jacoubi's home, she had no idea. Mrs. Jacoubi looked small next to her son, but Deana had never personally met her. She had glimpsed Edward at Jacoubi Enterprises on several occasions, and he reminded her of an older Ajai.

Dreaming about the Jacoubi family was nothing new for Deana. As a child, many times, she pretended to be a part of their family. To be a member of a rich, popular family who seemed to have no problems, was much more satisfying than being Deana Michaels. At home, her mother was beginning to visibly succumb to cancer. Deana did not have any idea how sick Colleen really was because her parents refused to discuss it with their daughter. Not until her father was forced to take a leave of absence from his teaching job to tend to Colleen did Deana fully realize her mother was dying.

Her father's study had been changed into a bedroom. It was on the first floor and the sun streaming through the bay windows kept the room warm during the afternoon. It was warmer than any other room in the drafty old house. Deana divided her time after school between keeping her mother company, doing homework and chores. Colleen read to her in a voice that became weak and wispy. Then Deana took over and read to Colleen.

Deana witnessed her mother slip further away from this life and into a peace only the virtuous and unselfish are allowed to enter. In the dim light of morning with only her husband at her side, holding Frank's hand, Colleen Michaels died as quietly as she lived.

Deana survived the final phases of her mother's death with a child's resilience. After her mother's death, the financial walls of the Michaels' world crashed. Terribly high medical bills had been piling up since her mother became sick. Frank was in shock and failed to remember things like the electricity bill and heat bill. Deana soon learned to collect the bills and help him keep track of when they were due.

When Frank reapplied for work, he found the district overrun with teachers. His only option was to start all over and begin substituting until a full-time position opened. For many years, the finances were a constant worry. Deana came close to selling Journey. The feed and upkeep of a horse was too costly. Deana went to Chip Davies at Jacoubi's stable to see if he was looking to buy any additional horses. Chip had a much different idea of what should be done and offered Deana a job. Eagerly, she agreed. The work was unimportant as long as it was with the horses. Deana learned that Chip had arranged for Journey to be moved over to the Jacoubi's stable. The deal included Journey's board. Deana thought she was in heaven. The heavy weight of guilt she felt about keeping the horse was lifted. She worked after school and weekends to keep up her end of the bargain.

Eventually Frank returned to full-time teaching, but Deana continued to work for Jacoubi Stables. She felt the satisfaction of earning money and helping Frank work their way out of the massive mountain of medical debt. Deana did not forget the lean years. She still gave her father half of her paychecks for the upkeep of the big old house and used the rest for her car and her horse.

16

The heat of the sun felt almost too hot. Deana silently watched the gray water of the lake from the top level of the parking ramp connected to Jacoubi Enterprises, while sipping from a bottle of Coke. "The sailboat races start next week," said Genie.

"I can't wait. The spinnakers look so beautiful when all of them are out there at the same time," Deana said eagerly. She turned from the wall and walked back to where Genie had a lounge chair set out next to her car. She was sunbathing fully clothed or as fully clothed as Genie ever was. Her arms, long legs and bare feet angled to catch the most sunrays.

"Your make-up is beginning to melt," Deana commented, taking a paper bag off the hood of Genie's beat up Buick.

Genie laughed, "You know me, I carry my entire make-up collection in my purse. I'll fix it later. One nice thing about working in the basement is we have that big bathroom all to ourselves. I just wish they'd installed a shower. Think of how much money I'd save if I could shower at work."

Deana grimaced when she imagined what damage Genie was probably capable of inflicting on a bathroom. She opened Genie's lunch bag to see if anything inside looked more appetizing than her lunch had been. A plastic container of yogurt was the only thing inside. "You don't have a spoon."

Genie looked at her, "Huh?"

"How do you expect to eat soupy yogurt without a spoon?"

Genie frowned, "I keep packing very little in my lunch hoping that Mr. Ajai Jacoubi will be asking me out to lunch one day soon."

Deana held her breath and then asked, "Has he?"

Genie scoffed, "I haven't seen him all week. I wasted my new spring wardrobe for nothing. I'm going to have to wear the same things next week. Two weeks and I've heard he hasn't stepped foot in the building. Do you think he chickened out and skipped town again? It seems that he's been doing that kind of thing all his life."

Deana added without thinking, "Not all his life, just since he became an adult."

"Really, how do you know that?"

"The same way you know he runs away from responsibility. It's too hot out here. I'm going in. See you later." Deana grabbed her things and walked away.

Deana flung her dark blue suit coat over her shoulder enjoying the coolness of the shadowed halls after the heat. The clock showed there was still a half hour of lunch break left. She walked to her office anyway, thinking, I might as well finish and go home early.

Deana draped the coat across the back of her chair and sat down. She touched the mouse pad and punched in her security code. The screen instantly filled with data. Deana stared at it for a moment. A movement in the hallway suddenly broke the silence of the room. A quick glance at the door showed nothing in sight. Her eyes moved back to the screen. Something just did not seem right. It was the third time this month the billing was low, much lower than she ever remembered.

"Hello, Deana," a tired voice said from the doorway.

Deana did not scream though she was startled enough. Slowly she stood, staring at Ajai. He sounded tired and he looked it. "Uh, hello," she finally said.

Ajai walked in the room and sat down in the chair across from her desk as if he'd done the same thing a thousand times before. Deana, dumbfounded by his unexpected appearance, stared at him. They stared at each other for a moment.

She asked, "Where have you been?"

Ajai grinned, "Why, that sounds like you've missed me, Miss Michaels."

Deana frowned and shook her head.

Disappointment crossed Ajai's face and he said, "I didn't think so. I've been down in the Cities. I had some unfinished business."

Deana suddenly wondered what she looked like. After being outside in the heat and the lake wind, she must look a mess.

"Why are you working through lunch? Or are you still avoiding The Patio?"

Deana smiled at the thought of their last meeting, "No, all is reconciled."

He nodded his head in approval, "Good, can I take you to lunch?"

"I've already eaten... thank you."

Ajai stretched his legs out and folded his hands in his lap, "So fast? It couldn't have been very much. You aren't doing something stupid like dieting?"

"Absolutely not,"

"You certainly don't need too. How about supper? Can I take you to supper tonight?"

Deana gaped at him. She searched his face suspecting he was teasing her.

With an expectant look, Ajai leaned forward. "You do plan to eat supper? I know a great place on London Road. Please, Deana have dinner with me or I'm doomed to dine alone."

Deana could not think of an answer. She looked at him again. He flashed a smile that reminded her of all the paparazzi pictures she had seen in the magazines and newspapers. He was doing it again, trying to charm her into doing something she did not want to do. His words and actions were so polished and smooth. She knew he must have used the same line many times before. "I have to feed my father." It sounded to her like Frank was a dog. With pink cheeks, she amended it to, "I mean fix dinner for my father."

Ajai shrugged, "No problem, invite him to meet us." He pushed the phone closer to her.

Deana remained motionless. She stared at the phone like she'd never seen one before. What was she supposed to do? This wasn't supposed to happen to her. Genie was the one who expected an invitation from Ajai. Why was he sitting here asking her?

"Perhaps I should call?"

"No!" She exclaimed.

"Perhaps you have another reason for not wanting to have supper with me?"

Deana's mind raced, searching frantically for some excuse. She did not want to go out with Ajai, even if her father went with them.

"This wouldn't be a date, Deana. I don't want to step on anyone's toes."

The time to invent a boyfriend would be now, but not a single name came to mind. Deana reluctantly shook her head, "I'll call my father."

Ajai leaned back in the chair and closed his eyes.

She watched him discreetly as she reached for the phone. He looked tired. Circles around his eyes made him look defenseless. His skin, for once, was not the bronze color Deana was used to seeing. He said slowly, "Ask him to meet us at the Bellows on London Road about five thirty." His eyes widened, catching Deana staring at him. They twinkled when he added with a silky tone, "Will you need a ride?"

Deana hastily shook her head no again, "I have my own car. I'll drive myself."

Ajai raised his eyebrows, "Of course, we could always stop back here to pick it up afterward, but no, I can see that won't do. Why don't you like me, Deana?"

Deana narrowed her eyes. Had she heard him right? "What?"

"You don't like me, admit it. I'd like to know why, when we don't really know each other yet. I have a feeling you didn't like me even before we met."

Deana's gray eyes widened in horror, "Of course that's not true. I'd have to be an idiot to dislike... my boss."

"Is that what I am, your boss? I'm not your neighbor? Or a friend of your father's? I'm the boss? Well, I can't argue that, though I've only been working here for a few weeks. That still doesn't explain why you didn't like me before."

Ajai stood and looked at her for a moment before turning away. He added in a pensive tone, "Well, I guess I'll have to be satisfied with that explanation, at least until later."

Deana watched him leave and shook her head at her own stupidity. Where was her cool self-control? For some reason, he brought out the worst in her. With a frustrated sigh, Deana sat staring into space until finally she dialed her father's number.

17

Deana drove slowly along the congested street watching for the restaurant sign and wondering if she missed the turn. She had told Ajai she knew the restaurant, which was true, but she had never actually been there. Suddenly, the sign was right next to her. Without time for her blinker, she pulled into the driveway with more haste than caution. Already late, she saw the time on the car clock said five-fifty. She'd stopped in the ladies room at work fiddling with her hair and make-up. She debated asking Genie for the use of some of her cosmetics, but decided that explaining would be way too much trouble.

"Besides, what does it matter? He's already seen me today," She argued out loud with her self as she found a parking place. Locking the car door, she hurried up the red-carpeted stairs and into the building. When she asked the hostess if Ajai was there, she was told, "No, but he has a reservation if you'd like to wait at the table."

Deana said a hasty no and sat down on the little bench to look around the entry area. From outside, the building was octagonal. The main building had long windows facing the lake and, from where she sat, she could see the dining area. Soft candlelight glowed from the crystal centerpieces on each table. The seating created intimacy whether it was wanted or not. Deana sighed and looked away. This meal was going to be much worse than she imagined. Frank could have saved her from this situation, but he refused. At times that man was so stubborn. She still did not understand why he thought she needed to get to know Ajai. She tried everything to get Frank here for dinner. Cajoling did not work, and she finally broke down and demanded outright that he do it. Nothing worked.

Frank's advice across the phone line had been clear, "This

is the perfect opportunity for you to get acquainted with Ajai. Instead of having to continue to believe all that nonsense the media prints about him, you'll be on even ground. You work together, you both enjoy horse back riding, I'm sure you'll have a lot to talk about." At the thought of her father's faulty logic, Deana ground her teeth in frustration. She looked around the waiting room. There was still time to just forget about the dinner and go home.

Somehow she could not do it. He already blatantly accused her of disliking him. Standing Ajai up, though tempting, might be going too far. How long could it take to eat dinner in a restaurant?

Deana silently watched as business people filed past the hostess stand and walked through the etched glass doors that led into the adjoining bar. She heard the sound of televisions blaring and laughter. That kind of noise was much preferable to the atmosphere of the dining room.

Ajai rushed in, "Sorry to keep you waiting." He slipped his jacket off.

Deana anxiously jumped to her feet and faced him.

Ajai barely looked at her, his distracted smile was the only change in his expression. "If you're ready, shall we go in?"

Holding two menus, the hostess watched them.

"Of course," Deana hastily agreed. Anything to get this over with, she thought.

The hostess, after giving Ajai the once over, led them across the restaurant to a table with an expansive view of the gray water and in the distance, the Aerial Lift Bridge.

"Is this table acceptable, sir?"

Ajai grinned, "More than acceptable, thank you. Will you please send a bottle of Chardonnay, preferably from one of the wineries in this area?"

The hostess nodded and hurried away.

Deana sat for a moment and then asked, "Why from a winery around here?"

Ajai shrugged and opened the menu, "It's better to support local people if at all possible. I was shocked to find out there's a winery as close as Carlton."

Deana nodded, though she felt his enthusiasm was a bit misguided, considering the precarious nature of the economy.

Ajai looked up from the menu at her. He said with a glimmer of a smile, "My father has always preached that supporting local businesses is important and I think the look I used to give him is the same expression as the one on your face right now."

Deana quickly tried to compose her features. "What's that supposed to mean?"

"Dad has always kept a certain number of employees working full time at Jacoubi. He believes that to keep a city in top form the local businesses need to hire the local work force. There is no better way to stimulate a local economy, even if it means keeping the profit level down."

Deana put her menu down to lean forward with interest. She interjected "That's a noble ideal."

"Very noble, too noble for an eighteen year old who wants to have a new sports car and any other toy that strikes his fancy. Only now am I able to appreciate exactly what my father was describing."

"And, from what I learned at college, when the economy is tight, a noble ideal lowers the profit margin by quite a lot."

Ajai hesitated. He glanced down at the table and then looked at her. "I wanted to ask you about something… if you aren't comfortable confiding in me, of course I will understand."

Deana felt a rush of cold anxiety run through her veins.

"Deana, I've been looking at the figures from the past year. Do you have anything to do with the outsourced services budgets?"

Deana shook her head even as she spoke, "Mr. Bascomb handles that."

"It seems that we're hiring outside businesses to do jobs that our employees used to do. Has anything ever been said about this?"

Deana searched his face and detected nothing dishonest in his concern. She frowned, "I'm sorry, Ajai. I don't know anything about it. The accounting department has been divided, so we basically don't have any idea what's going on with the business as a whole." She looked out the window and said, "My father did comment that when your father went into the hospital the stock took a dramatic dip. Of course, it's stabilized now."

Ajai gave a thin smile, "It's probably not important. Let's drop the business stuff. You haven't even looked at the menu and I think this might be our wine the waitress is carrying."

In an instant, gone was the concerned businessman. Ajai transformed into the charming man Deana recognized. She looked down at the menu and fiercely concentrated on reading the selections while Ajai spoke with the waitress. Was this why Ajai asked her to dine with him? To discuss business? She refused to mull over the brief but disturbing conversation. At least now she had a reasonable explanation of why Ajai unexpectedly showed up in her office and extended this astonishing invitation to supper. Nothing but work was on his mind. Deana did not know whether she should be insulted or relieved.

18

As the meal progressed, Deana experienced first hand what an entertaining host Ajai was. He kept the conversation light and enjoyable by asking Deana the right amount of questions. Before she fully realized how much time had passed, the waitress was ready to clear their plates.

"Would you care for dessert, or an after dinner drink?"

Deana looked away from Ajai. She remembered with a start exactly who he was and how dangerous it was for her peace of mind to spend time with him. Abruptly she stood, startling Ajai and the waitress. She exclaimed, "Look at the time. I really have to go."

Ajai turned to the waitress. "Could you give us a minute, please?" When she walked away he asked in a pleasant voice, "What's the problem?"

Deana, poised for flight, hesitated. She noticed how, even when he was clearly caught by surprise, he exuded self-confidence. Unnerved, she moved woodenly to look at her wristwatch, "It's late… later than I thought. I have to go."

Ajai stood next to her, reaching for her hand. He held it loosely, his fingers resting on her wrist, where her pulse pounded, "Please sit down for another minute. Why do you always have to rush off?"

Deana snatched her hand away and glanced around the room. While seated in the booth, she hadn't noticed that customers had filled the room. She knew the restaurant was set-up for intimacy, but she had been so engrossed in their conversation, she hadn't noticed any of the activity going on around her. Her irritation grew at how easy she made it for Ajai to manipulate her. Slowly, she sank back onto the seat. "How do you do it?" she asked him.

While re-taking his seat, Ajai gave her a slow look, "Do what?"

She gave a short laugh, "You're so accomplished you don't even realize what you're doing? Can I ask one thing?" Deana didn't wait for him to answer, "Why, me? Why are you wasting this... this seduction scene on me?"

"Is that what I'm doing? Trying to do seduce you?"

"Maybe not at first, but that's how it looks now." She waved her hand around the dimly lit interior, romantically glowing with the soft glow of candlelight. The dark silhouettes of other couples seated at the booths created a 1940s movie set appearance.

He chuckled, "It's a nice restaurant with good food. I didn't mean anything by choosing it. Is this why you hate me?"

"I don't hate you. I don't hate anybody."

Ajai leaned against the wing back of the booth to ask, "Then why are you so defensive?"

Deana nervously fidgeted, feeling the strain of his directness. How could she explain what she didn't even understand? "I... I guess, I don't know you well enough to speak so frankly."

Ajai shook his head, "Oh no, you can't get off with that lame excuse. I'm giving you permission to speak as frankly as you like. Come on. Lay it all out."

Deana picked up the cloth napkin and twisted it while her thoughts raced. Finally she spoke, her voice hesitant, "You're so used to having women fall at your feet. You're not interested in me as a person. Sometime tonight you forgot who I am. I'm not a pampered high society woman. I'm the girl who lives in a rundown house next to your mansion. I don't need special bottles of wine brought to the table. You really should try to remember you're back in Duluth, and most of the people who live here aren't immersed in their own importance."

Ajai ran his finger around the lip of the crystal wine glass while he watched her with a speculative look on his face. He said, "If I didn't know better, I'd think you were being a snob."

Deana's mouth dropped open and she squeaked, "Me? A snob? Hardly."

"You think that just because you live in a broken-down house that you can't be a snob?"

She snapped, "I'm not the kind of woman you're used to being with."

"That's not what I'm talking about. Nobody says you have to be high society. I've met people in very high places who were truly genuine and I've met people of very humble circumstances who are snobs. There's such a thing as reverse snobbery."

"Like who? Just who are these virtuous people?"

"One is a friend of mine from Spain. Alberto Casilda. And my parents, and the other you know very well, your father."

Deana's gaze fell to the tabletop. She suddenly found interest in the crumbs scattered across the hunter green cloth. Heat filled her cheeks. "I didn't mean to sound that way. I can assure you I'm not a snob."

Ajai looked amused, "I learned in a college psych class that snobbery's roots is prejudice. Everybody has their prejudices, we're all are plagued with some form of snobbery."

Deana jumped to her feet. She tossed the napkin back onto the bench before reaching for her purse. She snapped, "I've never understood all that psychology double talk. I just know that, with some people, a slight knowledge of psychology seems to give them the ability to twist anything a person says or does to fit into a convenient profile."

"Deana, I am certainly in no position to judge anyone."

"You're so... so overconfident, and I find that extremely irritating."

Ajai lifted an expressive eyebrow, "Hmm, so you don't hate me, you merely find me irritating. I'd say we've made some positive strides tonight."

Deana stared at him aghast. "Is there no end to your good opinion of yourself? I give up. It's like talking to a wall." She spun around and stopped herself just before she nearly knocked into a waitress carrying an overburdened tray. "Excuse me," Deana cried, flustered beyond feeling any shame. Hastily, she rushed out of the restaurant as the startled patrons watched.

19

Thunder crashed outside as a gust of wind blew rain drops through the open window fluttering the sheer yellow curtains next to Deana's bed. Deana sat up threw the covers off and reached over to pull the window closed.

The gloom outside made it easy for her to fall back on the warm pillow and pull the covers up over her head. Only minutes went by when the shriek of the alarm next to her ear sounded. "No," she groaned, "It can't be six o'clock already."

The sheets and the air were damp. It was a miserable day, but a working one. Deana pulled her jeans and sweatshirt on and left for the barn. Journey needed to be fed before she got ready for work.

Once outside, she slipped through the mud to the hay shed with Journey following on her heels. She fell twice. Then she dropped the hose and the spray caught her in the face. She rushed back into the house to get showered and changed for work.

Deana parked her car in the ramp at Jacoubi. The only spaces open were on the uppermost floor. She sat inside her car watching the downpour of rain. She had little hope that it would slow down enough to allow her to run into the building. After wearing her raincoat in the stable this morning, she left the filthy thing at home. With a cursory look through the back seat of her car she realized her umbrella must be in the barn too. With no raincoat or umbrella, she took a deep breath and made a break for it. Slowly she opened the door wide enough to stick her legs out and then, holding her purse under her suit jacket, she jumped out, slammed the door and ran.

She ran under the cement beam over the entryway of the

stairs as a gust of wind off the lake sent a sheet of icy rainwater on top of her head. "Ugh," Deana cried, ducking through the door. Shivering inside the glass-protected stairway, she brushed her coat off. Water dripped down her face and under her collar. The water seeped through her linen shirt. It was difficult for her to face the day soaked to the skin, but right now she had to get downstairs. Feeling the pressure of work and her personal life, she promised herself she would leave for home as soon as the morning work was done. She hurried down the stairs to her office.

The radiators that lined the hallway made it warmer than the stairs. In Duluth, even late spring was not the time to turn off the heat. Deana stopped under the heating duct to enjoy the warm air. The chill abated and she slipped her coat off to let the air dry her shirt. She grinned, thinking, this is way better than a blow dryer.

Partially dry, at least enough to tolerate the discomfort, Deana walked to her office. Genie's door was closed which meant she had not arrived. There was little noise from the offices located further down the hall. Deana unlocked her door and stepped inside. She took a hanger out of the narrow closet located behind the door and hung her still soggy suit coat. There was no convenient place to hang her coat next to the radiator, so she removed the framed picture of the Lift Bridge, standard issue for each office in the Jacoubi building, and twisted the wire hanger around the picture hook. With a satisfied sigh, she stepped back to make sure it did not slip off.

"Deana," Genie called in a loud whisper.

Deana turned with a smile. She walked over to the door and said, "Hey you, when did you sneak in? I just walked by your office and you weren't there."

Genie's face glowed with excitement. She glanced behind her and stepped closer to Deana. She kept her voice hushed, "You'll never guess what happened to me."

"Tell me. I'm terrible at guessing games."

"I met the greatest guy last Friday." Genie exclaimed, blissfully rolling her eyes.

Deana smiled, "Why did I say I couldn't guess? Go on, tell me where you met?"

Genie giggled, "Here, in this very building! Do you believe it! He's just been transferred upstairs from Minneapolis. I didn't even know there was a Minneapolis branch."

"It's smaller than this place."

Genie broke in, "Yeah, yeah, who cares. Listen because I haven't much time. His name is Matthew Reese. Doesn't that sound so classy? He asked me to join him after work for a drink at the Bellows. That's where all the execs from upstairs go to unwind on Friday nights. The place was packed with Jac. E. people. I couldn't believe it. And here I come walking through the door with an exec. Little ol' me from the basement, out with an exec. I have to tell you I loved every minute of it. Anyway we had to sit down at the bar because all of the tables were taken and while I'm sitting there this guy walks over and starts talking to me. I just about died when he sat next to me. I didn't know what to do. I mean anybody else, I'd just tell him to get lost, but not an exec. Pretty soon he starts asking about you." Genie laughed, "Here I am with some big ego trip and the guy is looking for you."

Deana was busy digesting the news that she and Genie had been in the same place pretty much at the same time and never saw each other.

"Well?" Genie demanded, "Isn't that unbelievable?"

Genie's high-pitched voice brought Deana's attention back, "Sure, who was it?"

Genie smiled at her, practically dancing with excitement. "This is a dream come true. Think of it, Deana, two guys from upstairs are interested in us. The possibilities are endless. Money, nice cars, dates with money. Going to places where you're not expected to go Dutch. I can't believe you can be so calm."

Deana laughed, "Slow down, Genie. I don't even know who it is you're talking about. I've never heard of Matthew Reese and you still haven't told me which exec asked about me."

Genie said, "This guy is our age and good looking."

"Genie, you think every guy in a suit is good looking. I definitely can't trust your judgment."

Genie gasped then grinned, "Oh, that's not true. For instance, I definitely don't think Julius Bascomb is good looking and he wears a suit."

Deana added dryly, "But he wears the same suit everyday. Does this exec have a name or not."

Genie hesitated, "Well, I didn't exactly catch his name and Matt didn't know him either, but I'll be able to pick him out. If we go to the Patio for coffee, I can show you who he is."

Deana held up her hands and declared, "No way! I will not go anywhere that's off this floor. Look at me, I've just had a fight with the rain and I lost. I'm soaked all the way through."

Genie looked her over, "You know you don't look that bad. Your hair looks kinda cute all soft and blowy like that and falling around your face. I know what's different. You don't look so efficient. That can be intimidating, especially for men, but you do need to put on some lipstick, and a little eye liner wouldn't hurt."

"Go away, Genie. I have work to do. I haven't even turned my computer on yet."

Genie gave her a look of disbelief, "So you won't come to coffee with me?"

Deana shook her head no. "If I'm still wet, I'm leaving during break to change my clothes."

Genie frowned, "Only you would pass up meeting an exec. Deana, he's gonna ask you out. Well, at least I'm pretty sure he plans on asking you out."

Deana walked away from Genie to the other side of her

desk, "If there really is someone who wants to ask me out on a date then I'm sure he can figure out where to find me, and now, will you please scram."

Genie, ready to argue, opened her mouth again, but quickly snapped it shut and stalked out of the room.

Deana sighed when she was gone and sat in her swivel chair spinning it to reach the computer's on button. The machine beeped and colors starting flashing on the screen. She watched the familiar restriction warnings come up and typed in her code to bypass each. Ajai's question came vividly to mind. Was it possible for her to find out exactly what services Jacoubi had passed on to outside sources? Deana waited for her entry code to be accepted and then accessed the history file. She checked the listing of services from two years ago. Deana pressed print and waited. She stacked the pages and slipped the bundle into her drawer. When she had time, she planned to look through the files and compare them to a list from five years ago. It was going to take time to go through the file, and might be a complete waste of time.

20

Genie never showed up to argue about going to coffee, so Deana worked through break. Her fingers flew over the keyboard, but the dampness of her skirt was distracting. She fidgeted in her seat, "I can't stand this. I'm going to have to quit early for lunch so I can run home and change," she said to no one.

The sound of voices in the hall caught her attention. Genie must be back from coffee break, she thought and, just as she jumped up, Genie stuck her head around the corner, "Got a minute?"

Deana stared at her. No pouting or nagging about how Deana had messed up her coffee break plans. That was usually the way Genie reacted when Deana did not go along with her schemes. Surprised, Deana asked, "How was coffee? Did you go upstairs?"

Genie was smiling impishly as she walked into the room. She said over her shoulder, "Come on in, Matt. Deana, this is Matt Reese. He's new here, only started last week. And this is David,"

Two men walked into her office and Deana did not know which of the two men was which. The man right behind Genie was tall, thin with closely cut dishwater blond hair. He looked similar to Ajai. The other man had a swarthy, complexion, dark hair and a moustache.

Deana smiled at them both, "I'm not quite sure who is who, but I'm Deana Michaels." Awkwardly they all stood staring at each other.

Finally, Mr. Dishwater Blond stepped forward and held out his hand, "Matthew, and I'll say it's a pleasure to meet you, Deana. Last week I rode from Minneapolis to Duluth with Ajai, and he spoke of you. You're quite an asset to this department."

Deana did not even attempt to hide her shock, "Thank you, though I'm not quite sure why Ajai would feel comfortable giving that compliment. He barely knows me or my work."

Matthew shrugged and stepped aside to allow the man behind him to move to the front.

He had a smile already in place as he stretched out his hand. His teeth were very white, "David Aniston, I work on the ninth floor. I've seen you around the building before, but until the other night, never knew your name. That is, until this little lady filled me in." He glanced at Genie and then stepped closer to Deana. "It was too bad you couldn't join us for coffee."

Deana tried to pull her hand away. It took several attempts before he finally let her go. He smiled and finally let go. She saw in his smile that he'd meant to fluster her.

"Since we missed Deana's company at coffee what do you say we all go to dinner tonight? How about it, a foursome?" David suggested. He first turned to look at Genie who was smiling and nodding her head wildly in agreement. Then he looked at Matthew. Matthew hesitated but then agreed, "If the ladies have no other plans?"

Deana opened her mouth to protest but Genie interrupted. "We would love to go out to dinner. Deana, you can change at my house after work and then we can be picked up there."

"My car," Deana managed to slip in while Genie took a breath.

Genie still smiling said, "Oh pooh, leave your car at my place. After dinner you can drive home from there. There that's settled. Won't this be fun?"

The men agreed, and left.

Deana was frozen with shock. She still was not quite sure how Genie had managed to maneuver the date so quickly.

Genie giggled with delight as she sauntered across the floor saying with satisfaction, "I can't believe it. We have dates with execs. Think of it! I've only worked here for nine months. I bet that's a record, for the accounting department anyway."

Deana hastily moved over behind her desk and sat down in her chair to say in annoyance, "You make it sound like the only thing women working at Jacoubi want to accomplish is getting a date with one of the guys who has an office suite upstairs. Not all of us are obsessed with money. At least I'm not, and what do you think you're doing, accepting a dinner invitation for me? I don't want to go out to dinner with two complete strangers. How dare you accept without giving me a chance to speak?"

Genie shrugged, "Because you always say no. You're so used to saying no you've forgotten about the word, yes. How do you expect to ever meet a guy or make any friends? You're what? Twenty-five, maybe six… your clock is ticking, Honey and it only ticks faster with every year that goes by. Don't you want to get married or have a family? You'd be a great mother or at least I think you will be. You certainly have the patience for it. Anyway, one date with a guy doesn't mean a thing. You don't ever have to accept another date after this one if you don't want to, but I need you to go. Matthew is a dream and not the usual type of guy I date. I'm scared stiff that I'll do something wrong and he'll hate me. If you're nearby I can watch how you act and hopefully pull the wool over his eyes about how I really am."

"What will you do when he does see the real you? You can't act like someone else for the rest of your life."

Genie gave a flippant laugh, "Oh by the time that happens he'll already realize he can't live without me and the rest will be history."

21

After Genie left, Deana tried to figure out a way to extract herself from the situation. She leaned down and rested her head on her arms closing her eyes. A sound from the hallway caught her attention. Feeling slightly dizzy, she barely lifted her head. A gasp of dismay escaped her as she sat up with a jolt. Ajai stood in the doorway with a curious expression on his face.

"What are you doing? Is this a new type of yoga or something?" He asked as tawny eyes slowly drifted over her appearance. He narrowed his eyes, "Why are you so, so rumpled? I've never seen you at work looking like this. What's happened?"

Deana jumped to her feet and crossed her arms feeling heat stain her cheeks. "I was caught in the rain. I'm sorry if I don't fit the Jacoubi standard of dress, I was going to change at lunch."

Ajai strode to her side, "You always go beyond the Jacoubi standard. That's not the only thing wrong. You look pale. Are you catching cold? Why didn't you wear a raincoat? It's been raining all morning."

Deana tilted her chin and met his stare. "I... I got it dirty this morning feeding Journey and I forgot an umbrella. It's not that big a deal."

Ajai grinned, "I can just imagine what happened to you in Journey's paddock with all this rain. Oh, what I would have given to witness that."

Deana made a strangled sound of frustration in her throat and stepped away from him. With a sigh she asked, "What do you want, Ajai? I have work to do."

"I wanted to ask you for dinner. I know how disappointed you were when your father missed out the other night, and

I've convinced him to have dinner at my parent's house to-night."

Deana gave him a quick look, "At your house?"

"Yes, my mother wants you both to join us. My father's doing so much better that he's chomping at the bit for company. He's driving my mother nuts. Frank has agreed to play a few unexciting games of chess with him in exchange for a meal. So what do you say? Will you come too?"

Deana was having a hard time sorting her thoughts from her emotions. To be invited to the Jacoubi's house, and by Ajai himself, was a dream she had kept close to her heart for all of her life, and now she had to refuse it. A stricken note crept into her voice, "This is unbelievable."

"That you're invited to dinner? Why I just invited you the other night. Which I might add, you accepted very unwillingly. Tell me what makes it so unbelievable today?"

Deana in a dull voice said, "I can't."

Ajai smiled, "I knew that's what you'd say first, so I have my mother waiting near the telephone line to personally invite you and explain I have absolutely no plans to seduce you. You see, it would be impossible, since the entire evening will be under the supervision of, not only my parents, but also yours. No matter what you've heard about me, even I couldn't accomplish a well executed seduction with that kind of distraction."

Deana laughed at his absurdity and shook her head, "I can't go. Genie asked me to double date with her tonight. She's in a complete dither because, a new employee who works upstairs asked her on a date. She'd never forgive me if I cancelled."

"Works upstairs. What does that mean?"

Deana realized what she said and began to fidget, "The executives all work upstairs," She explained awkwardly.

Ajai continued to look at her without understanding.

"From the fifth floor up, all the offices are suites. It's obvious they make more money than the ordinary staff."

Silence stretched between the two of them until Deana looked up and caught a glimpse of Ajai's angry frown. He carefully masked the expression when he spoke. "So anybody who works on one of the lower levels is referred to as an ordinary date? I thought you didn't date employees at Jac E?"

Deana was surprised, "Well, I don't but this isn't exactly my date. It's more Genie's date. This guy named David and I will just be tagging along."

"David? David who?"

This date of Genie's ruined what could have been a wonderful evening. A dream come true, Deana's annoyance was rising. "His name is David Aniston. That's all I know about him."

"I must say I'm surprised by this, Deana. I got the impression you didn't approve of meaningless flirtations. From the way you acted with me, I thought you'd be more selective about your dates."

Deana, without stopping to think snapped back, "Selective? What selection? There isn't any selection in my life? There's never been any man in my life until today. Oh, why did I just tell you that? Go away. You're making me forget where I am and who you are. This is crazy."

Though his face remained stony, Ajai softened his tone, "Well perhaps another time. I'm sure my mother will be willing enough to give you a rain check."

Deana shook her hair back, "That would be nice. I'd like that."

Ajai shrugged, "Then we'll have to arrange it soon. We'll leave it at that then."

"Please thank your mother for the invitation, Ajai. It's so generous of her, considering your father's illness. And I'm sorry, but I really doubt my father will come to dinner without me. He doesn't like to be away from home much."

Ajai gave her a long look and then unexpectedly laughed, "We'll see. My mother is a very persuasive woman. Goodbye Deana. Have a nice night."

22

When the two women arrived at Genie's apartment after work, she unlocked the steel security lock and pushed the door open. The shambles of the front room of the apartment caught Deana by surprise. She stumbled back into the hallway and gasped in dismay, "Oh no, Genie, you've been robbed?"

Genie pulled her key from the lock and laughed. Carelessly, with the side of her foot, she shoved a paper bag filled with garbage out of her path. She stepped over a pile of discarded clothing and shoes lying on the floor. "No, it always looks like this. I guess neither Phil, or I particularly care for house cleaning."

Deana's mouth fell open as she stared at Genie, "Phil? I didn't know you were sharing an apartment with a guy."

"Philomena, I knew that would catch your attention." Genie teased with a laugh as she disappeared down a hallway at the back of the room.

The living room was so cluttered it resembled a maze. Out of the odd array of furniture, Deana picked out several wooden straight back chairs and one wicker wing back with a stained orange cushion that sagged through a hole in the seat. Taking up most of the space sat an equally dilapidated couch. The chairs overflowed with junk, making it impossible to find a spot to sit. At the far end of the room stood the only uncluttered item, a shiny stainless steel super sized thirty-two-inch stereo television set. Wires snaked out from the frame and wound across the floor to a cube shaped box attached to several game controls.

Deana called to Genie, "What in the heck is this thing?"

Genie's muffled voice was heard from the back, "I can't hear you. Just wait a second."

Deana stood in the middle of the floor trying hard not to look at the clutter. Dirty dishes with dried food stuck to them filled the surface of the wooden crate next to the couch. Piles of magazines were stacked around the room and an over-filled basket of nail polish bottles teetered on the edge of a pile of glossy covered magazines. Deana leaned over and pushed it straight. Desperate to keep her hands to herself, and control the urge to clean someone else's apartment, she picked her way across the floor to the windows.

The old fashioned lead framed windows had panes of cut glass filling the delicate arches. The glass was dirt stained. Only a pale light shimmered through the filthy window. Distortions in the glass showed the age of the windows.

The apartment building was located in the old section of Duluth. Built in the 1890's, the building had originally been chateau style apartments. Then it was used for housing Villa for Scholastica students. Now, it was subdivided into thirty-two apartments and showed an impressive view of Mesaba Avenue and the waters of the bay area. The outside was an ornamentally carved brownstone building that caused people to stop and take a moment to marvel at the beauty and charm of architecture.

Deana looked out through the grimy windows at the grandeur of the harbor. She watched the road and the steady stream of traffic as it wound its way up and down the pavement of the major artery to and from Duluth's central hillside area. Deana swallowed hard when she realized that soon, the men were going to arrive and they would have to spend several hours with them. Two men, two strangers, she shuddered. She did not want to be here.

"You want to check your face again?" Genie asked as she walked into the room.

Deana slowly turned away from the view to give a mute nod and followed the direction Genie pointed out with her long manicured finger. The bathroom, surprisingly, was not as messy as Deana expected it might be. With her purse balanced on the edge of the sink, Deana applied some of the pale pink lipstick she preferred. Compared to Genie's crimson tinted lips, hers indeed looked pale. "I wish I was with my father going to the Jacoubi's house. Even though Ajai makes me uneasy, at least dad's familiar," she muttered.

"Deana, get out here. It's time to go."

Deana gave a quick study of her face in the mirror and then resigned herself to facing the evening.

"Will you hurry up? I don't want them to come up here and get a look at this place. It's a mess."

Deana followed Genie back out into the hallway. "Have you ever thought of cleaning it?"

Genie snapped, "No. Why should I have to? I'm not the only one responsible for the mess."

Deana silently raised her eyebrows in disbelief.

23

As they hurried down the stairs, Genie whispered over her shoulder, "Look, there's Matt. I knew he'd be the type to arrive at the door. He is such a gentleman and so cute."

Deana sighed and rolled her eyes thinking, this is going to be a long night.

Smiling, Genie raised her hand to wave wildly, "Matt, Matt, where's Dave?"

"Waiting in the car. Did you have enough time to get ready?"

"Of course, it only takes us a flash. Right, Deana?"

Deana glanced down at her own outfit. She had changed at noon with the thought of tonight in mind, so she had done nothing but comb her hair and put on lipstick. Genie was dressed in an entirely new outfit. At least it looked a bit more subdued than she normally wore.

Genie slipped her arm through Matt's and clung to him as they walked outside.

Just watching Genie with Matt made Deana feel old and washed up. Where is that feeling of excitement that Genie seems to find in dating? Whether the guy is special or not, with Genie, any date gives her a thrill. Why don't I feel it?

Determined to hide her trepidation, Deana greeted David with a buoyant hello as she climbed in next to him in the back seat.

David gave her a nod and a quick grin as he leaned forward to talk to Matt, "Did you ask the ladies where they wanted to eat?"

Matt shook his head no, "Let me get the car started first. Since I'm a newcomer to the area, I think we need to trust the judgment of a native Duluthian."

David snickered, "Is there anyone native to Duluth? I've heard they all move out after high school."

"I'm a Duluth native." Deana said in a small voice. "Born and raised in the same house I live in right now."

David raised his fine black eyebrows, "My, I'm impressed. You've been lucky enough to have access to this charm all your life. I should have recognized good bloodlines when I saw it."

Deana laughed at his flattery. She shook her head. "Not this country girl."

"A country girl," He said. His voice becoming softer, he said, "I am intrigued. If you're born and raised in Duluth, how are you from the country?"

Deana turned to find his face much closer to hers than she expected. Startled, she quickly turned away. "Oh, please... Nothing could be farther from the truth. I don't know any good restaurants in town. Except one, you know Genie, the one on London Road, the Bellows."

Genie cooed with excitement, "Oh, yes. That was such a nice place. Let's go there again. I never did get to try the food."

Matt lifted his eyes to look at David in the rear view mirror. "Well, what do you say, David?"

David shrugged, "Sounds fine to me. I've only seen the bar. It might be a good time to check out the restaurant."

Deana leaned back in the seat and stared out the window. Genie and David carried most of the conversation about the nightlife in Duluth. It was a topic Deana knew nothing about and had little interest in.

The restaurant was full and the hostess looked harassed as David asked for a table. She chewed on the end of her pen as she stared down at her table chart. "I'm sorry. It will be at least twenty minutes."

David turned to the others, "Are you okay with that? I'm sure we could get in right away someplace else."

Matt shook his head, "We'll wait in the bar."

Matt led the way, holding the door open for Genie. Genie looked like she was on cloud nine.

Deana smiled, it must be nice to have such simple expectations, to be able to gain such happiness from walking into a room with the right guy. Of course, Genie's right guy only needed to drive a nice car and work on a certain floor. The right man standing beside you could raise your spirits and brighten the entire look of the world. Deana glanced at David and wondered if he could ever be such a man for her.

By the time the foursome were shown into the restaurant, the ice had broken and friendly disagreements along with laughter filled the conversation.

Deana looked at the menu and realized how hungry she felt. Eating lunch in her car on the way home at noon to change clothes seemed like weeks ago. And besides, it was a hasty unappetizing peanut butter and jelly sandwich that was made more unappealing by her worry about tonight. The aroma from the grill brought her attention to the steak section of the menu, and she decided immediately what to order. She did not even realize that she planned to order the exact meal Ajai had recommended and ordered last Friday.

While she read the menu, Deana heard Matt ask, "What's the company picnic like?"

Genie said quickly, "I didn't start working at Jacoubi until after the picnic so I don't know." She turned to Deana. "You've worked there the longest. What's it like?"

Deana, already on edge, was taken aback by the sudden attention. "Th... the picnic for Jacoubi Enterprises? I can't really say. I've never gone."

David piped in, "Well then, it can't be much fun if the staff doesn't even show up."

"It's not that. It's probably loads of fun. Deana just doesn't get out much. She's always riding that dang horse. Last year it was held at Glensheen. The Jacoubi's rented the entire estate for the picnic. This year I heard it's supposed to be at the Yacht Club. Just think, a sandy beach or a swimming pool to choose from. That sounds like heaven to me. I'm going for sure."

"How do you know it's at the Yacht Club?" Deana asked.

David interrupted, "I heard the same thing. A friend of mine is on the planning committee. He said there's supposed to be a boat parade and then a regatta."

"A boat race," Deana said, "I wish I knew somebody with a sailboat. I've always wanted to sail on the big lake."

Matt said, "Sailboats always have full crews. They have to go out and practice a lot. I used to crew in Miami. When is the regatta?"

David answered, "The second week of July."

Matt turned to David. "Do you sail?"

David dropped his eyes and shrugged, "Well no, but I watch sailboat racing all the time on ESPN. It looks pretty complicated."

Deana remained silent. She knew someone with a sailboat, but she was not going to mention Ajai around these people. It would raise too many questions.

Ajai had sailed all during high school. He even competed in the local sailboat races on Lake Superior, winning several trophies. Usually the local paper didn't cover the weekly sailboat regattas, but, when Ajai won, the press was always there. Even when he was overseas, Ajai's picture was often in the local papers, whether he was in South America or Spain. He always had a smile on his face and a beautiful woman nearby. Deana glanced at Matt. How long had Matt known Ajai? She wished she could ask Matt about Ajai, but she was too afraid.

24

The foursome began to spend two and three nights together during the next few weeks. Every time Deana voiced any kind of reluctance, Genie quelled the objections with the well-placed barb, "You're going to become an old maid, Deana."

One Friday afternoon, David had announced that he was going to drive out to the house to meet Frank Michaels before dinner. When Deana told Frank that David wanted to meet him, her father reacted as if he didn't care who was dating his only daughter. Deana felt relief when David called at the last minute and cancelled the entire evening. It was the first and last effort David ever made to meet Frank.

After spending Saturday and Sunday blissfully free from the pressures of socializing with Genie, Deana was looking forward to a quiet Sunday dinner with her father. After dinner Deana found Frank out on the porch enjoying his pipe. Walking to the door, for a moment, Deana hoped Ajai might be with her dad. Her heart beat wildly at the thought. The last time she had spoken to Ajai was in her office when he had invited them to supper.

The swing creaked its usual song as her father pushed gently against the rail with one foot.

"What are you doing lurking in the doorway, Deana?" Frank asked. "Come out here and enjoy this beautiful night. The dishes can wait. For one so young you're too set in your ways, girl. But that's not your fault. You always did think I needed mothering after mom died. You've been a good daughter."

Deana frowned as she opened the door and walked over to sit next to her father. "Thanks for thinking I'm a good daughter, but what's all this about? I've never tried to mother you.

And I don't believe you've ever wanted me to mother you."

"Well then why are you feeling guilty about staying in town for dinner a few nights a week if you believe I can take care of myself?"

Deana stared at him, "How do you know that? I never said I felt guilty about leaving you."

"You don't have to say it in words. I think I've gained five pounds from all the cooking and baking you've been doing. I haven't prepared a meal for two weeks. If the Jacoubi's ran cattle I'd accuse you of rustling. I've never eaten so much beef before."

Deana smiled, "Its summer now. We are allowed to grill when we feel like it. And the clean up is so much easier."

Frank puffed on his pipe. He frowned, tapping the bowl against the palm of his hand. "I don't know why I waste money on tobacco. This thing will not stay lit."

"You're not going to tell me what you think about this situation between David and me?" Deana asked.

"Honey, I'm not sure what you want me to say. I'm not dating him, so it doesn't really matter what I think, now does it?"

Deana pushed against the wood rung of the porch and the chain squealed, "I just thought you'd be interested in who I'm spending time with. Aren't you the one who said dating is a preliminary to marriage? If I chose to marry this man would that cause you any concern?"

"Has he asked you to marry him?"

Deana gave a frustrated sigh, "Of course not, but if he did?"

Frank chuckled, "If doesn't mean anything. I'm not the one that would have to live with him every day for the rest of my life. You should be asking yourself that question, not me. It sounds like your imagination has jumped the relationship past a few dinners. Why not use some patience and take the pressure off yourself? Have some fun. It's warm outside, the nights are long and you're with people you like. Just let it be for now. Every single day of life doesn't have to be planned. The phrase, 'wing it' does have some merit."

"So, you seem to be saying that becoming twenty-six in a few short days should not cause me any kind of anxiety." Deana bounced off the swing causing it to jerk out from under her. "Somehow it isn't as easy for me to do as it is for you to say."

"I'm not telling you anything except, enjoy yourself. Do the things you like to do. If this guy fits in with those things then maybe he is the one God has chosen for you."

Deana tossed her hair back with a frustrated sigh. "Thanks a lot. Now I have to worry if God has chosen this man or not." She stalked back in the house to attack the dishes. She liked David, and the four of them did have a good time together. He was funny and energetic and, most importantly, he was not pushing for physical relations. They had exchanged a few light-hearted kisses that felt pleasant enough, but that was all.

Genie and Matt were getting along much better than that. Either Matt was an exceptional influence on her, or Genie was actually acting normal when she was out in public.

Deana went about the house finishing the weekend chores feeling frustrated with her dad. But the coming weeks of summer promised to pass quite pleasantly with a full social agenda like she had never experienced before. However, there was one fly in the ointment. David was funny about money. Whenever a waitress brought the checks, David always hesitated a moment before reaching for it. Furthermore, he would always examine it carefully before slowly taking out his billfold to reluctantly extract the bills to pay. Matt on the other hand grabbed his check the instant the waitress left. He slipped it off the table and into his lap away from Genie. The slip never was on the table again.

Deana tried to remember if David always paid the bill with reluctance. She hadn't really noticed the first few times they went out. His reaction was probably just a quirk about him. She decided he was just methodical about paying bills. Or, maybe he just wasn't Ajai.

25

"Matt says he was asked to crew for the regatta," Genie said from the chair opposite Deana's desk as she rapidly snapped her gum. Her long legs were stretched out as she relaxed, acting like the Genie Deana was used to.

The routine the two women had of sharing their coffee in Deana's office had significantly changed. Since Genie began to meet Matt for break in the Patio coffee shop upstairs, they met in Deana's office only once a week. Deana had quit going with Genie because sitting at a table with the two of them had become unbearable. She tried to stop watching Genie and Matt who were so close when they talked that they were almost in each other's laps. Deana found having coffee alone preferable to being a third wheel with Genie and Matt.

Deana dismissed the twinge of jealousy she felt with how well the relationship between Matt and Genie was progressing and said in a wistful tone, "The guys are being awfully mysterious about this sailboat race. Will Matt be ready to crew by Saturday? I thought they needed time to practice."

Genie stretched and yawned. "How should I know? But he said he would. What I can't believe is how I don't have a date now. What about David? Is he still going to be on the lawyer's boat crew?"

"Yes, but don't you have some kind of list of available dates? Call another guy to take you."

Genie shook her head vigorously, "I couldn't do that."

Deana lifted her head to give Genie a curious look. "Really, why?"

"'Cause I... I don't want to. I'd rather not go at all."

"My, I didn't realize your relationship with Matt was becoming so serious."

"You're right. I know it. And I know Matt doesn't feel the same way I do, but this time... I don't know this is different. Matt is really special. I've never had a guy treat me like I was... a lady before. He doesn't make fun of my mistakes. He calls me some nights just to ask if I got home all right. Nobody has done that since I moved away from home."

"Are you certain this has nothing to do with his nice car and salary?"

Genie became unusually silent at Deana's comment. In a quiet voice that sounded nothing like her, Genie said, "I deserve that." Abruptly, she jumped to her feet and leaned on the desk toward Deana to say earnestly, "I've been such a fool, Deana. I don't expect anyone, especially you, to believe this, but I wouldn't care if Matt worked in the mailroom. I don't want to be with anyone else but him."

Deana curbed her desire to laugh. Suspecting that Genie was smitten, not only by Matt, but also by his lifestyle and bright successful future, she studied Genie's expression realizing that Genie was acting different. Always, she'd been honest about her mercenary objective of dating and never wavered through the months they had known each other. This was an about face for her. Deana did not know what to think.

Genie sighed, "I can read your face. Deana, you're terrible at concealing things, and I feel the same way. I don't believe myself. I'm sure my attraction to him is affected by the money. I know myself too well not to admit it, but all of a sudden, I don't care if he takes me out. This weekend, I even broke down and cleaned the apartment to make him dinner. That turned out to be a total disaster. I'm completely lost in a kitchen, but for some crazy reason I wanted to try and cook a meal with my own two hands. Isn't that the corniest thing you've ever heard?"

Genie paused to give Deana a forlorn look, "Well, maybe not to you. You cook all the time, but for me it is. Everything was ruined. Finally, I had to give up. I was going to call the deli to deliver something edible, but Matt didn't care. The apartment was filled with smoke. The smoke detectors were all screeching. He came right in the kitchen and helped me. Together we managed to salvage part of the meal. Then, we cleaned up and, for the rest of the night, just sat around and played video games. Spending the night with him was better than going to any four star restaurant and dancing at a hot night club." She smiled then shrugged her thin shoulders and added, "This must sound silly especially to you. I figured out this is how you live your life. You like going home every night to cook for your Dad. You spend quiet nights and weekends at home doing simple stuff like reading and... whatever. I'm not like that. It's a whole new world for me. I think it's the kind of life that Matt likes, so I want to give it a try. I only hope he doesn't find out too soon how useless I really am and dump me for somebody like you."

Deana watched Genie's familiar careless wave as she left the room and felt thunderstruck. With Genie's heartfelt revelation still ringing in her ears, Deana murmured, "So this is love?" Suddenly, with crystal clarity she knew there had never been a love in her life like Genie described. Ajai was a crush. The few college dates she had accepted had dissipated soon after the class they shared together ended. David was already beginning to bug her. And now Genie was in love and it sounded like a perfectly wonderful relationship. With difficulty, Deana swallowed the lump of resentment that formed in her throat.

26

Genie's confession of love for Matt haunted Deana the rest of the day. On the drive home, while watering Journey and now, as she pulled weeds from the flower garden next to Journey's paddock, Genie's words replayed over and over in her head. A small black cloud of gnats clustered around her damp skin and face. Deana brushed them aside as she walked around the growing pile of weeds that far outgrew the meager flowers lining the freshly painted white fence. The cluster of trees nearby and the bushes surrounding the flower garden attracted even more annoying insects. Deana usually avoided working in the garden when it was this close to dusk, especially when the weather was as muggy as tonight. Her blood was feeding at least a million of the gnats and probably another million mosquitoes.

Deana paused when she reached the end of the fence. Frowning, she thought, it really isn't fair that Genie should be the one to stumble into a meaningful relationship. But there was an upside. If Matt and Genie became serious the four-some dates would end.

Deana had grown tired of David's financial games. She definitely knew there was nothing between them and didn't want to date him any longer. She did not want a confrontation. She had never ended a relationship in her entire life.

Deep in thought, Deana stumbled into a big thistle bush that had sprung up right in the middle of the flowerbed. With an angry shout, she kicked the thick clump. Pulling her leg back, she saw the clusters of thistles stuck to her pant leg. Brushing them away, Deana thought about walking back to the house to get her spade. Then decided it wasn't worth the effort. She slipped her leather gloves back on and with both hands grabbed the thickest part of the stalk and gave a heave.

The stalk broke off. Dirt clumps flew into her face but the root clump remained in the ground. With a grimace, she planted her feet, grasped the base and leaned backward. The remainder of the stalk snapped, sending Deana flying backwards into a pile of weeds. Journey lifted his head, sending out a loud whinny. Deana looked up to see him walk to the rail and put his head over it.

"You brute! Are you laughing at me?" Deana cried, throwing a clump of weeds at the horse's head. Journey jerked back and snorted.

"Get away from me, you mangy beast."

Journey whinnied again louder.

"Thanks a lot. I don't see you for a week, and you call me names, Miss Michaels, I must say I'm shocked."

Deana scrambled to her feet and turned to see Ajai sitting astride the flame colored gelding. He was grinning widely. His obvious amusement at her condition irritated her.

Deana waved her arms through the air trying to clear away the black cloud of gnats and mosquitoes that hovered around her head.

"Ajai!" she cried. She could not stop the feeling of joy that welled through her at the sight of him. "Where did you come from?"

"I followed this overgrown trail and found a... treasure at the end of it... you."

Deana laughed at his obvious flattery. This man's glib tongue was truly outrageous, but she secretly enjoyed hearing it, even if it was a gross exaggeration.

"It looks like that thistle is getting the best of you. Need some help?"

Deana hastily brushed her jeans off and shook her head no, "I give up. I'm being eaten alive, all for the sake of a bunch of weeds. He looks good." She said pointing at the chestnut.

"Yeah, he's turning out to be quite an enigma. I'm having

a hard time figuring out why he was brought to the auction. He's really fast."

"Then he'd make a good polo pony. That must make you happy."

Ajai hesitated before saying, "I'm not playing polo any longer. I don't plan on playing, ever again."

Deana looked at him wide-eyed, "You can't be serious? What made you decide that?"

Ajai swung his leg over the horse's back and jumped to the ground. He took a step closer, a lazy grin on his handsome face. He reached over and gently tapped her chin, "Close your mouth, Deana, or you'll make a meal out of those nasty no-see-ums."

Deana snapped her mouth shut, "You're just saying you'll never play again because right now you're sick of it. I bet in a year you'll be back."

Ajai shook his head. "That's a bet you'd lose."

"Ajai, no! You're one of the best polo players in the world. You can't give up. What does Chip have to say about this?"

"Chip's not going to say a thing."

"Well, Chip's been training him, hasn't he?" she nodded at the chestnut.

Ajai slapped the gelding's gleaming shoulder. "No, Chip hasn't been training him and no, Chip doesn't know I've quit polo, and thanks, if you think this boy looks like Chip's work, I must not be too bad a trainer myself. He's shaping up nicely, don't you think?"

"You're responsible?"

Ajai's Golden eyebrows shot upward. "You certainly do have a keen grasp of the obvious."

"Since when did you start training horses?"

Ajai lost some of his attitude, giving her a sheepish grin, "This is my first try, and Chip's giving me pointers. The gelding was pretty green but somebody taught him the basics. I really just have to smooth him out. Actually, I stopped by to see if you wanted to go for a quick ride. There's still a couple hours before nightfall."

Deana looked at the sky as she slapped a mosquito off her arm. "It looks like rain."

"Come on, you don't melt when you get wet, do you?"

"No, but..."

"Oh, then that horse of yours must melt when it gets wet."

Deana glanced at Journey who had stopped straining over the fence to meet the chestnut. It was tempting, but... Her dates with David had kept her from riding for several weeks... and, it did look like rain...

"You get Journey saddled and I'll go tell Frank we're going for a ride."

"Well, okay, but only for a little while."

Ajai swung himself back into the saddle and turned the gelding around on the path and called, "Come on down to the house when you're ready.

Deana climbed up and over the white plank fence dropping into the dirt on the other side. She spoke softly to Journey as she moved toward him and grasped a chunk of his spiky mane, "Come on, let's go for a run."

Journey followed her over the uneven ground. She led him into the lean-to stall attached to the shed. Her father had built the open-air stall as a shelter and Deana turned it into a saddling area. Before throwing a saddle over his back, she ran a soft brush over the big brown, black and white patches of Journey's coat. He stood stomping at bugs and swishing his tail in an even tempo until she set the saddle on his back and tightened the cinch. He jerked to attention and received the bit eagerly. Following her from the paddock, Journey whinnied a greeting across the yard to the chestnut that Ajai had tied to the front porch rail of the house.

Deana saw the gelding dancing at the end of his reins and yelled to Ajai as he exited the house, "If that horse jumps, he's going to pull the entire porch off its foundation." She wrapped the reins around Journey's neck and stepped into the stirrup.

Ajai hopped from the top of the rickety steps and called to her, "I was only inside for a minute. He's fine. You ready?"

Moments later, they trotted the horses down the road and turned onto the state trail. The leafy canopy above the trail was fluorescent green. They rode for five minutes in a silence that Deana wanted to ignore. She could not. Clearing her throat she asked, "So how do you find Duluth after the excitement of living abroad?"

Ajai's chestnut, a foot taller and with the long legs of the new style quarter horse, had moved ahead. He turned in the saddle, leaning back to face her with one hand on the cantle. "Duluth's changed. I can't believe some of the changes. But I hope the planning committees figure out how to encourage the tourist trade without selling the soul of the city and the waterfront in the process. Cape Cod and so many other beautiful places have been downright ruined by the tourist trade, like Atlantic City. It used to be so quaint. Now families don't feel welcome because of the shoddy atmosphere that gambling brought. When a place loses family visitors, it's a slippery slope."

Deana gave a short laugh, "And what do you know about families? From what the papers have been saying, you're always looking for places to party."

Deana met his tawny colored eyes.

Ajai frowned, "I'm the first to admit my failings, but I don't think I was ever selfish enough to overlook the importance of family. I might have been the typical disrespectful, know-it-all teenager, but who wasn't at some time? Anyway, I have enough faults to consider, without you adding to the list."

Deana tightened her grip on the reins making Journey prance under the pressure of the bit. She stared at Ajai hard, trying to judge whether this time he was being honest or just playing the game, like before. Suddenly she kicked Journey and the horse leaped forward past a startled Ajai.

Journey sprinted down the wide trail. It was a flat and fast track that Journey knew well and loved to run. He gave all he had. Deana felt him stretching out low to the ground. Sitting jockey style, half in the saddle, half across the horse's neck, her hair fell from the confined braid at the back of her head and flew out behind her like a thick black flag.

Deana didn't know if Ajai would take the bait. But, when she heard the thunder of the chestnut's hooves close behind, she smiled.

27

Ajai held the chestnut gelding on a close rein watching with great pleasure the sight of Deana and Journey pounding down the trail ahead. The bright colors of green that canopied the trail framed the slim girl... woman who rode high on the whither of her Indian pony. He shook his head at her unspoken challenge, prepared to take it, but he wanted to wait until just before the two disappeared around the corner. The chestnut strained impatiently and Ajai leaned his weight slightly forward. He felt the power of the horse bunch beneath him. He held a tight rein for another moment. He wanted to give the horse a try. Watching Journey and Deana race away in front of them flamed the fire of competition in Ajai and he hoped that the big chestnut would be just as inflamed. And he was right. With Journey in front of the chestnut's nose, it was obvious that the gelding wanted to run. When Deana and Journey vanished around the corner, Ajai held the gelding back just a few seconds longer, until the horse was barely controllable, then, with a yell, he slapped the reins on the horse's neck and gave him his head.

The gelding leaped a good foot in the air before his hooves touched the ground and they were flying.

The thrill of speed exploded in Ajai's head as he leaned into the flying mane that whipped his face. The thud of hooves on packed dirt, the squeak of saddle leather and the grunt of a horse moving with all the muscle in his body brought Ajai back to his polo days. His heart boomed along with the thunder of the horse's hooves. He became the horse, adjusting to each stride, feeling the movement and shifting his weight to keep balanced. "This is living!" Screamed in his brain. The horse moved alongside Deana and Journey, and Ajai tightened the rein to keep the two neck and neck. He looked at the rider next to him. Deana's fingers were wrapped in the reins and the long strands of the gelding's mane. No fear showed in her face, only a set look of determination as she glanced at him. Her gray eyes met his and then narrowed as she nudged Journey toward him.

The chestnut fought against Ajai's control and grasped the bit in his teeth. Ajai, feeling the change, looked ahead too late to see that the trail was narrowing where the trail crossed over a ravine. With no room for two horses, the chestnut lunged off the pathway and plunged down the embankment toward the silver culvert below. Ajai heard Deana scream his name before he flew head first over the chestnut's shoulder.

28

Deana reined Journey around and swung out of the saddle, her feet hitting the ground running before the horse stopped. The mud-caked chestnut lunged out of the ditch shaking its head and tossing clods of dirt everywhere.

Deana plunged over the edge of the trail and immediately lost her footing. She slipped to the seat of her pants, sliding part of the way down the steep embankment. She gained speed and lost control, tumbling the rest of the way to the bottom of the slope. At the bottom, about an inch of water pooled at the end of the culvert. Ajai was sprawled half in the water, half on the opposite bank. Deana stumbled through the water toward him. He sat shaking his head and rubbing the back of his neck. Deana hit a patch of clay and skidded through the water on her hands and knees. "Aaagh!" she yelled.

Ajai lifted his head as Deana floundered to her feet, splashing and slipping in the sloppy muck. He reached for her flailing hands and, grabbing one, hauled her out. Deana jerked away from his grip. Yucky water and grime streamed down her face and filled her mouth. She leaned over and spit it out with a strangled cry. "Ugh, that's disgusting." She didn't really want to straighten up and face him in this condition.

Putting her hands on her knees and breathing deeply, she asked, "Are you all right?"

There was no answer. Fearfully, she peeked around the mud-entangled hair hanging in her face. She brushed aside her hair. It only took a moment for her to realize why Ajai hadn't answered.

He was silently laughing so hard his shoulders shook. He was doubled-over holding his stomach.

"Well! I can see there's nothing too badly damaged from

your fall." And instantly she slipped on the greasy ground again.

Ajai reached out to save her from falling once more and he quickly regained his composure. His face was speckled with mud and his amazed eyes glowed with mischief, "Will you stand still before you fall flat on your back in that stuff."

Deana glanced over her shoulder and sidled away from the edge.

Grinning, Ajai said, "Now get over here and let me give you a boost. I don't know about you, but I've had enough of crashing around down here."

Deana felt strong hands on her waist as he shoved her up the hill. She grabbed at the long grass and yanked herself upward step by step until she flung herself onto the gravel at the top. The two horses were calmly munching flowers next to the trail.

Ajai flopped onto the ground next to her. He stretched his long legs out. His faded blue jeans were encased in a layer of red mud. He relaxed his tall muscular frame and rested his head back in the grass, folding his arms under his head. Sighing heartily, he said, "Wow! That was some ride!"

Exerting all the will power she had, Deana tried to stay calm. With Ajai this close, she could actually feel the heat radiating from his body. His eyes were closed. For the first time, she was free to look at every feature of his lean, handsome face without him watching her. He had a carefree boyish expression. Deana felt a strange tension growing in the pit of her stomach. Nervously, she jumped to her feet.

Ajai opened one eye, "Where're you going to?"

"I... I gotta go. I'm a mess. I'm riding back."

Ajai sat up, "Are you crazy? You'll wreck your saddle with all that muck you're wearing. Let it dry awhile before you ride. What's the hurry any way?"

"I've got mud in my mouth." She declared looking for something to wipe it away.

"And everywhere else."

Deana held her hands out and looked them over. They were covered with mud. Her sleeves and the front of her shirt were so muddy there wasn't a square inch to clean off with.

"Use this," Ajai called suddenly, as he tossed something white at her.

Instinctively, Deana reached up and closed her hands on the warm material. She stared at it, "What's this?"

"My t-shirt," He said. "At least it's cleaner than yours."

Deana looked up in time to see him pull his polo shirt back down over the smooth tan of his bare torso. She dropped her eyes to stare at the simple undershirt she held in her hands.

"Something wrong?"

Deana glanced at him. Yes, something was very wrong. Why did she think it was possible for her to spend any amount of time with him? How could she confess that she had to get away from him? The man totally unnerved her, and she certainly did not want to fall apart right in front of him. She said hastily, "Uh, no but I'm heading for the Hitching Post where I'll at least have clean water to use."

She spun around and tottered away. Her mud-sodden clothes were already beginning to dry, making it difficult to walk. She reached Journey, grabbed the reins and waddled down the trail.

A few blocks from the culvert on the edge of the state trail sat a small cedar shingled building. The gravel parking lot that could hold roughly five cars if none of them were pulling a horse trailer, was empty. A small neon sign with faded lettering hung from an old iron lamppost. It read, *The Hitching Post* and underneath, *Beer, Food.* Deana looped the reins around the short wooden hitching post that stood in front of the building, leaving Journey alone to wait for Ajai if he followed her.

Inside a narrow bar ran the length of the one room building. A pool table occupied the center of the room and a worn dartboard hung on the wall. At the far end of the room three small shelves created the atmosphere of a small store, carrying only the bare essentials. The smell of stale grease and cigarette smoke oozed from the wood. Deana never remembered it smelling any different, even though there had not been a working grill in the building for years. The only food offered now was frozen pizzas and hot dogs. The ten bar stools lining the bar stood empty. Without pause, Deana headed straight for the narrow cubby that was the women's bathroom.

Once the bathroom door was safely latched and she was completely alone, Deana leaned over and closed her eyes to rest against the small porcelain sink. "How can I be so dim-witted?" She whispered.

Looking into the mirror, she thought, I know full well what kind of man Ajai is, and now I've gone and done the unthinkable... I've let myself fall in love with him. I am the worst kind of fool. This isn't high school. This isn't a crush that he won't know exists. I work with this man. He's the neighbor who won't go away.

She shuddered at the sight of her reflection. "Not only am I a fool, but I'm destined to look like some gawky backward child whenever he's around."

Deana turned the faucet and rubbed her hands in the stream. It was icy cold for an instant then pleasantly warm, she scrubbed her hands then her face. When she saw the pink flesh of her face, instead of the red-brown yuck, she reached for the towel rack. The brown paper did little to absorb the water, leaving her distinctly damp. The tee shirt she had jammed into the waistband of her jeans was soft and cotton absorbent. She loathed using it as a towel. With a strange mixture of desire and reluctance, slowly she pressed the shirt into her face and inhaled.

The musky scent clinging to the material was all male. Whether it was from his cologne, deodorant or soap, Deana did not care, all that mattered was, this was Ajai. The way his skin smelled. The thought of the warmth of his body encased in the material sent a shiver through her. She rubbed it against her cheek before giving a sigh of regret. If only there was a chance for the two of them.

This is nuts, she thought. It's only a shirt! But it's Ajai's. She dropped her hands to the sink with a feeling of guilt. Hastily she jammed the shirt into her back pocket and reminded herself this was a man she needed to avoid.

As she exited the bathroom he was at the bar. He had no idea how much had changed in this short afternoon ride, but for Deana, chasms had opened between them, and she definitely wanted to avoid building any bridges, no matter how charming he was. As an afterthought, she raked her fingers through her mud-encrusted strands of hair and pulled it back into the usual ponytail at the back of her head.

Deana stepped into the dimly lit bar and scanned the room. It was empty except for Ajai and the figure of a tall woman standing behind the bar near the cash register. Nellie, tall, bottle blond, and rough around the edges, was half owner of the business. The other half was a brawny, tattooed, ex-trucker who, five years ago, pooled all of his money, asked his longtime sweetheart to marry him, and bought this place for their retirement. The two offered their patrons cold beer, conversation, card games at the bar, and good tunes on the jukebox. It worked and the place was packed most nights during the summer and always on weekends. Deana knew the place because it was the only bathroom with a flushable toilet on the entire State Trail.

Deana did not know if Nellie knew who Ajai was, or if she cared. The woman did not hold with much ceremony for anything. Deana heard her laugh and wondered if the line was drawn at handsome, rich, playboys. Deana was tempted to walk out the door, mount Journey and head for home, leaving Ajai at the bar. Why is it I have the urge to act like such a witch whenever I'm around him? That is so not like me, she thought. She squared her shoulders and walked across the scuffed wood floor to the bar. Like she always did, she ran her hand the length of the highly glossed bar until she stopped directly across from Nellie.

Nellie was holding something in her hands, and when she turned to smile at Deana, it was not long before she waved it under her nose. "Will you look at this? After all this time, the stud here finally stopped in and autographed this picture. It's been hanging on the wall since old Bill sold us the place. It's the last autograph we needed from the team."

Deana attempted to look interested by asking, "Team, what team?"

"Uh, I don' know. What kind of team is this? The uniform looks kinda foreign. Maybe it's that English football they play with a bat, or something."

Ajai laughed, "No, it's a polo team. The original Duluth Polo Team. I had the honor of playing with some of the best players we ever had, but I was too young to appreciate it."

Deana reached out and took the picture, her curiosity stronger than her resolve to have nothing to do with Ajai, crumbled. The faded picture was typical, for men. They stood in a semicircle with their arms around each other smiling. Deana recognized most of the faces, but there were some she did not know had played polo with Ajai. The uniform was familiar, the white shirts with royal blue stripes and royal blue pants. The central figure was a slim young Ajai, whose head of wild curly hair and cocky grin, as he stood holding a polo mallet in one hand and a polo ball in the other, was a marked contrast to the other team members. "What's the significance of that pose?" Deana asked handing Nellie the picture.

Ajai sipped his frosty mug of beer and shrugged, "I don't know, some meaning lost in time."

Deana glanced out of the only window in the place. It was situated behind the bar and resembled a long narrow rifle window like in fortresses. It allowed patrons sitting at the bar to judge the weather and the time of day until the sun set, but nobody could see inside the bar.

"Look at that sky," Deana declared, "It'll be raining before we make it home. Time to hit the road."

"As usual. The girl only uses us for the john. Someday I'm gonna start charging for bathroom stops." Nellie threatened.

Deana laughed and waved as she walked out. "So you keep telling me. Remember the check's in the mail."

Ajai drained the glass and set it back on the bar, "Best beer I've had in years, thanks." He slid off the stool and followed Deana.

Nellie chuckled, the sound rasping in her throat. She picked up the mug and saw the bill underneath. "Hurry back," she called out loud, "and thank you." She added in a mutter pocketing the five-dollar tip.

29

Ajai knew even before he opened the heavy plank door that Deana had left him behind again. Cooing at the chestnut and grabbing the reins, he tried to figure out what it was about him that irritated her so much, but was at a loss. Once in a while she seemed to forget her animosity toward him, but not today. Today, she was more jumpy than usual, and suddenly he realized what it must be. She was dating somebody from work. The date she had turned down his mother's dinner invitation for, he thought to himself. Everyone at Jacoubi was buzzing about Deana and Genie's double dating.

He grinned. No wonder she acted like she was sitting on a thistle bush. Their riding together was completely innocent. A neighborly, after work horseback ride. It made perfect sense to him. She had to realize he meant nothing romantic by asking her. Ajai chuckled. He almost forgot who Deana was. He doubted she realized it. It was obvious she thought he had no moral values. Deana thought he was a playboy always on the make for a woman. He should try to explain that he wasn't trying to move in on another man's woman. He grinned again. It was more fun to let her get all flustered. A woman innocent enough to be bothered by propriety was too much of a novelty for Ajai to resist.

He swung the reins around the chestnut's neck and felt wet drizzle run down his neck. I'll be soaked before I get home, Ajai thought as he swung into the wet saddle. The horse pranced as Ajai turned his collar up and headed back down the trail. Deana was nowhere in sight.

Ajai loped the chestnut down the trail. The overhanging tree branches provided some protection, but it wasn't complete. The rain was not only wet but cold. He shivered like a wet dog. Where the trail divided, one track leading north and the other to the Michael's property, he felt the horse tense and saw Deana. Under the protection of a copse of ancient pine trees with wide thickly covered branches, Astride Journey, Deana waited. He saw her looking down the trail and then saw her visibly relax when she spotted him. She lifted her hand in a brief wave of greeting.

30

Deana held the rein tight to keep Journey from moving off down the trail. He let out a soft nicker when the chestnut and Ajai turned the corner. Deana swallowed hard to clear her throat as she watched the horse and rider approach. She felt like a drowned rat and knew she looked like one, but worse, she was a coward. While waiting for Ajai, she rehearsed the explanation she wanted to give for ditching him, but knew it was useless. She knew the minute she opened her mouth something awful was going to come out.

Ajai grinned and saluted her as he joined her under the overhang, "You were right."

Deana smiled wanly and bit back the childish, I told you so she was tempted to say. "It didn't take you long to catch up. I thought I might make it home before the rain, but here I am just as wet as you are."

"I'm going to start wearing a cowboy hat."

Deana glanced at him with a mischievous grin, "A cowboy? So you're looking for a new image?"

"I don't need an image. It'll keep the rain off my face." He swiped the wet drips from the end of his nose and chin.

Wet branches slapped against her as she nudged Journey to fall into step with Ajai. "Did you ever name the gelding or do you still call him Boy?"

Ajai sat back in the saddle, "Yes, as a matter of fact I named him Second Chance. I figured this horse," Ajai patted the chestnut's shoulder, "needed a second chance, but I call him Chance. Well, mostly I still call him Boy."

Deana laughed, "Chance is a good name. I like it." Silence stretched between them. Deana reached under the pommel of the saddle and pulled his tee shirt out. Handing it across the gulf between them, she said, "Thanks a lot for letting me use this. The paper towels in the bathroom have no right being known as any kind of towel. They absorb nothing. This came in handy. I appreciate it."

Ajai took the shirt and wiped his face with it, "No problem. I'm glad you waited. I wanted to apologize."

Deana lifted her eyebrows.

Ajai continued, "I forgot something important when I asked you to ride with me today. Well, I've heard that you're," he paused and pulled his collar closer to his neck, "I just didn't want you to think I purposely put you in an uncomfortable situation. That wasn't my intention at all."

Deana silently contemplated his apology and wondered what it was he was getting at. She opened her mouth to ask, her curiosity getting the better of her determination to not speak unless she had to, when he added, "I'm glad you like the guy your friend set you up with."

"What?"

"You know the guy you're dating now."

Deana frowned, "How did you...?"

"I don't remember exactly. I heard it somewhere. I suppose you're going to the regatta with him on Saturday."

Deana saw the wooden plank fence that outlined the front corner of her property and gave a sigh of relief. She shivered from the wet, and cold. "No, no I'm not. He's already teamed with someone for the race, and there wasn't room for me."

Ajai's face brightened. He said quickly, "I have room on my boat. Would you like to go out on the big lake? Nothing can beat it. Not even the ocean."

They kept the horses at a walk up the driveway and stopped in front of Journey's paddock. Deana turned to look at him. Ajai's golden curls were plastered against his dark tanned face. His eyes squinted with small wrinkles at the corners when he smiled. He looked as carefree as a kid and so handsome her heart pounded all the harder. Without hesitating

Deana asked, "What if it's windy?"

"Then the lake shows an entirely different side. It's awesome, and, it can get rough. It isn't for anyone faint-hearted if it gets stormy. Oh wait, I've done it again. Will your... boyfriend understand?"

Deana looked to see if he was teasing her. She ignored the reference to David, "I'd love to go out on the big lake. What time and where?"

Ajai grinned, "I'll pick you up eightish Saturday morning. Bring sunblock and wear a sturdy pair of shoes that won't slip. See yah." He raised his hand in a salute and leaned forward in the saddle, kicking Chance into a canter. They splashed through the puddles in the yard and galloped around the backside of the house, disappearing from sight.

Deana sat in the cold rain that began to fall in huge drops. She said out loud, "I'm so confused. How is it possible to love someone that, most of the time, I don't even like and I definitely don't trust, and then he turns out to be so..." She lifted her face and hot tears mixed with the rain, as she wailed, "Why does he have to be so wonderful?"

31

Genie made Deana promise to wait for her at the main gate of the Yacht Club. When Deana had left the dock to go meet Genie and Matt in the parking lot, Ajai said, "We have to leave promptly. If you aren't back in time you'll be left behind."

Now Genie was fifteen minutes late. Deana paced the blacktop, looking through the shiny metal fence that bordered the marina. The warm sunshine and the gentle breeze made it a perfect day, especially perfect for a sailboat ride on big Lake Superior. The smooth surface of the water reflected the sapphire blue sky. Deana turned her face toward the sun, closed her eyes, and willed herself not to get impatient.

While her eyes were still closed, Deana heard, "What an absolutely fabulous day to go sailing."

Deana spun around and clapped her hands. "Where have you been? We've got to hurry or we're going to be left behind." Deana reached out and grabbed Genie's arm dragging her through the open metal gate and down the walkway that led to the docks. "Ajai's berth is at the end of the dock. Hurry!"

Genie, with a hand on her straw hat, ran as best she could in her high-heeled sandals. Twice she stumbled and cried out, "Stop!"

Deana dragged Genie forward without slowing her pace. As they hurried onto the narrow wooden walkway of the dock, several of the sailboats were already motoring out of the dock area, and Deana's heart raced in her chest.

"I've waited all my life to go out on a sailboat in Lake Superior, if I miss it now when I'm so close, Genie... so help me."

Genie panted, already out of breath from the short run, but she managed to gasp indignantly, "Are you threatening me? How can you be so heartless? Look at these shoes I'm wearing. I'm going to break an ankle the way you're man-handling me. If anyone has the right to be threatening some-one it's me."

Deana saw Matt standing at the end of the pier craning his neck to look in their direction. Deana waved her hand high and hoped he saw her. She sprinted, dragging Genie the re-maining half block. "Matt, Matt we're here." Deana cried out.

"Hurry, Ajai's already started backing out, but he's still close enough for us to jump on board."

Deana dropped Genie's arm and the other girl slowed to a stop. "It's your turn to carry her," Deana called to Matt as she sprinted down the dock. The boat shoes she'd bought espe-cially for today stopped her from slipping on the slick sur-face. As she reached the sailboat, Ajai stepped on the edge of the boat and held out his hand to grasp hers, and before she had a second to think, or breathe, she was in the air and then amazingly standing next to Ajai on the deck. Seconds later, Ajai was hustling her to the back of the sailboat where the tiller was.

He gave her a quick push and said quickly, "Slide over to the opposite side and sit tight in the stern until I help the others on board. Hold the tiller steady, like this, unless I tell you to move it." Ajai's words were rapid but clear, as he moved back to the railing.

Deana nodded and sat down, grasping the large chrome wheel and watching the bow of the boat. Her heart beat heavy with apprehension. How uncanny that she had arrived early with Ajai. He had taken almost an hour to check over the boat, and during the entire time he explained the parts of the boat and how to use them. As Deana concentrated on the or-ders she had been given, she found the slow speed made it easy to keep the sleek little vessel on course. There were shouts from the shore and a sudden jerk sent the boat skittering away from the dock. Deana didn't dare look to see what caused it.

She stared straight ahead, concentrating on putting the boat back into the proper position.

She hoped Ajai would return soon, because she saw the end of the pier directly in front of them. Several minutes later, Ajai scrambled across the deck and onto the narrow seat next to her. Watching the angle of the bow, he reached for the wheel and straightened the course. Deana gratefully relinquished control, rubbing her wrist while she took a minute to look around.

Jacoubi employees lined the length of the wooden docks with their families. They created a loud ruckus yelling to all of the passing boats and their crews. Ajai's name could be heard loud and clear. Deana glanced at him, wondering if there was anyone special waiting on the dock for him. He laughed and waved like the true extrovert he was and reached over to nudge Deana. "Wave, Deana!"

Reluctantly, she glanced over her shoulder and waved as she tried to pick out familiar faces. Suddenly at the end of the dock, she saw a bright sunflower yellow sun suit that looked like Genie's. Leaning forward, she shaded her eyes and stared in horror. Genie and Matt both stood on the end of the dock holding hands and waving. The boat slipped away from the pier leaving them behind. Deana half stood in protest causing the boat to rock. She turned to Ajai with a mystified expression.

"They missed the boat," he explained.

Deana sank back onto the seat and laughed, "How long have you waited to say those words to somebody?"

Ajai grinned, "I tried to get them on board, but Genie slipped in those ridiculous shoes she's wearing. Then there wasn't enough time. I warned Matt about the shoes."

Deana said, "She probably didn't pay any attention."

"Well, it's just you and me. That means, with only two of us on board, it will be a lot of work and not much fun."

"Aye, Aye Captain." Deana declared with a mock salute.

"I hope you're that keen on sailing after we're through. Wait, I almost forgot!" Ajai cried, and eagerly flipped open the top of the padded bench next to him. He pulled out what looked like a baseball cap, but with a much longer visor. He turned the beige hat toward Deana so that she could see the bold blue letters, CREW. "I brought one of these for everybody, but oh well." He handed it to Deana who slipped it on her head and tucked her thick ponytail through the gap at the back.

"Why is it like this?" She asked fingering the brim.

"Blocks more of the sun. It's good for water sports. By the way, you might want to reapply your sunblock. This may be your only chance."

"Hey your initials are the same as your name A and Jay, Ajai, cool."

Ajai grimaced, "I'd like to say that was one of my Dad's ideas of efficiency, along with a dash of his humor, except it happens to be a Jacoubi family name."

"Really?"

"I take it, by the question in your tone of voice, that you want to know why it's a family name. I'll tell you, but only because we have a minute. Every second generation of Jacoubi's takes it upon themselves to name a son Ajai. It dates back to when the family came to Boston and started up a shipping business. They say it originates from British South Africa in the early eighteenth century. One of my relatives left Boston to find his fortune in South Africa, probably hunting for King Solomon's mines. Instead of sending back a fortune in gold like he intended, he sent a son with the name Ajai back to America. For some reason, my relatives have held it near and dear to their hearts ever since. Here, hold the wheel for just a minute while I check the rigging."

"What did the first Ajai Jacoubi accomplish for the family?" Deana asked.

Ajai shrugged, "I have no idea."

"It sounds to me like you weren't the only adventurer in the Jacoubi family."

Ajai walked to the front of the boat. It swayed in the current sending up spray as the force of the waves hit the hull. When he returned, he said, rather breathlessly, "I don't really consider myself an adventurer, not like my ancestor, and I don't have the immeasurable treasure of a son to give back to my family. They got stuck with me." He took the wheel back again, "Once we get to the bridge, I'm hoping, it'll already be up so we don't have to hold our position for too long. That's when the sailing is going to get tricky with only the two of us. Sailboats don't like to wait. They want to be out in the big lake with the wind and the waves. Whenever they're made to wait they buck and rear worse than any horse."

As soon as they rounded the corner, away from the yacht club's final dock, the bridge came into view. Deana felt a thrill of excitement to finally see the graceful arch of the silver lift bridge from the water. All her life she dreamed of doing this, but especially since she began working at the Jacoubi office. Every Wednesday night, she watched the sailboat races from the top level of the parking ramp. As the trim, white sailboats dotted the bay, she wondered what it was like to be looking at the shoreline from the water, what it was like to see the beautiful old houses, not from along London Road, from out on the big lake without any obstructions.

It had always been a delight to Deana when, if the wind was right, the sailors unfurled their many different spinnakers. The designs and colors of the sails made a kaleidoscope against the water and sky. As much as Deana enjoyed watching them, she hoped she enjoyed sailing just as much.

Ajai stood and leaned his bare muscular legs against the side of the boat while holding the wheel with one hand and binoculars in the other. He watched the lead sailboats bob in the wavy water. A loud siren wailed above them. Red lights flashed from the bridge as crossing arms lowered across the

135

road and pedestrian walkway. Slowly the lift bridge began to ascend. The alarm sounded loudly as the heavy metal girders rose skyward while the massive chains holding the counterbalances drooped heavily.

Ajai's sailboat dipped crazily, making the confined area of the cockpit seem entirely too small. The bridge loomed up in front of them like an immense towering silver sentinel. Looking at it, Deana found it easy to picture the effect the Colossus of Rhodes must have had on the small ancient Greek boats that passed by the huge bronze statue. Here, the Colossus of Duluth is the Aerial Lift Bridge. It guards the channel that leads out of the protective waters of the harbor into the unknown, oftentimes dangerous waters of Lake Superior. Deana felt a shiver of expectation along her spine. They were so small, and the boat seemed defenseless against the immense forces of nature. It was apparent to Deana that the boats and their crews were at the mercy of the big lake.

Deana glanced at Ajai. He looked out past the channel at the wide expanse of water. A delightful grin played on his handsome lips. He turned and met her gaze, his smile widening. The sunglasses and sun visor hid most of his face, but she saw, almost felt, Ajai's excitement for what lay ahead. The tenseness in the broad width of his shoulders, the wind in his hair and his face, the grin, as he looked ahead to the deep black water was proof that Ajai Jacoubi was indeed an adventurer.

The blast of a horn from above caused the gathering of sailboats to motor into the choppy waters of the canal. Ajai sat down and stowed the binoculars in the case mounted next to the tiller. "Well, this is it. We aren't turning back now. Are you ready, Crew?"

Deana nodded, holding tightly to the side of the boat. Cold water splashed against her hands, a sharp reminder that this was real. "This is really happening to me! It's not a fantasy! This time it's real!"

32

In slow motion the boats moved forward and organized themselves into a line passing under the magnificent bridge. When they glided underneath the maze of metal girders, Deana stared above, amazed at what she saw as they passed beneath.

"Wave to the bridge operator," Ajai shouted above the sound of the alarm, sirens, boat engines and the slapping of the water against the hull.

Deana immediately lifted her hand, staring up at the small gray building. It resembled a small house suspended among the metal mish mash of rafters. It was like a crow's nest perched along the mast of a sailing ship. Deana anxiously watched the blank dark windows and wondered if she really expected someone to wave back.

The canal was lined with people watching the sailboats parade past. Tourists flocked to Duluth, and especially to the canal, during the warm months of summer. Those who lived in the vicinity of the lake tended to take the natural wonders of the area in stride. When visitors from the Dakotas or one of the other plains states came to Duluth and first caught sight of the freshwater lake, and how it vanished beyond the horizon, it always made a lasting impression.

For Deana, who lived inland, away from the lake, she began to notice how everything on the lakefront changed from year to year. More tourist attractions filled the already crowded area. When the tourists flooded the canal, it became more of a carnival atmosphere, filled with energy, and activity. The central hillside area of Duluth remained largely unaffected by the surge in tourism.

Deana smiled at the mass of different faces watching from the cement walls of the shipping canal. Some daredevils were hanging over the barriers waving. Deana waved back.

Ajai chuckled when he saw her.

"I don't care if I look silly," she cried defensively. "Just look at those little kids waving at us. See that one wearing the pink? She even has an American flag in her hand. Just like a picture post card. They're so sweet."

Ajai glanced at the crowd for a moment then turned to study what was ahead. The boat sailed smoothly past the tall lighthouse, that silent white and black guardian that announced their departure from protection. The heavy circular concrete walkway around the structure swarmed with people.

Ajai called to her, "When we move into the big lake sometimes there's a cross current. It can cause quite a jolt. Hang on tight, and don't get caught by the main boom, in case it swings over." He pointed at the thick wooden beam that held the mainsail.

Deana sank against the back of the sailboat and moved closer to the wheel, watching the mainsail suspiciously. Even though she was prepared, the force with which the small sailboat hit the heavier waves of the open lake sent her off the seat to the floor. For a second the boat felt airborne, Ajai kept a hand on the unfurled sail as the boat's motor carried them into the force of the wind.

"Hold the wheel steady while I unfurl," he called out. After the sail was free, he cranked on the winch, lifting the fabric slowly as the billowing material filled with air. The wind picked up the sail fast. The boat skimmed across the water. Ajai darted across the deck, moving like a madman. He trimmed the sail back to cut the speed and rewrapped the lines.

Deana's job was to hold the wheel and move it only when Ajai shouted directions. Soon Deana knew what was expected and was able to anticipate his commands, moving the wheel before he shouted.

Ajai checked the sail and the lines. He looked at the lead boats and darted to the back to stand next to her at the wheelsman position. His windbreaker wet with spray, his face red from his exertions, his voice quick with excitement, he said, "If we hold this tack, we can have a snack before the race." He pulled a box out from under the seat, opened it and handed Deana a wrapped sandwich. "Once we're racing there won't be any extra time. Can you reach that bench seat? Just lift the latch and it should open."

Deana crouched low and fumbled her hands along the seam of the seat until she grasped the metal latch. Inside were cans of pop covered with ice. She exclaimed, "This is a cooler?"

"Aye, aye," Ajai said, shoving part of his sandwich in his mouth.

Deana grabbed a Coke and held it out to him then, took another for herself. Ajai popped open the can and drained it in two gulps. He shoved the rest of the sandwich in his mouth and then jammed the can and wax paper into a small hatch in the hull. "That's where the garbage goes," he said. He kept one hand on the wheel and one eye on the boats out ahead of them.

Daintily, Deana opened the can and placed it in the holder on the rail next to her. With her hands free, she unwrapped her sandwich. She lifted the corner of the bread to see what was inside, "Peanut butter and jelly, my favorite."

"Mine too, but I packed them for the peanut butter. It stops hunger pains for hours."

Deana opened her mouth to take a bite as a wave splashed over the side of the boat. It doused her sandwich, her pop and her lap. Wrinkling her nose, she stared at the soggy mess and wondered if lake water made the food inedible. She took a tentative swig out of the can. The pop, unlike the sandwich tasted fine. She put the damp sandwich to her mouth as a screaming gull dodged past the mast and swooped down at the top of their heads. Another soon joined the lone gull, and soon more than a dozen circled and dove at them.

"Watch out! Those buzzards can see a speck of food from

anywhere in the sky. They're so gutsy they'll steal it right out of your hands," Ajai warned her.

Deana quickly tore a piece of the sandwich and stuffed it in her mouth as she shielded the rest of it from the greedy gulls. She finished her sandwich, all the while glancing over her shoulder for screeching, winged thieves.

After the hasty lunch, Ajai handed her a life vest.

"This warning is a little late, but don't take it off until we dock. We never should have left the pier without them on. You swim, right?"

"Of course I can swim," she declared. With a nervous glance at the cold dark water just over the side of the boat, she doubted her swimming ability would save her if she fell in out here. Hastily, she pulled the vest on over her cotton shirt and clumsily tried to clasp the fasteners together.

"Don't worry about trying to swim in this water, the cold will kill you first," Ajai said matter of factly. He moved closer to her. His height, and the width of his shoulders, covered as they were by a plain white tee shirt, seemed more pronounced on the confines of the narrow aft-deck. He brushed her hands aside chuckling, "Here, let me help. If the straps aren't adjusted right, and you do land in the water, you'll slip right out of it." His tan capable fingers moved over the vest in a professional, impersonal action.

Deana, flustered by the close contact, doggedly kept her eyes on the teak flooring, to keep from looking at his face.

Ajai stepped back, giving a sharp tug on the front of the vest, and nodded approvingly. "There, everything looks ship shape." He took the tiller again.

They were a two-man crew amongst the crews of no less than four. She expected that they would remain forever behind the pack, especially when she was a complete beginner. But, she watched as their boat sailed past vessel after vessel.

Ajai had handed her command of the wheel while he moved up the deck, then he came back and explained, "A lot of the people ditch the race and take a pleasure cruise and party. They're in for a surprise when the Coast Guard starts patrolling." Ajai pointed at one of the larger boats.

Deana looked over and recognized a group of Jacoubi Enterprises secretaries who were now scantily clad in bikinis and lounging on the foredeck of a large powerboat. They were holding tall drink glasses complete with paper umbrellas. While they were moving fast and passing a number of other regatta competitors, no matter how Ajai adjusted the sails, they could not catch the leaders.

Deana remained at the wheel watching and doing as she was told. When Ajai found the chance to pause and look around, he pointed out some of the interesting sites on the shore. Even without binoculars, Deana was able to pick them out.

She saw the Malt Shop on the Lake Walk, then Leif Erickson Park. The pavilion was easy to pick out from the water. Up on a hill, clearly visible from the water and silhouetted against the blue backdrop of sky, sat The Cathedral of Our Lady of the Rosary. The white steeple in the blue sky looked like a spire of ancient architecture.

Just as Ajai was preparing to turn around and head back, he pointed up the shore and said something to her. Deana tried to hear his words, but it was impossible with the wind in her ears and the constant splashing of the water. She looked at the shoreline and saw, jutting out into the water, a brick dock attached to a boathouse. Connected to it was a peaceful looking stretch of unoccupied beach. Deana realized it was the Congdon Estate, Glensheen. She squinted and wished they were going further up the shore so that she could get a look at the main house from this unique perspective.

Ajai had her turn the boat hard to port and soon the shoreline became an indistinct wall of browns and greens blending together. They followed the leading sailboats and Ajai began playing out the spinnaker as they sailed with the wind. The bright blue with red stripes snapped tautly in the wind as he trimmed the sail. Again the boat shot forward with a burst of speed. Deana followed Ajai's instructions while he attended the sails.

After a long run to the east, Ajai again commanded a port turn, and, after a while, the canal and the Lake Walk began to take form as they sailed toward the busy waterfront area.

Deana noticed that the sailboats nearest them had all hands on deck. The closer they all sailed to the canal, the busier the other crews were. Ajai moved non-stop as he began to lower the sails. Deana felt completely useless sitting in the back doing nothing to help. She wondered if the race was over and who won. Sailing in a race on Lake Superior was an experience she would never forget. It wasn't an event that she ever needed to repeat again, but it was something she'd remember forever.

33

Throughout the race, Deana had tried to keep track of how much water was splashing into the boat. How much water could a sailboat like this take on before it sunk? She thought. She hid her anxiety from Ajai and even smiled when she pictured how Genie might have dealt with the situation. It was certainly more rugged than either of them had expected.

Ajai tightened the last knot holding the canvas just as they turned into the canal. With his shoulders stooped to avoid the swing of the mainsail beam, he walked to the stern and leaned down to switch the motor on.

Deana held onto the wheel until he reached for it. He sat down next to her and wiped his face with his sleeve. He looked exhausted. While all she did was steer and watched him running ragged across the deck. How useless can a person be? she thought.

Suddenly, Ajai pulled off his sunglasses and leaned close to her face. He frowned and shook his head at her.

Deana backed away. She covered her cheeks with her hands and demanded, "What? What is it?"

"You're sunburned."

Deana stared at him speechless. Then she burst out laughing.

Ajai looked mildly surprised at her reaction. He said, sounding affronted, "Sunburn isn't funny. You're face will probably peel."

Her uncontrolled laughter was not about sunburn, it was the fact that they had returned to the canal safe and the ordeal was almost over and nothing dreadful had happened to either of them. Deana wiped her eyes, still laughing, "I... I'm sorry, but that sounded so funny."

"You should have put more sunblock on."

Deana sat rigidly on the narrow wooden seat and snapped, "I've just spent the afternoon in a complete state of terror, suspended between life and death, and you expect me to get upset because you're fussing about a little sunburn? As for sunblock it wouldn't have mattered if I had put it on. I've been almost drowned by the size of the waves splashing over the sides. The sunblock would have washed off. I'm surprised I didn't get washed off right into the lake."

Ajai declared scornfully, "Now that I think of it, you're right it's windburn. Sunblock wouldn't stop that. What do you mean life and death? Your life was never in danger. The waves out there today were nothing and they certainly weren't strong enough to knock you overboard."

"How was I supposed to know that? I've never been out there before. I've never steered a sailboat before. They can capsize. I know they can. And one of those times you were jibbing or keeling or whatever, what if the boom had knocked me overboard? How far would you have sailed away before you noticed I was gone? You told me the temperature of the water would kill me. How long does that take seconds? Minutes? Hours?"

Ajai pushed his cap up almost off his head. He had the decency to look ashamed. "Sorry about that. You were so efficient I forgot this was all new to you. You did a great job, Deana. I couldn't have asked for a better crew." He grinned. "But, if you were afraid of capsizing or falling out, why didn't you ask? I would have told you its pretty unlikely, novice or not."

Deana stood and stretched the muscles in her back and shoulders wondering why she was so sore. She rubbed her wrist, "I'm stiff and exhausted and I didn't do any thing except stand here the entire time. How do you feel?"

Ajai was busy watching the sailboats ahead of them. Content that they were continuing toward the bridge at the same pace, he shrugged. "It's almost over now. The bridge is already going up for the boats in the lead. You know what? I'm dying of thirst. There's bottled water in the cooler. Help yourself if you'll get me one too."

"I guess it's the least I can do since I've sat and watched you work for the entire day." Deana lifted the seat and pulled out two bottles that frosted when the heat hit the plastic. "This looks so good," she exclaimed opening the top and handing it over. She was just feeling too chummy with him. She put it down to the feeling of relief that she hadn't been the one to cause an accident today.

The crowd along the canal looked even more massive at this time of day. As they motored through the canal, she realized she had no idea what the time was. "What time is it?"

Ajai looked at the sun. "Around three, I guess. We have plenty of time. The dinner and dance don't start until seven. I think cocktails are being served here until five, and then its dinner and dancing at the warehouse. It's on the waterfront but on the Superior side. We'll have to take the bridge over."

Deana fell silent, sipping her water and watching the sun shining through the superstructure of the bridge, she said, sounding rather prim, "I had a lot of fun today. Thank you for inviting me."

"I'm glad. Did you get a chance to see your boyfriend?"

Deana gave him a mystified look, "Huh."

"I don't know how I'd feel about my girl spending the entire day on the lake alone with another guy."

Deana refused to look at Ajai, wishing he hadn't ruined the homecoming by bringing up David. Deana had no idea how David would react, but she found she didn't want to be bothered with him. She thought, how am I going to get myself out of this situation?

The sailboat directly in front of Ajai's turned into the dock and Ajai followed. The heavy smell of heat, gasoline, and stagnant water became nearly overpowering once they were in the confined area of the yacht club. Deana stood by the wheel waiting for instructions from Ajai when she heard a shout from shore, "Deana."

Deana looked around expecting to see Genie and Matt. They should still be hanging around having nice cold drinks delivered to them by waiters, while she felt like she'd gone through a gale.

But, it wasn't them. Standing on the dock next to a sailboat bigger than Ajai's, stood David. He wore such a look of surprise that he looked almost comical.

Ajai stepped from the side of their boat onto the dock and tossed his mooring line around a deck cleat..

Deana waved to David when the boat slammed against the old tires hanging on the dock. She fell backward grabbing the boom to steady her self.

Ajai jumped nimbly to the side of the boat and reached over to offer her his hand. Awkwardly, Deana grabbed onto him. Her legs were shaking when she stepped out of the boat onto the dock.

Ajai quickly reassured her, "It's only your sea legs, or in this case, your lake legs. Don't worry about it. The feeling only lasts a minute."

Deana moved away, "Thanks."

"No problem," Ajai said. He jumped back on the boat and handed over the duffel bag she had brought on board. "I've just got to lock up and then I'll be ready to go."

Deana sighed in relief, grateful for an opportunity to escape him, at least for a minute. She hurried to leave him and the dock.

David was waiting for her on the main dock. His expression was guarded as he approached her, "So, you were crew for Ajai Jacoubi?"

Deana wished for an escape, but there was none. "Yes, yes I was."

"You and who else?'

Deana started walking away from the area where Ajai would eventually appear. She did not want Ajai to hear their conversation, or, if possible, to talk to David at all. David followed close behind when Deana heard running footsteps.

"Deana, wait a second."

Deana looked to the sky in frustration, wondering what she'd done to deserve this. She had no experience with men, especially two men who did not know each other, and, as far as she could tell, did not seem to want to know each other. Genie might know how to handle this, but where was she?

Ajai bounded down the deck and stopped next to them, "Hi, David. I know we've worked together, but I don't remember if we've been introduced."

David slowly extended his hand, "Well, I have been at Jacoubi for over a year... "

Ajai interrupted, "On the ninth floor, I believe. I do know that."

And everyone fell silent.

People getting off the other sailboats lining the docks walked toward the boathouse where a bar and tables had been set out for the Jacoubi employees. Those who recognized Ajai, looked at him, and at the two with him. Their curiosity obvious, but they did not loiter long.

Deana murmured nervously, "I think we should move out of the way."

Men and women were pushing past them, barely able to keep their footing on the wooden planks.

"Yeah, you're causing a traffic jam," one woman said. She glared at Deana as she pushed past them. Her face looked more sunburned than Deana's felt.

David hesitated then asked, "By the way, how did your boat do?"

"I have no idea, but we had a great day. I'm sure we'll hear the outcome of the race at dinner tonight. Deana did an outstanding job, and this was her first time sailing. Is that why she wasn't on the same crew as you?"

David definitely looked uncomfortable. "Well, it wasn't my boat. I couldn't ask her to crew. Pete is a serious sailor, and he only wanted experienced sailors for the race. You knew that already didn't you, Deana?"

Deana felt like she was in the middle of a brewing storm and was helpless to do anything about it. She smiled wanly at David without answering.

Ajai said to David, "Then you must have done really well if all eight of you were experienced. That boat must have been flying when we sailed into that crosswind from the canal."

"How should I know? I don't know that much about sailing," David said and then his face fell, realizing what he just admitted.

"Oh," was all Ajai said. He pointedly turned to Deana, "Deana we have to get going home or we won't make it back for the dinner."

"I'll see you later, David," Deana called to him.

David simply waved.

As they walked away, Ajai made a move to put his arm around Deana's shoulders, then stopped himself.

She glanced at him in time to see him awkwardly drop his arm to his side and wondered what was going on. Was it her imagination? Or had Ajai just about put his arm around her? She pressed her fingers against her temple. A day like today certainly did not warrant any need for schoolgirl imaginings. Everything that happened was like a dream for Deana. Nothing real or lasting would come of it, but, if Ajai had even absently contemplated an expression of possessiveness toward her, well, it added a pinch of fairy dust to the dream.

34

On the way home, the scenery quickly changed from city to rural as Ajai sped down Jean Duluth Road. Country music, muted by the powerful car's motor, echoed from the rear speakers. They rode in silence until Ajai's voice practically exploded between them, "So, that's what new love is like!"

Deana glanced over and snapped, "What?"

"You and David. You haven't been dating very long, have you? I hope you're not offended that I'm asking. I'm only curious."

"Right," She muttered and turned away.

"No, really, I've never been in love before. I don't know if I'd recognize if I was in love."

In disbelief, Deana stared at his profile, "I don't believe you."

Ajai turned giving her a puzzled look, "Why would I lie?"

Deana looked down, "I don't know, but you've always had girlfriends."

Ajai chuckled, "Yes, I have, but that doesn't mean I've ever been in love with any of them. Love is the feeling that makes you want to spend the rest of your waking hours with only one person. I've never felt that way about a person before."

"Then how do you know the definition?"

He shrugged, "Song lyrics, poetry, novels, how does anyone know the definition of love? The women I've known want to steal a man's heart and put it in their pocket to keep as some kind of a trinket. No, I've never been in love, but I've watched my parent's. Their love has lasted for thirty years." He grinned, "I know because their anniversary is this December. My mother keeps reminding me."

Deana smiled, intrigued by the sheepish tone in his voice, "Isn't it customary for your mother to keep reminding your dad about their anniversary? Why is she telling you?"

Ajai fell silent, and Deana had the impression he was not going to answer.

"She's not hinting for a gift; She's reprimanding me."

This took Deana completely by surprise, "That doesn't make sense."

"If you knew my mother, it would make sense. She considers being unmarried a major character flaw."

"You're not that old."

His tawny eyes lit up when he grinned her, "Well thank you... I think. By the way, what time can you be ready tonight?"

Deana swallowed the sudden lump that blocked her throat, "I really am bushed after the boating today. I don't know if I'll be able to keep my eyes open for tonight."

Ajai laughed loudly, "That's the lamest excuse I've ever heard. No really, how long will it take you? I'm asking because my parents want to get there early. Then they can put in an appearance and not be late getting home, especially with Dad's health."

"Then why is he going?"

"He has to. People want to see him, and he wants to see all of them. If we take off early it won't be a problem for you will it? I'm sure if you do decide to stay, Matt's going to be around. He'll give you a ride, or I can always come back and get you."

Deana stared out the window and shook her head.

"Oh that's right, I forgot about David. I'm sure he'll want to drive you home."

"Will you stop arranging my life," she cried in exasperation. "I am perfectly capable of making my own arrangements to get home. If you have to leave early don't worry about me."

"Okay, okay. I didn't mean to arrange anything."

They both fell silent. The lack of conversation hung in the air until Ajai spoke again, "My mother is really looking forward to meeting you. After you missed out on her dinner invitation, she's been after me to invite you and Frank over again. She wanted to call you about tonight, but I convinced her that I'd ask you. Your father's last visit certainly lifted my father's spirits. They were friends you know, still are, so they were quick to reconnect. They said I was three so you must've been a baby. Our parents used to play cards together and barbecue. Your mom and my mom rode horses in the local shows. My mom was really excited when I told her you guys were riding to the party with us tonight."

Ajai drove up the driveway and stopped the car at the back door of the Michael's house. He turned to face her. One tan long-fingered hand dangled lazily across the leather-covered steering wheel. Deana stared at it. Then her eyes darted to his face before she looked away.

He said softly, "Of course, if you think David might object, then I completely understand. My mother will just have to be disappointed. If I was David, I know I wouldn't understand my girl getting a ride with another guy and his family."

Deana flung open the door, prepared to make a hasty departure. Hesitating, she turned. He might read the chaos of emotion in her face bright pink from windburn, or might finally understand how flustered he made her. To cover her confusion, she said quickly, "David isn't like that. I'll... I'll be ready at five-thirty."

She slammed the car door and ran up the back stairs and into the house. The screen door banged shut behind her. She leaned against the door to take a deep breath. Her heart raced against her ribs. What irony that Ajai would ask her advice about love!

35

Deana twisted to see herself in the ancient mirror that hung in the bathroom.

"Why didn't I just tell him I couldn't go? This outfit is totally unsuitable, but I have absolutely nothing else to wear," she said. Staring at the faded reflection, she brushed her hair back from her face.

The blue silk skirt that floated around her ankles was old. So old, she thought, that the style has already returned to chic. She had worn this sapphire blue skirt and matching sleeveless top for the high school graduation. She'd kept it around for one of those few special occasions that unexpectedly popped into her life like tonight. She pulled at the top. It looked snug, but there was nothing to be done now. The sandals she'd bought for the outfit eight years earlier definitely did not fit, so she wore a pair that were newer but still out of date.

"Wow, you look like a knock-out." Frank stopped in the hallway to look in at her. "Who are you all dressed up for? That fellow from work?"

Deana's hand paused before she touched the curls around her cheek, before she reluctantly answered, not quite sure what the truth really was, "I don't really know. This is the only suitable dress I have. Is it too dressy, do you think?"

"Too dressy? Certainly not, you've worn it before but for some reason it looks different tonight. I know what would go perfectly with that outfit, come here, Dee."

Deana, her curiosity sparked by her father's sudden animation, followed close on his heels. Frank opened the cupboard of his armoire and pulled out a jewelry box that Deana recognized as her mothers. He opened it and took out a velvet box. With a flick of his finger, the lid sprang open revealing a string of pearls, each pearl identical in size and color. In silence he stared at it and then, as his voice strained, he said, "I gave these to your Mother for a wedding present. I don't know why I never passed them on to you before this. Rather silly of me, but I forgot they were here, until I saw you in that dress. You look so much like her tonight, Deana. It takes me back years."

Deana barely breathed as she turned and lifted her hair. She felt her father's hands tremble against the back of her neck when he placed the necklace against her skin. "I'm sorry it's taking me so long. The clasp is tricky," he muttered hoarsely.

Deana brushed the wetness that strayed down her own cheeks, placing a smile on her lips, as she slowly turned around. Her eyes shining with tears, she said, "Thank you." She fingered the silky texture of the pearls and pressed a kiss to his warm, rough cheek before hurrying back to the bathroom to look in the mirror.

"They're perfect." She called out to him.

"So, who is picking you up?" Frank asked following her back to the bathroom.

Deana glanced sharply at her father, "Who else would be picking me up?"

"You haven't mentioned David lately. I thought some other man at Jacoubi might have noticed the jewel in his midst. Not that I'm complaining at the nearsighted group you work with. Your mother was just such a jewel, and I thank God every day, that I was the one he chose to recognize that treasure."

Deana laughed merrily. "Aren't you full of talk tonight? Tell me more about you and mother."

"Don't change the subject. I want to know your plans."

Deana stomped her foot, "I can't believe that tonight, of all nights, you want to know details. Why? You haven't questioned me like this since I graduated from high school."

He stood inside the door and watched her. "Actually, I

was invited to go with the Jacoubi's tonight. If you were going with them I planned to accept."

Deana was stunned. She stared at him then, a slow smile brightened her face, "How wonderful. Of course that's who I'm going with. And with you along, he can't be the one in control of the night."

Frank frowned, "What's that supposed to mean? Who is this he you're referring to?"

Deana shook her head and tried to move around her father. Frank was a big man and when he blocked a doorway, the doorway remained blocked.

"It doesn't matter. Get out of the way. I have to use the phone. I'll be riding into town with you instead."

"I'm not moving. We need to talk. I just got off the phone with Ajai. He said he was picking us up at five-thirty. The way he said it, I thought you already knew."

Deana shot him a look of surprise. "It'll be easier if we drive ourselves. We'll save them the trip over here."

Frank stared at his daughter in amazement.

Deana pleaded, "Why don't we just drive ourselves, Dad? The Jacoubi's will have plans of their own for tonight. Then we can leave whenever we want and we don't have to inconvenience them."

The look Frank gave his daughter stopped her babbling. He said, "Who cares about all that? I'd much rather ride in a decent vehicle than my beat up station wagon. I can't imagine why you wouldn't want to ride along with the Jacoubis. Is there another reason?"

Deana dropped her eyes to the floor and nervously chewed at her lower lip. "I know it sounds silly, but arriving at a Jacoubi event, in Edward Jacoubi's car… It's going to cause plenty of gossip, especially after I was the only passenger on Ajai's sailboat this afternoon. You can imagine what people are already saying."

"Since when are you worried about what people say?"

"Oh Daddy, how can you ask me that? This isn't high school. This is my job and the people I work with. Plus Ajai's my boss."

"What do you mean Ajai? I thought Edward was your boss."

"Okay fine, he is, but Ajai's the boss's son. It's just as bad."

"I'd think being seen with Ajai would be a confidence booster. He isn't old or ugly or broke. He's good-looking and sociable and nobody would dare snub him or his date."

Deana spun away from him, "That's just it. I don't want to be associated with people who snub other people. And when Ajai loses interest in the girl next door, because that's all I am to him, where will that leave me? The laughing stock of Jacoubi, that's where. I'll be pitied and whispered about." She covered her face with her hands. "I couldn't stand it, Dad. I really don't think I could stand that happening."

"That's a mighty fine argument, but I have to say I disagree with you."

Deana sighed giving him an exasperated look, "Why am I not surprised to hear you say that. Fine, you disagree, but before you try to explain, the Jacoubi's are arriving at five thirty and I'm not ready yet."

Frank asked, "Am I to understand this is a dress-up affair?"

Deana shot him a horrified look, noticing for the first time his wash-worn short sleeve shirt and patched khaki pants. "Of course it is. You need to change, and don't you dare try to tell me you haven't got a suit coat and tie, because I know better."

Frank held up his hands in surrender. "I wouldn't dare claim any such thing. I'll meet you downstairs when you've finished primping."

"Hurry," Deana cried before slamming the bathroom door in his face.

36

Ajai piloted Edward Jacoubi's big black Buick down the freeway toward Superior. Edward turned to look in the back seat. Next to his lovely petite wife, dressed in a lavender pantsuit, her favorite color, sat Deana and Frank Michaels, two people Edward had wanted to bring back into his life for a long time. Deana, at this age was the exact image of her mother. Her looks, mannerisms and the melodious sound of her voice reminded Edward of Colleen Murphy Michaels.

When Edward first met Colleen, he was a freshman in college. The gray-eyed Irish beauty had a dedication to knowledge and energetically pursued her studies. She also pointedly disdained individuals, like Edward, who took a good education for granted. Now, many years later, he saw a lot of himself in the wild antics of his son. Just when he was beginning to despair that Ajai would never grow up, Ajai surprised him and returned home declaring he wanted to take a serious part in the family business.

Edward glanced over at the handsome profile of his son, and smiled. He felt the pride of a father. He looked at Deana again. It was also apparent to Edward that Ajai had overlooked the excellent qualities of the girl in the back seat. The apple doesn't fall far from the tree, he thought. Edward wanted to point out the excellent qualities of Deana Michaels to Ajai, but he knew it was a waste of time. Edward had never listened to his own father where women were concerned.

At the beginning of his college years, Edward had been easily distracted by how women threw themselves at him. He knew one big reason for his popularity was his money. He was also handsome and witty. The combination attracted all kinds of women. He made the mistake of overlooking the fineness of a woman like Colleen Murphy.

Colleen had never approved of him. She accused Edward of being a playboy and taking his privileged life for granted and that he never had to work for anything. Colleen was the first woman who sparked both his intellect and his libido. In his senior year, at the College of Saint Scholastica, Edward realized he and Colleen would be parting ways and had a hard time understanding his feeling of loss. By the time he realized what a treasure of brains, natural charm, and good sense mixed in with sound judgment resided in Colleen Murphy, it was too late. She had fallen in love with someone else. He was a studious man and as poor as a church mouse. Frank Michaels had a lot of brains, but no capital, and very little drive to achieve the status money and power could give. He was content researching and teaching. With his simple ways and simple talk, Frank had taken over, and asked Colleen to marry him. Colleen accepted his proposal.

Edward never knew if Colleen realized how deeply he had loved her. She was the first woman he had ever wanted to marry. He left Duluth and moved to Boston. Edward's main purpose in moving to Boston was to work hard, make a lot of money, and forget Colleen. He succeeded in doing both, but it took time.

While in Boston, he met his wife Patricia. Patsy Louise turned out to be a woman like John Adam's, Abigail. She encouraged him, advised him and also insisted he work to help the community and local charities. She was a better woman than he deserved.

Edward interned for Virgil Paxton, Patsy's father. Virgil Paxton, a shipping mogul in Boston, worked with his father's family. At the time, Edward worked for his own family's business but soon found he was more interested in the shipping industry and left his family business to work for Virgil Paxton full-time. Patsy's family was built of old Boston money. They were raised to understand the importance of donating much of their time and a chunk of their yearly earnings to charities along with adding money to the family coffers. Virgil Paxton passed on his belief to Edward that businessmen are responsible, to a large degree, for the success and unity of their community. The experience helped him to develop a program to train young people from the high schools in area businesses. Then an apprenticeship was established at the college level. Job opportunities grew within the business community and kept young families from leaving the area.

Edward met Patricia Louise Paxton many times during the months of socializing in Boston. Never did he seriously think of dating her until a friend, her older brother Lane Paxton, Edward's classmate, encouraged him to ask Patsy on a date. Even after that one date, Edward continued to think of her as a friend until several years later.

Edward left Boston to begin training at the Jacoubi Technology business in Duluth. He realized after three short months that his love for Colleen had been wiped away by a deep love and admiration for Patsy. Edward asked Patsy to marry him. It surprised both of them, but Patsy knew what she wanted and it was Edward. She said yes immediately.

When Edward and Colleen's paths did cross again, he found he still wanted the best for Colleen, which included her husband. They were looking for a house and Edward offered them the old estate manager's house that stood on the outskirts of the Jacoubi's land. The house had been empty for many years and was in desperate need of attention. The Michaels loved it. Colleen was a busy, handy person and Frank quickly learned the finer points of plumbing and carpentry. Little by little the two of them fixed the old place up. Edward knew they were happy there. Unfortunately, the happiness was short-lived. Colleen Michael's death, at such a young age, was a tragedy they all felt.

37

Thin white clouds swirled designs upon the pale blue sky as the sun faded toward the west. Cars zipped across the bridge from Duluth to Superior. Deana scanned the blue waters of St. Louis Bay through the window of the Buick. Two huge ore boats were docked at the Superior elevators. Gulls circled the sky in large groups. A small island in the middle of the bay looked white from the terns nesting on its surface.

Ever since they got in the car, Edward had remained oddly silent, lost in thought, Deana guessed. Ajai had tried to keep the conversation going, but it was difficult until his father snapped out of his reverie and began answering Ajai's questions. Patsy too had remained quiet when the Michaels' first got in. Deana wondered if everyone felt uncomfortable.

"Deana," Ajai said.

Deana jumped. She saw Ajai's tawny eyes looking indirectly at her through the rearview mirror. "Look, that's the boat we saw out on the lake this morning. It was just coming into view from the North when we were on the lakeside of the bridge, remember?"

Deana looked out of the window. The big red and white boat loomed above the dock. Its long metal flanks were streaked with wide paths of rust. The slight breeze ruffled the Canadian flag flying from the top of the ship's smokestack. She stared at it with no recollection of seeing any boat while sailing. "Really," she murmured.

Why didn't she seem able to give more than monosyllable answers?

Patsy Louise turned to her and asked, "How did you like sailing? Ajai told us this was your first boating experience on the big lake."

Frank chuckled, "Her first boating experience ever."

Deana smiled wanly at her, "It's an experience I'll never forget."

Ajai broke in laughing, "That's the only comment I've heard from her about it. I'm not sure if that's a good sign."

Deana surreptitiously looked at the mirror and saw he was watching her again. Turning away, the warmth in her face deepened. At least with this sunburn, he couldn't tell every time he made her flush.

"I tried to convince her that I'm an extremely capable captain, Mother, but I don't think she believes me."

Patsy Louise smiled, "I don't see why not."

Edward said, "Perhaps it might be caused by her introduction to the sport. From the very first, when you dragged her off of the dock onto the deck of a moving sailboat, and then left the other half of your passengers stranded, she was not getting a good impression. Besides the fact that you joined a race you couldn't possibly win with a crew of only two in the busy shipping lane of Lake Superior, one of the most dangerous of the Great Lakes. I believe she had good reason to be nervous." Edward's dry tone caused them all to laugh.

Ajai added, "With a beginner, don't forget. And I believe I was the one taking the risks. Deana had no idea how difficult it would be with only the two of us, but we completed the course and returned to the dock safely. That's quite an accomplishment."

Deana listened gratefully, letting the talk flow around her. She appreciated that the long awkward silences when she was slow to answer, had been replaced with lightheartedness. Since she couldn't think of any intelligent conversation to add, it was nice to enjoy the others.

Immediately after they crossed the Highbridge, Ajai turned off the main road to follow a narrow side street. The street was clean but oddly empty. There were no pedestrians, no parked or moving cars. The road led them past several large brick buildings with windows boarded up with plain white planking. They left the nameless businesses behind and entered an open area where Lake Superior spread out before them. Blue water sparkled with white sunlight. The dark blue outline of Duluth across the water looked like a Mediterranean seaport.

Ajai pulled up at a large white metal building next to the waterfront. Behind a wire fence, at the back of the building, gleamed a row of semi tractor-trailers painted bright red and white. Parked cars lined the curbs all around the large parking lot. A small lot in front of the building was also packed with cars and trucks and SUVs. Ajai pulled in front of the double doors leading inside the building and stopped. He turned, leaning his arm across the back of the seat, "You guys get out here. I'll drive around and find a parking spot. I thought for sure we'd get here before everybody else."

Edward shook his head, "I told you, son. It's been years since you've been at one of these. This group of employees really knows how to enjoy a party."

"Okay, okay Dad, whatever you say. I'll catch up soon."

Opening the door, Frank said, "Everybody out." He held his hand to Deana. She scooted across the seat and stood. The breeze warmed her skin after the car's air-conditioned interior. Frank patted her bare arm and then helped Patsy Jacoubi. She stood next to Deana and looked her up and down.

"My goodness, you are so lucky to have such long legs."

Deana smiled. She liked Patsy's tone of voice. It was bubbly and warm, not at all what she expected. "Thank you, but I'm wearing heels."

The woman was not short by Deana's estimation. The top of her head reached Deana's shoulder, but she carried herself in such a stately way, that somehow, she looked taller. Whatever it was, she was a woman you noticed. Her hair was a chin length bob of auburn waves. The features of her face were marked from ordinary by her delicately curved chin and high cheekbones. Deana could not decide whether she was pretty or striking. Mr. and Mrs. Jacoubi certainly dressed like most of the other people Deana knew. They wore casual but stylish clothes without a lot of shiny jewelry. Patsy wore a thin strand of pearls similar to Deana's. Her wedding ring and slim gold watch were her only accessories. The jewelry was better quality than usual, but it wasn't meant to slap any-one in the face.

Frank and Edward stood together quietly talking when Patsy walked over and slipped her hand through her husband's arm. He looked down at her with a tender look. "Are you ready to go in?"

Patsy turned to Deana and asked, "Are you coming with us, Deana?"

Deana hesitated.

Frank asked quickly, "Are you meeting your friends?"

Deana shook her head, "I'm not sure."

Edward and Patsy walked away.

Frank held out his arm. "Come and have a drink with us. I'm sure you'll see them just as easily from the bar."

Deana looked through the open doors of the cavernous building, scanning the crowd moving inside. "I think I'll stay out here for a little while. Then I'll come in. The weather's so beautiful, I hate to go indoors."

"Ajai should be here in a few minutes. You can come in-side with him," Frank said.

Deana gave her father a narrow look, "I'm not here with Ajai, Dad. I told you that before."

Frank looked surprised. "I didn't mean to imply that you were. We're all in the same car. I just thought…"

"I know exactly what you're thinking and stop it. You'll only be disappointed. I mean nothing to Ajai and he means nothing to me."

Frank nodded toward the Jacoubis, "All right. But, I don't think I'm the only one thinking you and Ajai would make a good match."

Deana frowned, "The Jacoubis? No way!"

Frank said nothing.

Deana kept her voice low, "Well, all of you should be ashamed of yourselves. Arranged marriages are a thing of the past, and I have a hard time believing the Jacoubi's would approve of me as a match for their golden son."

"You say that because you don't know the Jacoubi's," Frank said. He gave her a disapproving look before he leaned over to kiss her forehead. "I'll be at the bar if you need me." He turned and took a few steps, then paused to say over his shoulder, "If that young man of yours is here I'd like to meet him."

Deana gasped, "David! I completely forgot about him. And Genie and Matt too. This has gotten so complicated."

Deana nervously played her fingers along the ornate metal clasp of her handbag as she watched her father and the Jacoubis disappear inside. David! She knew the night would get complicated. She should have broken it off with him before this. From behind, someone took hold of her arm. Deana swung around.

David, a sullen frown on his face, demanded, "Did I see you getting out of the Jacoubi's car?"

Deana winced at his grip and said, "You're hurting me."

He let go.

"Was that Ajai Jacoubi driving?"

"Yes," She stated coldly.

David's frown dissolved into anger. "What's going on? First you were on his boat at the race and now tonight."

"It's nothing, David. We're neighbors. Our parents are old friends. My Dad decided to come along and the Jacoubi's wanted him to ride with them... so I rode along." Deana tried to keep her tone light. She glanced around at the people walking past. They did not attempt to hide their curious stares. "Can we discuss this someplace else?"

David was obviously displeased. "Yeah. Over there," he nodded toward the lake. Deana set a brisk pace because she wanted to get away from the entrance of the building and Ajai's eventual appearance.

The sidewalk next to the narrow beach held several groups of people. They were dressed in party clothes but seemed intent on taking advantage of the sunset and balmy weather.

Deana, caught by the sight of the rosy glow of the setting sun over the bay, paused to enjoy the unexpected beauty. "Isn't this gorgeous? I never imagined what this side of the lake looked like."

David grunted in response, but did not slow to see what she was talking about.

For a moment Deana had forgotten whom she was with. Disappointed that she was not with someone who appreciated simple pleasures, she sighed.

He turned to face her. He crossed his thick arms giving her a hard stare.

Deana looked at his darkly tan arms and his Ralph Lauren polo shirt, his Tommy Hilfiger khaki pants and turned to stare at the water. Even watching the gulls was preferable to facing a disgruntled David.

"Well? What's going on here?"

At his tone, Deana felt heat flow through her veins until her face began to redden, "Excuse me?"

"I want an explanation."

Deana gave a sarcastic laugh, "Exactly what kind of explanation are you looking for?"

"Why are you hanging around Jacoubi? Has this been going on since he started at the office? Have you been chasing him behind my back?"

"Me? Chasing Ajai?" This time she did laugh. It was too too funny. All her life she'd been chasing Ajai, except for now, and here was David accusing her of doing just that.

David's eyes narrowed, "I don't like to look like a fool, Deana."

Deana tossed her head defiantly and looked him in the

eye. "The only one who can make you look like a fool David, is yourself. I owe you nothing, least of all an explanation for my actions. Since you don't appreciate this spectacular view of the sunset, we should go to the party."

David glanced around, "Don't raise your voice. It's embarrassing. Everybody would love to see some dramatic scene from us."

"Nobody cares about what's happening between us."

David shook his head. "Deana, I'm an important man. People at Jacoubi recognize me. There's no way they don't care."

This was certainly a new twist on how David felt. Deana knew he liked his position as a lawyer, but she didn't realize that he thought position made a difference. She raised her eyebrows, "If you say so."

They retraced their steps in an uneasy silence.

Deana, lost in her thoughts, berated herself for not telling him off, and adding with gusto, that she never wanted to see him again. And she would, but later. Why? Because she needed David to keep Ajai away. With David's accusations and her father's insinuations about the Jacoubi's, this friendship between Ajai and herself had gone too far and was becoming too Hollywood. It needed to end now.

38

Inside the cavernous building, the music played loud and fast. The tempo kept everybody on the dance floor, even though it was hot and humid among the crush of twirling, gyrating bodies. Deana slipped out of the room into the fluorescent twilight. The sound of the water, as she walked alone toward the lakeshore, soothed the pounding in her ears. The dampness on her skin dried, causing goose bumps along the flesh of her arms. The glow of light from the last rays of the sunset made her wonder about the time. Inside the building, with the flashing lights, the music, the chaotic movements of dancing and the roar of the band, made her lose track of reality. The neon lights that lined the boat docks gave an odd glow of orange to the sky. Mosquitoes slowly found her unprotected skin. The buzz around her became troublesome as the insects followed her leisurely gait.

Only a few yards away from a crowd that had to number 300, the night turned into something so peaceful. Deana had been waiting for an opportunity to slip away alone. David's attitude, when she first arrived, kept her from truly enjoying the short walk they took.

Couples with hands intertwined swayed slowly as they walked close to where the tide moved stealthily higher. Deana remained on the sidewalk and kept her own steps slow. She watched the couples with envious eyes. How nice to have someone special tonight. Someone you wanted to enjoy moments like this with. Alone in the darkness, Deana smiled at the nonsense of her thoughts. Ajai is the one she wanted to share a night like this with. It was entirely likely that Ajai's reaction to a romantic scene would be the same as David's. Men created romance, but many forgot how to enjoy the natural elements that enhance it.

Deana heard footsteps behind her and realized she was

standing completely motionless in the middle of the sidewalk, just staring. At least I'm facing the sunset so I don't appear to be a complete simpleton, she thought. Impatiently she swiped at a mosquito that found its mark and then turned around.

A deep voice said behind her, "I've finally found you."

Deana jumped and exclaimed, "Why are you always sneaking up and scaring me."

Ajai looked her over and said softly, "I didn't realize I was. I'm sorry."

She shrugged impatiently, "It doesn't matter. I was just going back inside. The mosquitoes are feasting on me."

"It's that soft skin of yours. They can't resist."

"Oh, right." Deana snapped, edgy that once again he caught her dreaming about him.

"I was looking for you. My parents are ready to leave."

"Oh, I was just wondering about the time. It has to be later than nine o'clock."

"It is. The folks were having fun and decided to stay. I think my Dad is about maxed out. So what have you decided to do, stay or ride home with us?"

"I'll have to ask. If Genie... or David... can't drive me home then I'll go with you."

They walked toward the building. Deana nervously asked, her words disjointed, "The party... It's um... great and still looks like it's going strong."

"Yeah and your friends are going strong too. They'll probably stay until the very end. It looks like they're having fun. I can't say the same about you."

"What does that mean?"

"Exactly what I said. You look sensational in this blue thing you're wearing yet you've never danced once. I've seen wallflowers at dances, but never to this extreme. Doesn't what's-his-name dance?"

"David," she corrected him automatically. "And mind your own business."

"I'm not sorry that I'm being pushy, Deana. Somebody has to speak up and tell it like it is. We've had a great day together, so I feel I have that right. As a matter of fact, we've had a lot of fun over the past few months and I thought we were at least friendly neighbors. You've ignored me all night. Your date hasn't asked you to dance once, yet, when I asked, you refused, and acted like I'd insulted you. And now, now you're making it obvious that accepting a ride home from me is the last option you're willing to take. So, I have a very valid reason to be involved with your business."

Deana nervously glanced around. None of the couples were close to them. She kept her voice low, "Ajai, I..."

Ajai interrupted, "See? There you go again. You're acting like this is a clandestine meeting. Did David blow his cool when you showed up with us? He doesn't own you. You aren't married or engaged or really dating as far as I can tell, by the way the two of you act. He has no right to get upset about you getting rides from other people."

Deana tried to keep her temper under control by staring at the streetlights above his head. She could never tell him David was only an excuse. "Yes, he did say something."

Ajai gave a derisive laugh, "I knew it. When I saw the two of you strolling away when we first got here, it certainly didn't give the impression of a lover's stroll."

"You were spying on us?"

"In a public place in broad daylight, that hardly falls into the spying category."

Deana said in a stiff voice, "Well, you were watching us when I didn't know it."

"Only until I could escape inside and get my hands on a strong drink."

"You've been drinking? You can't drive home if you've been drinking."

"One drink four hours ago, I'm well under the limit. Let's get back to the subject." he suggested in a silky tone Deana did not trust. "Tell me. What did dear David say?"

Deana suddenly stepped around him and hurried her pace, "All he said was he didn't understand why we were together so much." Deana skipped David's accusation that she was chasing Ajai.

Ajai clenched his jaw, "Did you ask him why he hadn't offered you a ride?"

Deana glanced at him, "No, I never thought to."

"Well, I thought about it. What kind of a guy asks a woman out yet has never been to her house? He's never met your father. Don't bother arguing with me, Deana. Frank already told me. I know what kind of guy does those things. One who isn't giving you the kind of treatment a girl like you deserves."

Deana, shocked that he was defending her, felt a rush of warm satisfaction, but she also reminded herself that Ajai was a master flatterer and got out of many close calls with the use of his well-oiled tongue. She replied flippantly, "I can take care of myself. I always have."

"I know you can, remember I'm the one you and your horse pushed into a ditch. Listen to me, Deana. When a guy takes you for granted right from the start, think of how he'll act in the future."

Deana had thought the same thing about David many times, but she forced a light-hearted laugh, "I don't see any reason to worry. Tell me, how do you treat your girlfriends from the start?"

"I don't remember. It's been so long since I've dated anyone for any length of time. Not since high school. You know I've been moving around a lot."

"So you're more experienced in one night stands than in any kind of a real relationship."

"I learned from watching my parents. They're still in love with each other after thirty years of marriage. I think that's a pretty good model to have, just like your parents."

Deana fell silent.

Ajai touched her shoulder. His long fingers smoothed across the silky material of her blouse. Deana's flesh tingled. She nonchalantly moved away before he noticed how his touch affected her.

"I'm sorry, Deana, I didn't mean to remind you of your mother. Why is it when I'm around you, the worst in me comes out?"

Deana held up her hand to stop him and said quietly, "It's not my mother I'm upset about. You reminded me of something my father said to me when we first got here." She paused. It sounded too conceited to say her father and his parents were hoping the two of them would end up involved romantically with each other, so she decided to play it safe and just stick to Frank's opinion. She kept her head lowered. She needed to hide her own feelings from his probing eyes. In a monotone voice she said, "My father, earlier tonight, insinuated that, that... he was hopeful you and I might eventually become involved in a... a romance. I have no idea where he came up with the idea or why he would suddenly care. It's a ridiculous idea and I told him so." She ended in a rush and held her breath, wondering what he would say.

"I know why he thinks that."

Deana lifted her head, "You do?"

Ajai smiled and reached out to take her hand. "I warned you about all of this before. Do you really think your father came up with the matchmaking idea? No way, but unfortunately, it has the clear signs of my mother's touch. She's been waiting years for an opportunity like this. Imagine our very neighbors to have such a lovely, charming daughter and she's so intelligent," He mimicked. Then he grinned, "It doesn't mean a thing. Just ignore them."

Deana blinked, uncertain if he was serious. "Ignore them? I can't ignore my father and now it's your parents, my dad, and David, and who knows who else? There's too much talk. After today I don't know what kind of stories will be going around the gossip chain at Jac E."

Ajai frowned. His eyes swept over her face. "You're upset by it?"

"Of course I'm upset. People are gossiping about us when there isn't any us." She sighed, "You couldn't possibly understand. How could you? All your life you've been the center of attention. I've never been a person anyone notices. That was before you showed up. Most of the people at the party tonight thought I'd just started working at Jacoubi when you arrived, and I've been working there longer than any of them."

"That's your fault, you know," Ajai said softly. "If you ever dressed like you did tonight, nobody could overlook you."

"Not exactly the outfit recommended for a working atmosphere," she retorted. "I know you're right. It is my fault. But I wanted to be a professional, working in a plush office. The work I do for the company is serious and I wanted to be taken seriously. I'm still waiting for that to happen."

Ajai frowned. "Who doesn't take you seriously?"

"It doesn't matter."

"Well, it does to me. If there's any kind of discrimination going on at Jacoubi, my father will want to know about it."

"It's not discrimination. It's more like the paranoia because of the difference between men and women and nothing can change that. The more a company spouts off about sexual discrimination, the more everybody focuses on those very differences that cause chemistry. Nothing can get rid of that chemistry. I get paid as much as the men. I get the same benefits, the same privileges and that's the equality."

"Then what are you talking about?"

"I'm trying to tell you. It only happens when I'm with you."

"Chemistry?"

Deana stopped talking and blushed to the roots of her hair. Aghast, she stammered, "A... A... Absolutely no, this has nothing to do with chemistry. I... I'm talking about the attention. I'm not used to it, but when I'm with you, I'm constantly in the limelight. Not just because you're Ajai Jacoubi, but also because you're the kind of person that acts like a natural light bulb. You attract all of the moths, and you don't even realize it." She had no idea if he understood what she was trying to say as she studied his handsome face. She always felt his magnetism, but refrained from saying so out loud to preserve what little pride she had left. I'm one of the moths who are afraid to follow your light because I know eventually it'll singe my wings and then I'll fall to my death. Then what will I do?

Ajai shoved his hands in the pockets of his pants. "So you're telling me because I enjoy life and do things to enjoy life, which, unfortunately, includes being with other people, we shouldn't do anything together because you don't want to be noticed or talked about? Nor should we be seen together by people at work, or by our families, because it too will cause talk. That's crazy, Deana. You can't live your life worrying about what other people think or say. All of that is their problem."

His words sounded incredibly harsh. Deana fought away the guilt, "Don't you see, Ajai? The only way we're going to stop the gossip is to stay away from each other."

"Who cares about the gossips?" Ajai demanded and frowned, "And how do you know anyone cares what we do? You've always given me the impression that none of this mattered to you. You always look to the positive. The important things in your life are family, a happy home and peace. Am I right, Deana? Aren't those the things you think are important?"

Deana stared at him. Her mind raced. What he said was true. She demanded, "Who told you that?"

"I don't have to be a mind reader to understand you. What you want is a simple, uncluttered life filled with contentment."

Ajai's right, she thought. That's exactly what I want, but

darn him. Why is he the one to notice? Suddenly, Deana knew for certain Ajai was the one who would enjoy walks in the twilight. He was the flesh and blood man of her dreams not just a crush she'd obsessed over in the flux of being a teenager.

39

Deana looked away from Ajai. No words could get past her tightly constricted throat. They were standing in front of the open doors and the rock music had stopped. Suddenly, the overhead lights went on, flooding over them in a harsh glow. Matt pushed through the edge of the crowd running toward them. His face strained.

Just then Deana saw David walking toward them from the other direction. He looked annoyed and Deana knew why. She stood helplessly, watching, wondering why the events slowly unfolding before her eyes looked like the climactic scene from a black and white movie. The two men arrived in front of them at the same moment. Matt blurted out breathless, "Ajai, you're father's collapsed! The ambulance is already here. Your mother's looking for you!"

Deana gasped and Ajai looked at her. When their eyes met, the look of stark desolation on his face gave him a vulnerability Deana did not expect. Instinctively, she moved toward him to offer comfort. He took a step toward her, and opened his mouth as if to say something. His eyes flicked toward David, and he tightened his lips. His face lost all expression. "Let's go," he said to Matt. The cold look of dismissal he gave her before silently following Matt left Deana feeling like she'd done something wrong.

David hissed in her ear. "We need to talk."

Deana shook her head no. Already her eyes scanned the people around them. "No, I have to find my father and see what's going on."

"You heard Matt. They already loaded him into an ambulance. How long ago did the two of you sneak off together?"

Deana barely looked at him. "Where is Frank? Poor Ajai, he must be frantic." she murmured.

"There's nothing left to do here," David said. "We might as well go. I'm sure it won't be long before the party breaks up, and I want to get this straightened out between the two of us."

Deana, exasperated by his lack of concern, insisted, "I can't leave without my father."

David grabbed her by the arm and spun her around. His eyes were cold and black as he stared at her. She smelled the liquor on his breath and wondered if he was drunk. His thin upper lip lifted in a sneer. "You don't think I know what's going on, do you?" She felt violated by his irrational accusations. "I know exactly what you're up to. What you've always been up to. You've been using me." His fingers tightened around her arm.

Deana, astonished at his echo of her exact thoughts from this afternoon, merely stared at him. Guilt flooded through her body. Not the same guilt he implied, but guilt all the same.

He gave her shoulders a shake. "I knew it! You thought by stalking me you'd cozy up to Jacoubi!" He gave a bitter laugh, "You think Jacoubi would ever be interested in you? What a laugh. That friend of yours, Genie, might be his speed, but definitely not you. His taste is for beautiful, sexy women. Nobody wants a woman with all brains and nothing..." Insolently his eyes looked her over, "nothing else. He'll be moving on soon. There's certainly nothing in Duluth to interest him. Once old man Jacoubi is back at work, he'll get out as fast as he can."

Deana gritted her teeth, lifted her hands, and pushed against his chest. With the strength from years of lifting hay bales, she sent him staggering backwards. Her body trembled with anger as she faced him, "How dare you touch me. There is nothing we have to discuss ever again, there is no us, and never has been." Other words of contempt crowded her mind. Deana, unable to speak again whirled on her heel and ran inside.

40

Fleeing David's mocking words, Deana rushed into the crowded building to search for Frank. Suddenly the lights went off and the music resumed blasting. Deana stumbled over something, but didn't stop to look as she disappeared into the confusion of people and away from David's painful accusation.

With hair flying, her color high, and her anxiety increasing with every step, she hastened past groups of women and men. Thoughts that family and friends had deserted her became stronger as she stopped by the dance floor. The band was in front of her against the back wall of the building. She could go no further and still she saw no familiar faces.

She turned and looked behind her, wondering if she missed them in her rush. Someone touched her arm and Deana saw Matt looking down at her with concern. "Deana," he shouted, "Are you all right?"

Deana nodded yes.

Matt grabbed her gently by the same arm David had, and lead her away from the giant speakers through the crush of dancing people. She allowed herself to be lead until he pushed open a side door. The door slammed on the music so at least she could hear.

"Ajai asked me to find you. He didn't want you to worry. He went with his mother in the ambulance and your father insisted on driving their car to the hospital."

"Is... Is there any word on how Mr. Jacoubi is doing?"

Matt shook his head. "All I know is he was conscious and mad that they insisted on calling an ambulance. I think that's a good sign."

"I've got to call a cab and get to the hospital. I don't want Dad to sit there alone."

Matt smiled.

Deana noticed how comforting his presence was. It was nice of him to have taken the time to find her and explain everything,

"Ajai told me to tell you he'll make sure your father gets home. He'll call you as soon as they hear any news."

Deana frowned, "Oh he did, did he? Well I…"

Matt interrupted, "He also told me how persuasive you can be about getting your own way and asks you please just go home and get some sleep."

Deana had to smile. She asked pertly, "And what if I still don't obey the mighty Ajai?"

"Then I'm instructed to say pretty please."

This time she laughed. "It seems Ajai is more persuasive than, he's had a lot more practice getting his own way."

"I'm sure he has. Can I drive you home, Deana?"

"Of course. It will be a pleasure. Where's Genie?"

"She's sitting in the car. It's right over there."

Deana walked beside Matt across the gravel drive. They were on a side road that led to a ramp and big double doors. They pulled up to the buildings delivery entrance. She was grateful for the respite from David. How many people witnessed their dramatic scene, she had no idea. At the time she had been too angry to look around. She remembered little until Matt found her. With a sigh she brushed the tangles of hair that had gone completely wild. What was the use of trying to be stylish? David was right. Ajai was out of her league.

"It's been a crazy day," Matt murmured sympathetically as they stopped at his car. The engine was running and Genie opened the passenger window just enough to say, "Hurry up and get in. You must be getting eaten alive. The mosquitoes are everywhere." She closed the window.

When Deana climbed in the back and settled herself against the seat, Genie was watching her. "Are you all right?"

Deana nodded. "Tired, but I'm fine."

"How terrible about Mr. Jacoubi. Ajai was so upset. I think it's kinda sweet how worried he gets about his dad."

The ceiling light flashed on, attracting the bugs to it and Genie reached over to swat them against the ceiling. "Ugh, that's disgusting," she exclaimed. She reached under the seat to pull out a small container. "Want a moist towlette?" she asked Deana, handing the box back to her. Genie wiped her hands and then the plastic cover on the light.

Deana asked curiously, "Why do you have these?"

Genie laughed and looked at Matt, "The second time I rode in this car I dropped my lipstick on the leather seat. This is the cleanest car I've ever seen. It's kinda scary how clean it stays. The only way it's going to stay spotless with me around, is if I clean up my own messes."

Deana smiled and opened the box to take a few of the moist sheets and wipe her hands.

Matt protested, "I don't care if the seats get dirty. I told Genie it's only a car."

"Deana knows that, silly. She's seen my office. She knows exactly how messy I am."

Deana added, "Not to mention her apartment."

Genie turned in the seat to look at her over the tan leather back. "Hey, don't go telling secrets. I've been trying to keep my apartment clean."

Matt put the car in gear and said, "You mean it looks worse than what I've seen?"

Deana laughed, "You can't even imagine."

"Okay," Genie broke in and said dryly, "You've both had your laugh. Deana, what happened to David? Why didn't he give you a ride home?"

She gave a careless lift to her shoulders, "He was busy."

"Well that wasn't very nice of him, especially considering what happened tonight. He must've known you were upset." Genie glanced at Matt, "Don't you agree?"

"He knew what was going on." Matt said, "I don't think

that was his biggest problem tonight."

Deana looked out of the window. This was a conversation she definitely did not want to encourage. Though it was comforting to hear that someone beside herself thought that David acted like a complete jerk, Deana realized they did not know what had happened between them.

Genie turned forward and the song from the radio filled in the silence.

Matt never asked for directions. When they passed the driveway that led to Jacoubi's, Matt looked at her in the rear view mirror and asked, "Ajai said your driveway is about a mile past his. Can you be more specific?"

"The street sign up ahead that says 'No Passing' is directly across from my driveway."

"Thanks," Matt said, flipping on the blinker.

Deana leaned back against the seat, letting her shoulders sag into the comfortable cushion. Throughout the ride, she'd been expecting Genie to bring up the subject of David. Now it was over. She knew that good manners dictated she should offer Matt and Genie a nightcap, but felt quite beyond voicing the invitation.

As Matt stopped the car next to the front porch, Genie stretched yawning, "I don't know why I'm so beat tonight. It's still early."

"Imagine how exhausted Deana must feel, after all that fresh air on the sailboat," Matt teased her.

"Deana, don't invite us in. I'm sure Matt's right. You have to be bushed. I'll see you at work on Monday."

Relieved, Deana piped up, "Are you sure? I feel like I'm cheating. You drove me all this way and now you have to turn right back around to go home."

"Don't be silly. Although I do expect to be invited to your house sometime. We talked to your dad tonight. He's great, isn't he Matt? And so are the Jacoubi's, I never expected them to be so normal."

Deana nodded, "Let's plan a barbecue and then I'll be able to introduce you to my favorite boyfriend. Thanks so much for the ride, Matt. See you Monday."

She slammed the door and waved until the car disappeared down the driveway. As she walked to the side door, she heard Journey's soft call. Deana hesitated a moment then kicked off her dress shoes, left the sidewalk and walked around the corner of the house through the wet grass to the paddock. Journey, with his head hanging over the top plank, whinnied loud this time.

"Hey, you," Deana said. Sharp rocks bit into her feet. "Ouch," she yelped hopping across the grass. Journey jerked his head at the unexpected cry. Deana grabbed the strap of his halter, "Don't you recognize me in this get up?" she asked when he pulled away. "Of course not. I smell too pretty for the likes of you." She patted the hard bone of his cheek while listening to the sounds of crickets, the whine of mosquitoes, and the quiet hoot of an owl.

"Oh, Journey, I'm so confused. Why can't I just learn my lesson the first time? Oh no, I have to fall head over heels in love with Peter Pan himself. The boy who never wanted to grow up, and I'm certainly no Wendy. I won't clean up after lost boys. I don't want to learn to fly. What am I saying? I've always hated that story."

Journey nuzzled her side, searching for a treat. Deana pushed the horse's nose away. "Get your nose out of there. I don't have any pockets in this skirt. Why am I bothering to tell you my problems? You certainly never gave me any good advice before."

With a final pat to the paint horse's shoulder, she stepped away from the fence. Though her body ached from the unaccustomed exercise of sailing and then high heels, she checked the water in the trough and then returned to the silent house.

The light above the sink was the only glow in the darkness of the kitchen. She left the door unlocked and, with her head throbbing, walked wearily up the stairs.

The chipped blue and white tiles on the bathroom floor felt cold on her bare feet. She scrubbed the make-up from her face, brushed her teeth, and left the bathroom to hang her dress-up outfit in the back of the closet. Never did she plan on wearing it again. She slid her plain cotton nightgown over her head and climbed into bed. She left the door open so she could hear if the telephone on the table in the hallway rang.

Prepared for a sleepless night, even though she was so tired, she stretched out under the cotton sheet to stare at the shadows on her ceiling. The open window allowed the night sounds inside. They usually helped her fall asleep, but not tonight. Tonight, her active mind mulled over the events of the long day. The day seemed like a week, not one day.

David's unusual insolence clearly had to be alcohol driven. She tried to overlook his cruel words. It was Ajai's that plagued her. He acted like she'd hurt his feelings.

David had been right about one thing, she thought. Ajai will never look at me after the beautiful women he's used to dating. Deana remembered the pictures of Ajai and one beautiful woman or another in the newspapers and magazines.

The ringing telephone disrupted her thoughts. Deana scrambled from bed and rushed to the hall, grabbing the receiver. "Hello," she said softly even though she was nervous.

Her father's voice, dim and broken, came through, "Deana, it's me, Dad. Edward is fine. Turns out it was just a case of indigestion. We're ready to leave the hospital. I shouldn't be long. Get some sleep, Honey. I'll see you in the morning."

Deana held the receiver staring at it, overwhelmed with disappointment. She had wanted to hear Ajai's voice. After what had been said between them tonight, she probably would be the last person he'd want to talk to. She set the receiver back in the cradle and went back to bed. As she closed her eyes she remembered to be thankful the trip to the hospital had been a false alarm.

41

The quaint one-room wooden church's bell echoed across the sleepy summer Sunday morning. A white picket fence encompassed the churchyard and the small cemetery next to it. Parishioners who were delaying going inside the warm interior of the church, now hurried up the front steps.

Inside, narrow aisles lined with wooden pews were filled with people absently waving paper fans. Wooden ceiling fans slowly sifted the air around, but did nothing to relieve heat in the main area. The organ music sent out a welcoming crescendo, bringing the congregation to their feet. In the side pew next to an open window, Deana and her father rose to sing the opening hymn. After the breezy day on the lake yesterday, the humidity in the room was stifling. While she sang, Deana waved her mother's fan. The one lined with stiff black lace and a picture of the Madonna imprinted into the fabric. When the last chord ended, in the brief silence before the priest began to speak, the sound of footsteps on the tile floor caused several heads to turn. Someone was arriving late for the nine o'clock Mass. In such a small congregation, tardiness was frowned upon.

Deana heard her father's whisper, "Will you look at that."

She moved her head just enough to see Ajai slide into the pew next to his mother and father.

"I don't believe it," Frank said with a soft chuckle.

Deana couldn't believe it either. Years had passed since Ajai had made an appearance in church. Except for the token Christmas Eve and Easter Mass required for Catholics, Ajai had stayed away. Deana looked at the altar. Despite her attempts to concentrate on the priest's homily, she found it hard. She usually enjoyed the sermons because Father Jim was a good speaker and the subjects he talked about fit into her everyday life.

Her lips twitched at the irony. It was here in church she had first noticed Ajai. She pictured that day when the fifteen-year-old Ajai walked into the little church with his parents. Back then the slump in his shoulders and the defiance in every movement of his body made it obvious he did not want to be with them. And then after church, Deana happened to overhear Edward and Ajai arguing. She remembered Ajai saying too loudly, "This is stupid. I can talk to God anywhere. I don't need to listen to some old man telling me how I should think and what I should feel. If God created everything, then he already knows how I feel. It's a waste of time, and I'm not coming back."

Deana did not remember how Edward Jacoubi responded. She was too busy watching and listening with fascination to the openly defiant Ajai. Good looking and tall, Deana never remembered Ajai going through an awkward stage. It was his belligerence that caught her attention. Ajai dared to defy, not only his father, but also God. She decided then that he must be crazy.

Deana's faith was a part of her and she never thought to question it. God was the Father of everything. That's the way it was and always will be. She wanted God to be a part of her life so she went to church and followed the Ten Commandments. There were times when she felt lazy, and following the rules irritated her, but she did it anyway. Her mother was in Heaven and remembering that kept her faith steady.

Deana never found any reason to argue with her own father. Frank was not one to fuss about the proper way to do things, it was Deana who was the conventional one. After her mother died, she pretty much stepped into her mother's shoes and took over the duties of caring for them both.

Today in the heated interior of the church, Deanna actually felt electricity shoot along her nerves caused by the golden- haired man sitting across the room. Why did she have to fall in love with the boy who never wanted to grow up? I've always hated the movie *Peter Pan*, she thought disconsolately.

During the rest of the service, Deana suffered under the weight of speculation about what might happen after Mass if Ajai spoke to her. After the last verse of the last hymn, Deana slipped the music book back into the holder and picked up her purse. She lifted her eyes to see Ajai and when their eyes met, he smiled. Then, as fast as it appeared, his smile faded. He nodded stiffly, lifting the corners of his mouth at her, then deliberately smiled at Frank.

Deana felt like a physical blow hit her chest. She turned away and hurried down the aisle and outside. This was much worse than she expected. Several parishioners bid her good morning. Deana forced a smile, said cheerful hellos and walked quickly across the parking lot toward the cemetery. The brown/green grass was scattered with tombstones, white daisies, and yellow buttercups.

Deana stopped at the gate and reached down to pick up the small bouquet of pink and white roses tied with a silk ribbon she had left there before Mass. She had picked the flowers from her mother's rose garden. She stepped through the gate holding the folds of her simple yellow skirt away from the rusty gate. She picked her way across the rough path to a single marker. Deana knelt in front of the white stone etched with a carving of the Sacred Heart of Jesus. She brushed away the leafy debris. Written across the bottom were the simple words, "Wife, Mother of Unselfish Nature/Rest With Jesus." She folded her hands and bowed her head. As she had in the past, her mother would listen to her woes about Ajai.

42

Ajai watched as she kneeled in front of a headstone and bowed her head. Her black hair waved free to her slender shoulders. The ebony tendrils contrasted with the buttercup yellow shirt she wore. The sapphire blue of the July sky radiated serenity. The surrounding wildflowers and sweet-smelling pasture grass enhanced Deana's Irish beauty.

Standing next to Ajai, Edward said, "Every Sunday she visits her mother's grave. She never fails. Even in winter. Father Jim shovels the snow from the walkway just for her."

Ajai frowned. He said roughly, "I guess after all these years she should move on. Living in the past isn't any way to live. It's not healthy. If her mother was half the woman everyone says she was, she wouldn't be too happy with her daughter."

"I've never had the impression that Deana lives only in the past. What makes you say that?"

Ajai shrugged unable to tear his eyes away from the field and the charming picture Deana made, reminding him of a Monet watercolor. "She's afraid to live. She told me so. What kind of life can you live with fear like that?"

Edward shot Ajai a quick look. "Don't judge too harshly, son. But for the grace of God..." Edward paused then added, "It was nice of you to come to Mass. You made your mother and I very happy."

Ajai looked down at the ground, "Things that used to be important don't matter anymore. I admit that what you've been telling me all along has begun to make a lot more sense."

Edward slapped Ajai's shoulder and said jovially, "I appreciate you admitting that, son, but you don't have to. I said the same things to my father and lived to retract every one of them. The past is best left where it belongs."

"That's easier said than done. What if some… someone who knows your past is frightened of it? And I don't know what to do about it. I don't know how to change it. Even God can't change the past so how is it possible to show you've changed."

"You mean your reputation? This is the first you've cared about your reputation. What's brought this sudden attack of conscience?"

"Huh? Conscience, no that's not what I'm talking about," Ajai changed the subject. He thought he'd told his father too much. He looked at the cars pulling out of the parking lot and speeding down the highway, "Why are we still hanging around here? I'm starved."

"Your mother has invited Frank and Deana to brunch. After last night, it's the least we can do."

Ajai glanced out at the field with renewed interest on his face. "Does she know yet?"

"No, that's why we're waiting. Frank has to make sure she hasn't any other plans for the morning."

"How long can she stay out there?"

Edward shrugged, "I don't think it would be considered an acceptable question, for starters, she doesn't know we're waiting for her."

Ajai shoved his hands in his pockets and began to walk across the parking lot. "Well, I think she should know. I'm going to tell her. Tell Frank she can ride with me? If she has other plans I'll drive her home."

Gravel crunched under his dress cowboy boots until his steps became muffled on the soft ground. He stepped through the open gate and quietly crossed the field. Deana remained on her knees. Ajai watched her. The sun burned hot against his back. Many fat, black and yellow bumble bees droned past while he waited

She opened here eyes and carefully arranged the flowers on the stone and stood, stepping away from the marker. Leaning over, she brushed the clinging grass from her skirt and with the back of her hand hastily wiped her cheeks. She turned and looked up. Astonishment flooded her face when she saw Ajai standing a few feet from her. Then she looked distinctly uncomfortable.

"Good morning," he said.

Deana glanced nervously behind him, "Good morning, if you'll excuse me, my father is waiting for me."

Ajai did not move. "No, he isn't."

"What?" Her voice rose slightly. Deana leaned to look around his tall frame at the parking lot.

Ajai turned and pointed to where only his sports car remained in front of the church. "As you can see, your father has left with my parents. It seems plans were made for you both to brunch at our house after church. If you have someplace else to go this morning I'll be glad to drop you off at home."

Indecision clouded the thickly lashed gray eyes that flicked over him. She quickly looked back to the parking lot.

"Isn't this a lovely view?" he said keeping his eyes on the creaminess of her skin and the light sprinkle of freckles across her nose.

Deana paused to shade her eyes and looked at the narrow crescent of the lake visible from this elevation. It was miles away, but the cemetery stood alone on a hilltop and the view stretched all the way across the fields of grass and trees to the lake against the horizon.

He added, "It's a lovely day, but I miss the breeze we had on the lake yesterday."

She glanced at him with a frown of consternation that marred the delicate arch between her brows. In a quick movement she side-stepped around him and began to walk toward the gate. Ajai followed a few paces behind, enjoying her confusion.

"The inside of the church was stifling," he continued.

She walked on without replying.

"It usually is this time of the year. If only the building was turned the other direction, then the windows could catch the breeze."

They left the field and Deana walked toward his car.

Ajai asked, "Why doesn't Father Jim put in air conditioning?"

Deana laughed, "Because it costs too much." She stopped next to the passenger side and waited for him. "You left your windows down."

"It's too hot to keep them rolled up all the way." Ajai stopped behind her and thumbed the keyless entry. At the click he reached over and opened the car door, holding it for her. Deana sat down but kept her head lowered so he could not see her face. He slammed the door and hurried around to slide into the driver's seat. Then he turned to face her. "Well, where do you want to go?"

Deana looked quickly out the side window and sighed.

"You're not still afraid of me, are you?"

"Afraid of you?" She cried in disbelief swiveling in the sseat to glare at him.

Ajai grinned, "You are so easy to rile up."

"Only around you."

"Because I'm such a bad influence?"

Deana turned her face away. After a second of silence she said, "I never said that. Quit putting words in my mouth."

Ajai started the motor. He put the car in gear and pulled onto the main road. As the car picked up speed, he asked, "Are you going to tell me where to go, or should I just head straight to my house?"

"I haven't any plans except taking care of Journey. He's not going to be happy waiting for his breakfast," she said woodenly.

"He can miss a meal or two. You feed him well. It won't hurt him," Ajai said dryly.

"Why are you doing exactly what we decided we shouldn't do?"

Ajai glanced at her, "Driving together?"

"Yes, being together when our parents are trying to be matchmakers. It isn't fair to make your mother hopeful when I'm certainly not in the running to be her future daughter in law. I think you're being unnecessarily cruel."

"And what do you suggest I do? Refuse to give you a ride to my house when they ask? Tell me what excuse I can give to satisfy them that I find you completely unattractive?"

Deana's face flushed red. She said indignantly, "Well I certainly don't think I deserve that."

"I only repeated what you said."

"That's not what I said. I'm not unattractive. I just don't measure up to the kind of women that you usually date."

"And what kind of women would that be, Deana?"

"I'm not sure. I've never met any of your girlfriends, but I have seen pictures of them in the newspapers."

"Those rag sheets. Deana, the pictures were probably set up by some photographer."

Deana shook her head, "It doesn't matter, Ajai."

Edward Jacoubi's dark blue Buick was parked in front of the Jacoubi's house. Frank's dusty beat up station wagon was parked next to it. Ajai pulled up right behind Frank.

Before he could say another word, Deana threw open the car door and bolted out of the seat. Ajai watched her slender bare legs as she ran in high heels to the front door. Without bothering to knock, she threw the door open and vanished inside. He leaned back against the seat and ran his hand over his forehead, thinking, how in the world does one deal with a nice girl?

43

After brunch, Deana, exhausted, sank into the plush pillows of the contemporary style couch. The high peaked ceiling of the Jacoubi's living room reminded Deana of pictures in skiing magazines of a Swiss Alps chalet. The view of the living room from the front hallway was deceiving. A dividing wall hid the length of the room. From the fireplace, the large area spread out like a fan, leading to many intimate alcoves furnished with comfortable chairs and convenient tables.

Patsy Jacoubi and Ajai insisted on doing the kitchen clean-up and Deana had no idea where her father and Edward had disappeared to after they cleared their plates from the table. Patsy had waved her away with an airy, "Go explore the house and the gardens if you like, Deana. We'll be done here quickly and then join you."

With the other parts of the room spread out before her, Deana, attracted by the lovely leather volumes that lined the shelves of the alcove, stood and made her way across the lush carpet. The books were bound in rich-colored leather of forest green, burgundy, and royal blue. The colorful volumes were the timeless classics everyone should find time to read. Deana read the familiar titles *Pride and Prejudice, Dr. Jekyll and Mr. Hyde, Ivanhoe, The Scarlet Pimpernel,* and *Peter Pan,* along with countless others.

Deana frowned at the remembrance of her comparison of Peter Pan and Ajai. She looked at the rest of the shelves. Intermittent among the impressive books were mementos. Figurines, some as fine as Dresden, others chipped and scarred, could only have sentimental value. Seashells of different kinds and several chunks of rock sat next to exquisite china. Deana smiled as she fingered bindings, her eyes rested on the shelf holding many well-read children's books. Arrayed amongst them were grubby, well-loved stuffed animals and toys. There were titles Deana recognized. She wondered which Ajai had read, if any. *The Little House on the Prairie, The Black Stallion,* and a tattered Cub Scouts Guide Book. The furniture looked perfect for curling up with a book. Short backed, overstuffed chairs with homemade afghans thrown across them, short-legged tables next to the chairs. Deana turned to look at the view out the big bay window directly across from the chairs. The shining sun lit up the green of the steeply sloping hill of Jacoubi property that led to the Michaels property. It was an area Deana often rode in. All the while she had done it, she knew she was trespassing but thought the Jacoubi's would never find out. And it turned out that the entire area was in full view of anyone who happened to be in this part of the house. Deana drew back from the window. The entire family must have known she had been trespassing ever since she was eleven-years old. How embarrassing, she thought.

Hastily, before anyone found her in this secluded part of the huge room, Deana hurried back to the couches that encircled the large gray-stoned fireplace. Primly, she sat on the couch until her breathing returned to normal. Anxiously, Deana listened. No sound was heard from the others in the house, so, until they joined her, she looked over the rest of the amazing room.

Cream-colored wooden beams of wood lined the ceiling. Deana never knew cream-colored wood existed in nature. She put her head back and studied the ceiling, the walls and the furnishings. If Patsy Jacoubi decorated this house, she had impeccable taste. Deana admired the vibrant colors and the openness of the beautifully furnished home. The room was not only beautiful, but also relaxing and comfortable. Deana slipped off her high heels and buried her toes in the plush carpet. The white marble fireplace mantle highlighted the gray stones. The fireplace itself was big enough for Deana to crawl inside. The whole house lacked dust or disorder in any form.

Deana pictured her house with her father's packets of junk stacked in every available corner, and smiled. How long would it take Frank Michaels to joyfully fill this place, knowing his pack rat ways? Deana sighed and rested. The room remained cool even with the sun shining through the big windows. Right outside the patio doors, in the backyard, a pool sparkled under the sunlight. Deana jumped up, leaving her shoes under the couch. She stood in front of three shining clean plate glass windows. A swimming pool was such an extravagance, as were windows this clean. Deana wondered if they had hired a cleaning person.

The patio area was spotless. Several round tables surrounded the pool. Thinking of Duluth's climate, the accountant in Deana came out and she cringed to think of the cost. In this part of the Northland the swimming season was so short, the cost could not be worth it. Unless you considered just one day. A day like today. The smooth glass-like azure surface of the pool was too much to resist.

Deana tentatively pulled on the sliding glass door and it moved. With a quick glance behind her, she wondered if she needed to ask permission. Deciding to take a quick peak, she slid the door open enough to glide through and then shut it as quietly as she could.

44

The heat on the tiles burned her feet. Deana jumped quickly to the grass that lined the patio. It was a small pool, the narrow end was deep and then it widened into the shallow area. Spacious steps lead into the shallowest water, making it perfect for small children to play in. Deana skipped quickly from the cool grass across the hot tiles and stepped onto the first step. Cool, blue water swirled around her ankles. Holding her skirt in one hand, and stepping lower, the water was deliciously soothing.

She had never been in this part of the yard, even when Journey boarded with the Jacoubi's. The pool area was secluded. Trimmed hedges lined each side of the yard, hiding the barn that was just below the hill, closer to the road. From where she stood, only the green-peaked dormer with the glinting copper polo horse and rider weather vane on top were visible. Flowers bordered a small building painted white and green that might easily be a bathing house.

Deana looked down at her legs half in the water and had a horrible thought. My wet feet on the beautiful beige carpet in the living room, ugh. She stepped quickly from the water and walked on tiptoes through the grass, hurrying back to the house. When she stopped in front of the glass doors, her feet were now, not only wet, but also covered with grass clippings. Deana reached down and tried to brush her skin dry. Her skirt fell and the hem stuck to her wet ankles dampening the material. "Oh, dear, this is going from bad to worse."

Suddenly, the glass door opened with a bang.

"I didn't sneak up and scare you that time." Ajai declared.

Deana looked at him and then at her feet and frowned. "Yes you did, and now look, I'm covered with grass."

"Were you wading? The pool looks great. Care for a swim?"

Deana missed his teasing tone and took him seriously, "I don't have my suit."

Ajai's eyes twinkled, "Well, that's not a problem for bad boys."

Deana stepped out of reach and gave a nervous laugh, "Oh, stop it! I don't think you're a bad boy. You're just more of a free thinker than I am."

"I thought you said free-doer. Nothing was ever said about thinking. As a matter of fact, you said it was the things I do that make you nervous."

Deana laughed again, a high-pitched twitter that sounded panicky. "You're putting words in my mouth again. Now help me dry off so I don't mess up your mother's carpet."

"You don't have to worry about being watched. There's nobody around out here. We're miles from the gossips at Jacoubi."

"But not your parents!" she reminded him sharply. "Nor mine. They probably think we're having some sort of interlude out here. We should go back inside, so we don't mislead them any more than we already have. I think it's time we went home anyway." Hopping on one foot to brush off the grass she tried to look at her watch and tipped forward.

Ajai jumped and grabbed her shoulders to steady her, "Mmm, you smell good," he said holding her.

He was so close Deana could pick out the different colors highlighted in his hair. She pushed him away, "I smell like sausage and bacon," she said tartly.

"And syrup," he added, laughing. He held on, and wouldn't let go. He looked into her flashing gray eyes and said, "I really want to throw you in the pool now."

Deana gave a genuine laugh at his humor. "You are such a tease."

Letting her go, he said, "Then why do you keep taking everything I say and do so seriously?"

Deana sobered and brushed at her skirt and what was left

of the grass on her legs. She straightened and reached for the door handle, stopping to give him a look of regret, "Because I don't know where to draw the line. You're such a good actor."

Shaking his head, Ajai said, "Then try taking everything I say as a joke."

Deana shook her head, opening the sliding glass, "When it comes to you, I can't make that mistake ever. There's too much at stake." Horrified that she revealed too much, she added, "I've never had a boss like you and my job is important to me and my father. We depend on you to pay our bills."

Ajai fell silent.

That put him in his place, she thought. He probably forgot that I'm poor and he's rich. It's a good thing I reminded him. Besides, I can't afford to get caught up in all of this attention. She left the door open as she tiptoed across the carpet to where she left her shoes.

"What in blazes are you doing?" Ajai demanded from the doorway.

Deana did not stop on her way to the couch. "I don't want to get the carpet dirty."

Ajai laughed, "Deana, my mother raised one boy, had about ten nephews visiting here all the time, and their friends too. She's used to a dirty carpet."

"Look at this place. It's spotless. This must be new carpet and furniture."

"No, it's the same stuff I grew up with." Ajai followed her across the floor and stood above her. He blended in with the creamy colors of the room in his khaki and cream colored shirt and trousers.

Deana sat on the edge of the couch. Without taking her eyes off Ajai, she fumbled under the couch to find her shoes. "I don't believe you. How would you even know if your mother remodeled the entire house? You've been gone for years."

"Yes, but I have visited…often. I'm surprised you didn't know that."

Deana picked up one shoe and fidgeted with it, trying to slip it over her damp toes, "Why would I know about your visits?"

"You seem to know a lot about me that isn't common knowledge."

Deana paused, "Really? I don't know why. Unless it's because I pay attention when the Jacoubi name is mentioned…because I work at Jacoubi." Her words faded.

Ajai knelt down on the carpeted floor directly in front of the couch and in front of her. He reached under the couch for her other shoe the one she could not reach.

"Ajai, what are you doing? Get up, don't you dare…you're not thinking of… helping me," Deana squeaked. She giggled, but could not ignore the flutter of her pulse. What would her senses do if he actually touched her bare skin? She pulled her bare foot out of reach and moved as far against the back of the couch as possible. "I'm quite capable of putting my own shoes on, thank you."

"I have no doubts about your proficiency, Deana. You've proven yourself on many occasions. I only wish I could say the same about myself."

Deana sobered, "Oh no, Ajai. Don't say that! You've accomplished so much since you've been back in Duluth. Just think how quickly you picked up the work you're doing. And look at how happy you've made your parents. It's obvious you're on the right track. They glow whenever they look at you. Your mother mentioned how important it was to them that you came to church and how pleased she was that you almost made it on time."

Ajai, still on his knees fishing under the couch for the other shoe, looked up and said, "You little minx, you just had to get that jab in there about being late. I noticed you didn't turn around to give me a disapproving look like all the others, and for your information, I would've been early if the Mass schedule hadn't changed by a half an hour. It's earlier than it used to be."

"How many years ago was that?" Deana taunted him. She said in a honeyed tone, "I like looking down at the top of your head, it gives me a feeling of power."

"Deana Michaels, power hungry? I never would've guessed." He reached out for her hand and gently pulled her closer to him. "I'm beginning to believe you really do have no idea how powerful you are."

Deana was speechless. She stared into the liquid gold of his eyes and enjoyed for just a moment, the feeling that nothing but the two of them existed.

45

The clatter of metal bouncing on tile and the shattering of glass brought Ajai to his feet and a gasp from Deana. In the doorway leading to the kitchen stood a flustered Patsy, her mouth covered with her hands. Her eyes were wide and shock filled as she stared at the two of them. In a stricken voice she cried, "I... I'm so sorry, I didn't mean to interrupt you." Then she spun on her heel and ran back into the kitchen.

Deana gave Ajai an inquiring look.

He shrugged, "I have no idea."

Deana grabbed her shoe out of his hand and shoved her foot into it. "She's going to need help cleaning that glass." The two walked around the couch to survey the damage. Liquid spread across the ceramic tile of the walkway. Broken pieces of china were strewn everywhere, the half of a lovely blue and white teapot leaned forlornly on its side against the mopboard.

"I'll get the garbage," Ajai said walking to a small alcove near the front hall and pulled out from under the entry table, the most ornamental garbage can Deana had ever seen. "The broom and dust pan are in the kitchen. It'll only take me a second," he said, handing her the can and walking into the kitchen.

Deana sank to her knees and began picking up the larger pieces, wondering if there was any chance it could be glued. Patsy Louise appeared and said, "Deana, please do be careful. Broken china is so sharp."

Deana smiled as Patsy knelt with a roll of paper towels in her hand. "What do you find amusing?"

"That was such a motherly thing to say. It's been a long time since I was mothered."

Patsy smiled and the look in her eyes was a mixture of confusion, tenderness, and sadness.

The two women set about their cleaning and, after a moment Deana asked, "Did I offend you?"

Patsy sniffed and pressed her fingers to her eyes. "To hear you say that breaks my heart." She smiled, "When he was only thirteen, my Ajai told me not to mother him. I had a hard time stepping back. Some mothering I can never stop and don't plan to."

"Like worrying," Deana said, "I suppose you can never stop worrying about your children." She frowned at the lovely china she was throwing into the garbage. "I'm sorry the teapot can't be saved."

Patsy waved her hand, its perfectly painted fingernails fluttering, "Don't worry dear, it's not like the set was a family heirloom or anything."

"But it looks like it could be your wedding china."

Patsy laughed, "Ajai and his cousins took care of breaking that many years ago. I learned to replace things that broke, not mourn over the pieces that did. I've always felt like Wendy in the *Peter Pan* fairy tale. I've been taking care of lost boys all of my life. Edward will never admit it, but when we first met, he was a lost boy. I took care of him like I did all my brother's friends. You see, I'm the only girl in a family of five."

"You have four brothers?"

Patsy laughed gaily, "Yes, and a rowdier bunch you'll never meet anywhere. Now my brothers all have boys of their own, but I wouldn't trade any of them. A daughter would have been nice, but I'm still the only female in the family. The hardest time I had was when my own Ajai was having such a difficult time. He pushed me away. He wasn't sure where he fit in. He didn't want to be saddled with stepping into his father's shoes and being just a businessman. He thought that living a rough hard life filled with excitement was what he wanted. Even excitement becomes tedious after awhile. I knew eventually he'd come home

Picking up the last of the china pieces, Deana grabbed some paper towels and swept the remaining small shards into a pile.

Patsy exclaimed, "Goodness, you get me talking and then you end up doing the lion's share of the work. Let me finish. Edward and Frank are in the game room. Why don't you go and see what they're doing?"

Deana picked up the garbage can and asked, "Where should I put this?"

"Just set it on the counter in the kitchen. The game room is just past the kitchen. You can't miss it."

46

Deana scanned the empty kitchen and set the garbage can on the counter. She followed the hallway to a grand staircase with oak banisters. A crystal chandelier with at least five tiers of crystal droplets hung above the alcove. The beautiful exterior oak door accented the rich feel of the room. Deana wanted to explore further but instead hurried down the windowed hallway, enjoying the view across the sprawling fields that led to the tree line.

She recognized the pastures where the horses grazed. When she had ridden along the tree line and across the fields and glimpsed the house, she never thought she'd be inside looking out. Deana walked along the hallway to a large room with a big-screen television in one corner, an ornate pool table in the center, and several small card tables along one wall. A small bar, with the same fleur de leis carvings as the ones on the sides of the pool table was at the back of the room. Dark tongue and groove ash paneling lined the walls, decorated with old-fashioned photographs of past presidents and famous events in the history of the United States.

Hesitantly, Deana stepped into the room and saw her father sitting at one of the small tables across from Edward Jacoubi. The two were concentrating on a chess game. Ajai was not in the room. Deana walked across the dark hunter green carpet. The room reminded her of an old western movie set, "Who's winning?"

Frank looked up and smiled at her. A vacant look remained on his face. A look Deana recognized from years of interrupting her father in his study when he struggled with something he needed to solve. "Hello dear, at this point I can't honestly tell you which one of us in the lead. I thought for certain I had the game, until his last move."

"Edward," Patsy called from the hallway.

The men's attention returned to the chessboard.

"Edward!" Patsy called again, and Deana heard a hint of excitement in her voice. "I have something very important to tell you."

When Edward did not respond, rapid footsteps echoed down the hallway and Patsy rounded the corner. At the sight of Deana, she stopped. Her expression changed and she collected herself, controlling her tone of voice, "Deana, you found them. I'm so glad."

"What were you saying?" Edward asked as he moved a bishop. "Check, Frank."

Patsy shook her head, "Nothing, I don't want to bore the others. I'll tell you later. Where's Ajai? I expected to find him in here with you."

Edward shook his head. "Haven't seen him since brunch."

Patsy said, "Oh, dear. I left the lemonade in the kitchen. Deana, do you mind?"

Deana stepped forward, eager to have something to do. "Of course, I don't mind. Just the lemonade? I don't need to bring glasses or ice?"

"No, everything we need is in here," Patsy smiled, "You just bring the pitcher. Can you find your way back?"

Deana nodded, "I'll only be a moment."

Patsy took a quick intake of breath and Deana had the distinct impression that she was very excited about something and trying to hide it. "Is everything all right?"

"Of course everything's fine. Just bring the lemonade," she hesitated and added, "and Ajai, if you happen to cross paths." Her smile almost jumped out at Deana it was so animated.

Deana left, wondering what Mrs. Jacoubi was so excited about. Wandering down the hallway, still puzzled, nothing looked familiar. Have I taken a wrong turn? She thought, disgusted with her lack of concentration. She turned around and examined her surroundings. This hallway looked almost identical to the one she'd left, but this one smelled of damp earth. Continuing in the same direction, soon Deana detected the heavy scent of flowers.

Turning a corner, Deana walked into a solarium. It looked like a rain forest. A lovely arbor of vines framed the entryway. A medley of pots overfilled with flowering geraniums, hibiscus, and impatiens lined the walkway. Deana saw a row of potted roses and moved toward them. Wild roses were her mother's favorite flower. Deana, attracted to them, fingered the blossoms of a bright pink rose. She smelled the heady fragrance and moved to the next pot. Ferns hung down in cascading waves of green leaves, the tips brushed the top of her head. Thin stumpy trees with miniature oranges in the boughs caught her attention next. Deana reached the back of the glass room and turned around to find her way out and back into the hallway.

The hallway curved with a natural arch. Discreet lights recessed in the walls gently lit the amber painted walls. Pictures of the family decorated a section, most of them showed Ajai in various stages.

"Deana," a muffled voice called.

Deana looked around to see a small box attached to the wall that looked like an intercom. Deana remembered that when she worked with Chip, the stable had intercoms throughout. She walked over and pushed the talk button. "I'm here, stuck in the hallway and I can't get out."

Ajai's laughter came clearly through the line. "What part of the hallway?"

"I just passed the indoor garden," Deana replied.

"Keep walking. You're almost to the kitchen."

"Thanks I'm on my way." She walked into the kitchen and saw Frank, Edward, Patsy and Ajai waiting. "What a great house to play hide and seek," Deana said, not feeling embarrassed that she was lost in the Jacoubi's house. "This place is like one giant cornfield maze."

Frank picked up his suit coat and slung it over his shoulder. "Now that you've been found, we best be heading home. Thank you Patsy, Edward."

The three glanced at Ajai and Deana. Patsy's eyes practically glowed when she looked at Deana. "I'm so happy that this is something we'll be doing much more in the future." Her voice held the same tremor of excitement that Deana had heard in the game room. The whole scene had an unreal feel to Deana. What's going on here? she thought.

Edward grasped Patsy by the arm and firmly turned her around, "Why don't we walk Frank to the car. I'm sure Ajai will escort Deana."

Patsy smiled happily, "Take your time, you two. We'll be chatting at the car… no hurry."

Turning his back on Deana, Ajai opened the refrigerator door, looked inside and said, "I have beer and fruit punch and 20 ounce bottles of pop. What'll it be?"

"Nothing, I'm fine. I'm going home. I should never have come here. You really should pass out maps of the house whenever you invite anyone over," she shot over her shoulder as she followed their folks into the hallway.

Ajai strode along with her cracking open the twist top of a Coke, "I'll keep that in mind." he said.

Outside, Deana saw a new look on Patsy's face, a look of disappointment. "Ready so soon, Ajai?"

Ajai, who had remained standing in the doorway, held his half-empty plastic bottle and absently twisted the top. A slight smile played on his lips, "Yes, mother why what did you expect?" He did not look in Deana's direction again.

Deana wondered what she had done to offend her hostess and wished she had the courage to ask her what it was. Instead she said, "Thank you very much for the wonderful afternoon." Deana walked to the passenger door and got in.

From inside the safety of the familiar car, she turned to

look at the group of people gathered at the end of the side-walk. She felt like she was back in high school and was being excluded from the fun. She wondered again. "Why is every-one acting so weird?

Edward and Patsy stood next to Frank who, as he talked, was leaning against the open car door. Ajai slouched against the kitchen doorway and averted his eyes when she looked at him. As her father shook Edward's hand and hugged Patsy, Deana thought, what a horrid way to end a nice day.

47

Monday morning, Deana squinted as she looked out the windshield wet with torrential rain. The windshield wipers slapped on high speed the entire drive to work. Deana's wipers slapped then squeaked, slapped then squeaked. The noise made Deana wince. She hated using the wipers.

Once she parked the car, she raced across the parking lot and into the office building. In the empty corridor, her shoes left wet prints on the shiny linoleum. Deana wondered if Genie had arrived yet.

Genie was not the frequent visitor to Deana's office that she had been in the past and Deana missed her company. No longer did she see her for their fifteen-minute coffee breaks. Genie had told her that she stopped taking coffee breaks so she could have a longer lunch with Matt.

Deana didn't blame her. Matt was one guy in a million. With a sigh, Deana shook her raincoat out and hung it up. She shut the door and stared at her reflection in the mirror, thinking, damp is not a good look for me. The skirt of her dark blue suit was wet from running across the lot to the building. Her tidy hair now curled in wet tendrils around her face. She found satisfaction in the tan she acquired from spending the day on the lake in the boat race.

Deana pushed the hair behind her ears. She said to herself, "Oh well, it doesn't matter how I look. Ajai won't be visiting anymore."

The day's work ahead stretched in front of her and filled her with as much gloom as the rain had brought. When break time came around, Deana spent it in her office at her desk. She decided it was time to go through the company files to find any discrepancies. She found nothing in the first filing box full of papers.

Deana did go upstairs to the garden room for lunch since she had forgotten to fix her usual bag lunch the night before. The girls from the secretary pool crowded around her when she stood in the buffet line, their excited chatter about Edward Jacoubi's collapse and the sailboat races and Ajai lightened Deana's mood. She added nothing to the conversation, but enjoyed hearing their speculations about what had happened, about Ajai, and the unspoken questions about her involvement with the Jacoubi family. Deana looked around, feeling uncomfortable about seeing David. Luckily he never made an appearance.

The lunch made Deana feel more hopeful about the day and the week ahead. Maybe she had been wrong in warning Ajai to stay away from her because of the gossip. The girls she had just been with seemed rather pleasant. Not catty at all. Deana settled down and accomplished more than usual. At five she closed her office feeling proficient. It was an uplifting feeling she took pleasure in

48

Two days later, the hallway leading from Deana's office into the basement was silent when she left at five-thirty. Exactly at five, Genie had stuck her head in Deana's office to say a quick goodbye. Deana was not surprised to be leaving work alone. Exiting the elevator Deana stood in the enclosed entryway and studied the steady rainfall. Just like Duluth to rain for three days straight, Deana thought. Deana paused to slip her arms into the black raincoat and pull the hood over her head before she stepped out into the parking ramp. A warm breeze made the rain less miserable. Deana walked up the steps to where her car was parked. She jammed the key in the lock and turned it. The familiar click sounded, along with the sound of her name.

Deana saw nothing in the gloomy interior of the parking ramp. She walked out into the middle where stone pillars did not block the view. Only a handful of cars remained on this level of the ramp. Who could have called her name?

Suddenly a long-legged figure ran toward her. Each footstep created a splash as he dodged the puddles. "I checked the place out to be certain we were alone," Ajai said slightly out of breath when he stopped next to her. "There isn't anyone out here but you and I, so we should be safe for a few minutes of conversation."

Deana barely controlled the urge to punch him right in his square, handsome chin.

Ajai reached over and pushed the rim of her rain hood off of her head. He stared down at her and then stepped closer. His big body leaned against her. One long-fingered hand reached up to cradle her chin as he leaned over and pressed his lips against hers in a kiss filled with fire. He released her suddenly and stepped back.

Stunned, Deana wondered if she'd imagined it. The tingle on her face from the roughness of his chin added to the ache of her lips.

In the shadows of the gloomy day, Deana stared at him as her world burst into the brilliant colors of complete and utter joy.

Ajai gave a deep sigh, "So, are you going to yell at me? Maybe a slap? Or a kick in the shin?"

Deana touched her throbbing lower lip with her fingertips, "What was that for?"

Ajai gave a moan and swung away from her, shoving his hands in the pockets of his overcoat. "Why would you ask me that? Don't you realize how hard it is to explain? Okay, because it's you, I'll tell you. I kissed you because you probably won't ever speak to me after today, and because you looked so much like the true professional, no nonsense, don't-mess-with-me Deana, I just couldn't resist."

Deana glared at him. He was making fun of her. She knew it. "What does that mean?"

"I don't know exactly, but I thought we were making progress and that you didn't dislike me as much as you did before. Until of course, you told me to stay away from you. Then last Sunday you were... ah forget it. Nothing it means nothing. Deana, I don't have much time and I have two things to tell you before I leave. You're not going to like either one."

Deana said in a flat tone, "Then just get it over with and say it."

Ajai hunched his shoulders, "David has asked for a transfer back to the Saint Paul office. The transfer has been approved to take place immediately. Deana, I'm so sorry. I feel I'm responsible for this happening. I never meant to cause you and David any problems. Please believe me that wasn't my intention, ever."

Deana fingered the cold metal of her car keys. She really did not feel much besides relief hearing that David was leaving Duluth, "I don't believe even David knew why he transferred to Duluth. He never liked it here. He likes the big city. He'll be much happier there."

The rain began to splash through the openings of the car ramp and Deana pulled her hood back over her head. "Hurry up. What next?" She said, edging toward her car.

Ajai frowned, "If you remember, I warned you this would happen. My mother has this fear that no woman will ever marry me without her help. This year she's been planning my future, and she's chosen you as the perfect bride for me. She doesn't realize she's giving me way too much credit. She actually thinks I deserve you."

He paused, looking uncomfortable, "You're not going to like this, but there's no way to put what I have to say delicately. My mother thinks I proposed to you in the living room."

Deana felt her knees go weak. "I don't understand."

"You remember when she dropped the tea tray? Well, she thought I was on my knees proposing."

A feeling of complete and utter joy hit the pit of her stomach. She thought, Deana Michaels engaged to Ajai Jacoubi? For one second the thought of how glorious life with this man might be overwhelmed her. Then common sense crowded in. Deana struggled to keep her knees from buckling. She kept her head down, clenched her eyes shut and gasped for breath.

Ajai touched her shoulder. "Are you okay? You're not going to faint or be sick?"

She heard the strain in his voice and gave a quick negative shake of her head.

"You know, girl, you're unbelievably brutal on my ego. I've always hoped that when I mentioned engagement to a woman she would at least act like she was thrilled, but the first girl I say it to almost keels over."

The raw ecstatic emotion that had fired through Deana completely dissipated. Feeling capable of maintaining her composure, she straightened and reluctantly faced him. The heat in her cheeks continued to burn. She stared at him for a second before blurting out, "This is unbelievable. I can't understand how this can be happening. It isn't some silly fabrication you've come up with, is it?"

"No! Of course not, why would I do something like that?" Ajai paused, then said, Oh yeah. Now I remember. You think I'm incapable of telling the truth. The only reason I'm here is to let you know Frank probably knows about the engagement too."

"Stop saying that."

"Stop saying what?"

"Engagement."

"Okay, fine. Whatever you want. Let's call it the fabrication. In case Frank mentions something about *the fabrication*, you can set him straight. Tell him it's all my fault."

Silence fell between them.

Ajai said softly, "I don't know what I can say to you, Deana, except that I only wanted you to know what's happened, and once again you've proven you're the most exasperating female I've ever known."

Deana gave a bitter laugh pacing to her car and then stalked back. "At least this... this mix-up explains why your mother treated me so strange. I thought I'd insulted her. But, what the truth is, it turns she couldn't hide her disappointment that you picked me."

Ajai reached to take a hold of her icy fingers, "Has my mother done something to offend you?"

Deana mouthed a silent no as she turned her face away.

"No, I didn't think so. Then how can you have any doubt that if this was real, she'd be thrilled. On Sunday, I didn't see disappointment on her face when she was constantly pushing us at each other?"

Deana snatched her hand away and glared at him, "Quit patronizing me. Any woman you asked would agree to marry you. You know it, and your parents know it too. At the moment, I'm just the one conveniently available, but when it comes down to an actual engagement, they will expect you to marry someone in the league of the Jacoubi family. Somebody to make you happy but also somebody who fit into their world. I'm not that somebody."

Deana desperately wanted to disappear, but she had to ask. She had to know what happened next. "What did your parents say when you told them what really happened?"

Ajai's lips tightened in a grim line. "Well, the truth is I haven't exactly had the chance to tell them."

Deana gaped at him. Then blindly reached out and socked him in the arm. Her knuckles stung. She glowered at him, rubbing her hand. She was ashamed of her lack of self-control and she bit out, "I'm sorry. I shouldn't have done that, but how could you? If you never explained what happened they think... tell me they still don't think we're engaged."

Ajai gave an unimpressive shrug of one broad shoulder. He said, "Everything happened so fast. When I tried to explain, my father jumped in and told her not to put me on the spot. He said the whole thing was between you and I, and they would have to wait until we were ready to announce our engagement. Then the two of them started to argue and I quit listening after that. I do know I never came right out and actually told them we aren't engaged." His voice didn't sound apologetic nor did he look it.

"Ajai," Deana shrieked. "You go home right now and tell them it's a mistake. This minute do you hear me? Or better yet, call them right now on your cell phone."

"Sorry, I can't. I'm on my way out of town. I've got a late meeting in St. Paul tonight. The company helicopter is waiting for me up on the roof. After the meetings I'll talk to my father and explain the whole thing. It's probably better if I tell him first. He'll know the best way to break the news to Mom."

"Ajai don't you dare leave town without resolving this."

Ajai pushed up his coat sleeve and looked at his watch, "Sorry there's nothing I can do about it now. The helicopter's waiting. Goodbye, Deana." He hesitated, and unexpectedly leaned forward to capture her lips in a kiss that was brief, but the impact shattered Deana. With a mocking salute, he turned and darted toward the elevator at the other end of the ramp.

Deana watched with mixed feelings. "Coward," She yelled half-heartedly after his retreating figure. Gingerly, she touched her lower lip and couldn't suppress a smile.

49

A week later, sitting in her office, Deana struggled with the memory of Ajai kissing her. It had been a week spent constantly worrying about her future at Jacoubi Enterprises and jumping from the feeling of delight at what happened to a feeling of abject fear.

Without confirmation that Ajai had spoken to his parents and stopped the rumor, she didn't know what was happening outside of her small perimeter, her home and her office. She resigned herself to the fact that she wouldn't know anything until Ajai returned to Duluth. There wasn't another soul she could talk to about this, not even her father.

Deana had asked Frank if the Jacoubi's had told him that she and Ajai were engaged. "It's between you and Ajai," is all he said before walking out to the porch to smoke his pipe.

The coolness that had kept the July heat bearable changed into heavy humidity the first week of August. The only relief Deana found from the sweltering conditions was in the basement of the Jacoubi office building.

With Ajai out of town and Genie constantly absorbed with Matt, Deana found time to sort through the employee files in an effort to figure out why the company was paying so much money for services that were previously offered within the company. The results she found in those files enlightened her more than any of the other files she'd gone through. The services previously available within Jacoubi were now being sent to local outside sources, costing the company hundreds of thousands of additional dollars. Yet, the service departments within Jacoubi had never been downsized. Why was the company paying double for such services?

At the end of the day on Friday, after meticulously filing away her paperwork, Deana dusted her desk and the wall of file cabinets in her office. She worked slowly because she didn't look forward to the sticky damp humidity that was waiting for her at home in the old house.

As she was giving the desk a swipe with the fleece dust wand, she heard the click click of high heels on the linoleum outside her office. Deana looked up expectantly.

Genie stepped inside with a grin and asked, "Hey stranger, got a minute to talk?"

"It's five o'clock and you're not running out of here to be picked up by Matt. What's up?"

Genie suddenly became agitated, as she swept into the room. Deana noticed other changes in her. Her clothes, although not exactly conservative, were not as outlandish as before, and she wasn't wearing as much make-up.

Deana studied her for a moment. "Hey, what's with the outfit? That certainly isn't your look."

Genie sauntered to the chair and sat down with a sigh, "I'm an absolute wreck. You won't believe what Matt's asked me to do. He wants to take me home to meet his parents."

At the horror in Genie's voice, Deana laughed. "I thought that was a good sign that he's getting serious. You don't feel the same way?"

"I know I know...I always figured I'd feel that way too, but I don't. Yesterday, he told me this is the weekend. Help me, Deana. I have no idea how I'm supposed to act. I wish I were you. You're the kind of woman any mother would approve of for her little boy. I'm the type that makes a mother shudder and roll her eyes."

"How do you know what Matt's mother approves of?"

"I don't, but this has never happened to me before. No guy has ever wanted his family to meet me. This is worse than when I was sixteen and had to take my driver's test."

"What does that have to do with meeting Matt's family?"

"I was terrified to take my driver's test. I flunked three times and I think the only reason I finally got a passing grade was that the instructor felt sorry for me because I was sobbing all over the steering wheel."

"Whatever Matt's parent's think of you won't affect Matt's feelings."

"Do you think so?" The depth of Genie's anxiety was apparent in her face, Deana felt a stab of jealousy. To openly show how much you adore the man who fills your life and not have to constantly be hiding your feelings, Genie doesn't know how lucky she is, Deana thought. "Look at you... wrapped up in one man and not prowling around the local hot spots any more. I'm jealous."

"No way. Your life is great. You're always happy."

"I am?"

"Except about David... that was a mistake. I should've known right away. You two were so different. And when he left town so suddenly it was so strange. It could have been because he couldn't bear to stay here after you broke up with him. That's romantic, isn't it? For a man to leave town because he can't bear to be without you."

"There's nothing romantic about him. He couldn't move up the corporate ladder fast enough here so he went back to the Cities. Greed is the reason he left, not romance."

"Ouch, that's a rough way of looking at it. Just tell me one thing. Why does Matt want to complicate our relationship this way? We've been having so much fun."

"Matt inviting you home with him is a compliment not a complication."

"Unless he likes tormenting his mother."

"Matt doesn't seem like the type."

"Okay, okay, you're right. I don't want to think about it anymore or I'll go crazy. Just tell me again that I'm going to be okay whether they like me or not."

Deana smiled, "You know that already."

Genie straightened her shoulders and took a deep breath, "You're right again. Thanks, Deana. I'll fill you in on all the grisly details Monday morning. What are your plans for the weekend?"

Deana said dryly, "I'm not going to start painting the outside of the house, that's for sure."

"Why not?

"In this humidity, it would be miserable."

"I'd be relieved to put it off. Hey, if you're not busy, do you want to go with me and Matt to his parent's place? It's only for overnight."

"No way."

"What kind of friend are you? Thanks for nothing."

After Genie left, and quiet spread through the room once more, Deana considered the question. 'What kind of friend am I?' Genie was being flip but after the fiasco with Ajai the thought continued to nag at her.

50

While Deana was driving home through the heavy Friday night traffic along Woodland Avenue, a strong wind brought thick billowing clouds scudding in. They soon piled up, completely covering the translucent blue sky and blocking out the sun.

Once she pulled up the gravel driveway and parked the car, Deana glanced at the menacing sky and the wildly pitching branches on the trees. Deana tossed her purse onto the back porch and raced out to the paddock. The feeling of electricity in the humid air warned that a storm was brewing. Thunder rumbled in the distance as Deana led Journey inside the shed. The hope of taking a late ride had died with the change in weather. She slammed the gate shut, double wrapping the chain around the post. Then she ran across the yard and up the back stairs into the mudroom off of the kitchen. She kicked off her leather work shoes, noting that they'd need a polish before Monday.

The telephone was ringing. In stocking feet, Deana skidded across the linoleum to pick up the receiver, "Hello, Michaels residence."

"Deana," static clouded the line. "Deana, this is Chip Davies."

"Chip, what's going on?"

"I'm out at the Barnum race track, there's a storm kicking up out here. I might lose the signal."

"I can barely hear you."

"Just hold on," The line broke to dead air. Soon the static returned with Chip's voice. "Deana, say something if you can hear me?'

Deana found herself shouting into the telephone, "I can hear you but barely."

"I can hear you fine so don't shout," Chip said, as his voice faded in and out.

"Ajai registered Second Chance in the qualifying race tomorrow and he's still out of town. I hate to scratch him. You wouldn't believe how this horse moves."

"So what does that have to do with me?"

"Ajai suggested I call you and ask if you'd be a substitute jockey for him."

"He did?"

"Of course he did. What do you think? Can you do it? First race is at eight am sharp. Think you can make it?"

Deana felt her stomach muscles clench into a tight knot. Fiddling with the telephone cord, her mind raced as she paced back and forth through the kitchen. "I don't know. A race track, I've never raced except for fun."

"Ajai told me about the race you two had a couple of weeks ago. He thinks you have racing potential, and I've seen you ride on a polo field. I know you can do it. Ajai says you can do it, but if you don't want to that's okay."

Deana thought fast. I really don't want to do this... I really, really don't want to do this. But she said into the receiver, "Fine, Chip, if you want me. What time should I be at the track?"

Static hit the line.

"Deana, what did you say?"

"I said I'd do it. I'm not sure if I can, but I'll try." And I'm probably going to die trying, she thought.

"I've got the Jacoubi's horse trailer set up on the South side of the fairgrounds. You'll be able to see it from the road. Be here about six thirty. Then you can take a trial run on the track."

Deana hung the phone back on the wall and tried to bury her fear. I don't want to take a trial run on any track, especially not a muddy one. She looked out and saw a curtain of rain plummeting past the kitchen window.

219

Saturday morning, with the windshield wipers making their familiar slap/squeak on the windshield, Deana exited at Barnum. The fan was blasting on defrost but her windows were still fogging up. She followed the exit ramp and passed the restaurant. The next road led to the Barnum County Fairgrounds. The entire town of Barnum gave Deana the sense of a by-gone century. Life seemed to move at a slower pace along the quaint tree-lined streets. The small houses with neatly mowed lawns were decorated with children's toys, swing sets and plastic wading pools. Some of these had bright, white fences surrounding them and huge shade trees.

When she turned off the paved street and down the gravel road that led to the racetrack, she expected to see Andy and Opie walking by carrying fishing poles. People were walking toward the fairgrounds. Some waved to her as she passed. The little red car splashed through puddles and muddy tracks, and the number of people multiplied the closer she got to the fairgrounds. They walked in groups carrying big black umbrellas, wearing mud boots and rain slickers of every color. The rain wasn't going to keep the locals away from the big annual horse races that had been going on in Barnum for fifty years.

Deana shuddered. By the condition of the road she was driving on, she knew the racetrack must be deep in black oozing mud and treacherous. A horse would have to be strong to make it through this stuff. She wondered about Second Chance. Ajai had saved him from the meat man's hatchet, but did he have what it takes to make a show on the track? She was going to find out whether she wanted to or not.

Slowly, she maneuvered around the deep grooves made by the big trucks and horse trailers until she saw the Jacoubi's trailer. The horse trailer was parked under the protection of a huge elm tree with wide spanning limbs, heavy with leaves.

51

Deana parked the little red car under the tree. Big raindrops fell from the leaves but the drizzle had stopped. She turned the car off and reached into the back seat for her rain boots and slicker. The sky looked brighter toward the east. Hopefully, that was a sign that the clouds were going to clear away. She pulled on her boots and pushed open the door, her step making a sloshing sound into the rain sodden ground. Pulling her raincoat over her shoulders, she ran to the trailer and knocked. The door opened, the smell of coffee and the feeling of warmth radiated around her, enveloping her in its hominess.

Chip was in stocking feet dressed in rain pants, and a Jacoubi Stable polo shirt. He grinned down at her while he munched on a bagel. His gray hair, wet and slicked back against his head, showed the deep lines in his tan face. "Deana, you made it. Come on in." He backed from the doorway to give her room in the narrow area.

Deana remained standing in the mud. "I'd rather keep my gear on. I'll start grooming the horse until you're ready."

"He's already groomed and saddled. I put him in the trailer to keep him dry. Would yah look at that? Over there, blue sky. It just might clear up. You want some breakfast?"

Deana's stomach was already wound into knots. She gave a definite shake of her head, "No, I'd rather take a look around."

Chip nodded, "Don't go too far. We should see how Chance reacts to a muddy track before too many people are around."

Deana walked away muttering, "I'm the one in the mud all ready to go, Chip, so you hurry up."

The racetrack was located in the center of the fairgrounds

about a half a block from where Chip had the Jacoubi rig parked. The circular racetrack enclosed by wooden rails did not look as large as she thought it would. Next to the gate where the announcers sat during the events was an elevated wooden structure with a roof over it. The center of the arena was covered with freshly mown grass.

The black track had been used since the rain because there were hoof marks in the mud. Deana climbed up the wet wooden plank in front of her and looked around. She watched as a few saddled horses, led by people covered in rain gear and tall rubber boots, were led inside the enclosure. The horses walked easily through the mud track, but the people slipped and slid as they crossed through it. Deana studied the area and noticed there weren't any sharp turns. In this mud, turns would be a hazard. These looked gradual enough.

Deana hopped off the rail and returned to the trailer. Second Chance stood outside cross-tied with his head hanging. When she walked up, he lifted his head to sleepily blink his big brown eyes.

"You look like you're raring to go, sleepy head," Deana spoke softly while she moved closer to the horse's muzzle. She leaned her shoulder against the trailer and looked him over. Chance blew at her then shook his head. His bridle jingled as the stream of warm breath hit her, "You remember me. I'm the one who knocked your master into the ditch. We won't ever tell him how funny he looked. That'll be our little secret. I just wanted to remind you that today we're on the same team, so be nice. And by the way, I think Journey can lick you in a fight, so if I get hurt today you better watch out because he'll be out to get you."

Chip leaned out of the open window of the trailer, "I don't think threatening the horse will help you win today, Deana. Come inside, I found a uniform with the Jacoubi colors that'll fit you, and a helmet with goggles. I think you're going to need them."

Deana reached over to gently scratch Chance's velvety nose and she gave a sigh, "Oh great, I'm not going to be able to see anything either. I hate those riding goggles you have. They never stayed on when I played polo."

Deana left Chance and walked over to the metal steps leading into the trailer. Chip opened the door.

"You know the best way to keep your goggles clean," Chip said jumping down to stand next to her. "Get in the lead and stay there."

"Like that'll happen with me as jockey."

He laughed at her, "Don't be so nervous. Chance is a big horse. You'll be sitting high and he's a mover. If you're behind it won't be for long."

"Thanks Chip, but I don't feel a whole lot better. If I'm taking a practice run I'll wear these clothes, then the silks won't be dirty for the race. I've got my own boots."

"Then get 'em on girly, we got some racing to do."

Deana sat on the trailer's metal step and slipped off her mud caked rubber boots. She set them aside and wiped her hands on her jeans before putting on the leather riding boots. It was an old pair she had used for polo. The boots were half a size too small so her toes were squished in the front, but as long as she didn't have to walk, she'd be okay.

The stirrups were high on the saddle. Chip leaned down and cupped his hands. Deana stepped in and he boosted her up the horse's back. She grasped the English saddle and swung her leg over. Quickly, she positioned her feet in the stirrups and adjusted her seat. She gathered the loop of thick leather reins into wet hands.

"Did you bring gloves?" Chip asked, as he checked the cinch and straightened the reins. "The leather's wet. There's a chance your hands might slip."

"No, I forgot."

Chip frowned. "Hold your hand up." He looked at her soiled palm that was already becoming white from the cold and shook his head. "I don't think I have a pair that small, but I'll look. I don't want you losing your grip. I have no idea how Chance will react to a loose rein."

Deana briefly closed her eyes. This is getting very scary.

Chip clipped the lead rope on the bridle and led Chance down the path to the track. They met up with several other horses and riders. Except for a brief hello there was no small talk.

When they arrived at the track, a few horses were already being worked. The jockeys looked like they were keeping the horses at a slow pace and testing the turf.

Deana said, "It looks like I'm not the only one nervous about the mud."

Chip kept silent. At the entrance, he unclipped the lead from the bridle and said, "You walk him around in there and try to find a comfortable seat. Don't worry so much about Chance. You're the one I want to get a feel for how the horse moves through the mud, and keep firm contact on his mouth."

Deana nodded, and with a nudge of her knees, she urged Chance through the open gate. They walked toward two horses already walking on the same path. Chance lifted his head and moved toward the strangers. Deana turned him away toward the outside of the track. She didn't know how he would react around strange horses. Chance eagerly stepped out along the track. The mud gave him no cause to hesitate. In no time, he broke into a long-legged jog that quickly became a slow rolling canter.

For several long strides, Deana bounced along in the saddle until she adjusted her weight to the height and length of Chance's strides. Compared to Journey's short choppy gait, it was easy for her to find a comfortable position. Feeling her body relax as the horse moved smoothly along the track, she leaned forward and stood up in the stirrups. Chance felt her movement and increased his speed. Head high, his big ears turned forward, she felt the muscles in the horse propel them swiftly through the mud. Deana smiled and crouched lower into his neck. Riding this horse was like being on a carousel. The gaits were so smooth she barely felt the increased speed. She kept the reins taut, and Chance shook his head fighting for slack. Deana held him in a slow canter. He shook his head again and hopped. Deana laughed and said, "You devil, don't you think for a moment you're going to get away from me." Then she turned him toward the gate and slowed him to a fast trot.

Chip waited at the gate, a smile on his face. "What do you think?"

"His gaits are a dream. He's so smooth. He wanted to run. Did you see him buck?"

"He's a handful and don't forget it. He's still just a diamond in the rough. And if he gets any leverage, he'll take off on you. How was his footing?"

"He never slipped once."

"He's big and his weight will give you an advantage the lighter horses don't have. Plus he's got big feet. Let's get back to the trailer. Look at the mud on this horse. While you change, I'll try to clean him off."

"Why bother," Deana said as he led her across the ground.

"He wants to look his best for winner's circle."

"We can only hope," Deana said. They walked up to the trailer and Chip helped her dismount. Deana pulled off her boots and hurried up the steps inside the trailer.

With fifteen minutes until the start of the first race, Deana emerged in the Kelly green and white silks of the Jacoubi stable. Suddenly, the gray that had covered the sky as far as she could see became streaked with brushstrokes of yellow and orange. As if painted by the hand of God, glowing sunrays filled the clouds over the racetrack. Deana's mood immediately became brighter.

Chip, holding a bristle brush, labored on smoothing Chance's unruly mane. A group of people stood watching the grooming. Chip fielded their questions as they admired the fine animal. Once Deana appeared in the doorway of the trailer, all eyes were on her. Chip smiled at her then tossed the brush into the bucket at his feet. He raised his voice using the clipped professional tone Deana knew well, and he said to the group, "Excuse me, I need to get my horse and jockey out to the track or we'll miss competing in this race."

The people did what Chip expected them to do, they quickly dispersed heading toward the racetrack.

"Where did they come from?" Deana asked pulling on the boots.

"They're out checking on the competition. It happens at every race. I hope that sun doesn't stay out too long."

"You can't be serious?"

"Of course I am. It only makes it muggy, and brings the flies out. I prefer cool, wet weather."

"Well not me," Deana said, "And the sun might dry the mud. That would help."

Chip shook his head and boosted her onto Chance's back, "Can't dry it enough to do you any good," he said looking up at her. "You need to pull your hair back and stick it inside your shirt. If it gets in your face, it'll blind you."

Deana twisted her hair with quick efficient movements and shoved the coil down inside her collar knowing it wouldn't stay. She wondered why Chip suddenly sounded nervous. Funny, she didn't feel nervous any more. She pulled the plain black helmet over her head and slid the chinstrap tight.

"Pull your goggles down. How do they feel?"

Deana wiggled the goggles into the curves of her face. They felt heavy, but stayed in place. "This is great. I can barely see, and I'm sure I look like some kind of alien."

"Don't worry, you'll be able to see the track in front of you. This isn't a polo match. You don't have to watch a ball on the field and you're gonna look much worse when the race is finished."

"Thank you very much, Chip. You say the nicest things."

"Watch it Deana or I'll think you're starting to enjoy yourself."

"I am enjoying myself. I think seeing the sun did it."

"Tell me about the practice run. Did you feel comfortable? Chance listened to you?"

"Yes, I didn't think he'd stop, but he did."

Chip untied the lead rope from the trailer and once more they moved across the gravel walkway to the racetrack. "You can see that they don't use any kind of starting gate," Chip explained. "No wire, no nothing, these races are based on the Irish and English version of a county race. Four horses in a row, the gun sounds and you're off. If the horse you're riding freaks out, then that's your problem. We've been using a starting pistol around Chance for a couple of weeks now so he shouldn't get too nervous from the sound. The other horses are my biggest concern. He isn't aggressive toward new horses, but who knows in this situation? With the slippery ground, remember to be prepared for the unexpected."

Around the racetrack there were crowds of spectators dressed in rain gear with umbrellas. A vendor meandered through the crowd holding mammoth bunches of different shaped Mylar balloons that bounced wildly in the wind. The cluster of nervous horses inside the ring pranced around in tight circles. Chance walked calmly past it all. He never looked at the balloons or the people crowding around the rails. He saw the other horses and moved quickly through the mud towards them. Deana kept a firm grip on the reins as he chewed the bit. Deana detoured the big chestnut away from the other animals and kept off to the side while they waited.

The loud speaker went off and the announcements began, "Horses registered for the eight o'clock race line up at the starting line. Welcome everyone for the running of the Barnum Derby Races. We have a great first prize this year. The winner will receive a check for $2,500. That should keep everyone on the track energized. In five minutes the starting signal will be given for the first race of the morning and it's going to be a muddy day, folks."

Deana's heart pounded faster. Her clammy hands clutched the reins tightly. She glanced over to where Chip was standing and saw his encouraging thumbs up signal and thought, this is a nightmare. What am I doing out here on Ajai's horse putting my life in danger all for a silly race? I must be crazy.

52

A t seven fifty-five Saturday morning there was a row of constantly moving horseflesh around the starting line. After the officials stepped in to organize the group, four horses with riders perched on their backs were assembled waiting for the pistol shot.

Deana sat stiff-legged in the stirrups. Her knees almost rested against her rib cage. She glanced warily to either side at the prancing, pawing horses surrounding her. A brown and white paint with one blue eye kept baring his teeth at Chance whenever he moved too close. On the other side, danced a beautiful bay horse with long tapered legs. The jockey held a crop in his hand and seemed to enjoy flaying the weapon through the air. The whip didn't bother Second Chance but it caused the bay to swing around and push them closer to the paint. Deana wanted to avoid being kicked or bitten in the starting line.

A shot sounded. A scramble of hooves, and flying mud ensued. Deana froze. She gave no command. Chance stretched out his neck, clamped the bit in his teeth and with a giant leap jumped away with the group. The horses were off. Soon riders were whistling and chirping to their horses, urging them to run faster. Deana just held on.

Chance kept the bit in his teeth and ran against the tight grip on the rein. Mud flew in clumps, hitting Deana in the thighs, face, arms and chest. She crouched closer to Chance's muscular neck and loosened the rein. With her head low to protect her face, she lifted herself off the saddle and allowed the muscular horse to move. Several seconds passed before she realized the muddy assault on her body had stopped. With Chance's thick mane blowing in her face, she lifted her head and saw the only thing in front of them was the track. They were in the lead. She dared not move her head to see if any-body was next to them and only seconds later the roar of the crowd filled her ears. Emotionally numb and still holding tightly to the reins, Deana reined the horse in to a slow trot. She looked behind her to see the other horses slowing as their jockeys turned them toward the exit. Deana sat down in the saddle and pulled on the reins, turning Chance toward the exit, wondering who won.

The gate area was packed with people and horses. Deana whipped off the mud-spattered goggles and helmet.

"Whew, now I can see," Deana said. She caught sight of Chip moving around the crowd toward her. Deana guided Chance to him when the officials, two men dressed in long red coats wearing black pants and helmets riding in western saddles, stopped in front of Chance. They smiled in unison, "Congratulations," the man on a flashy chestnut said to her.

Chip appeared next to her and said, "Deana, you won. Congratulations." He reached up to grab Chance's bridle.

"Miss, you will sit out the next race and then you will ride against three new horses."

Deana listened then nodded, "Can I return to my trailer?"

The officials glanced at the other and said, "The races run on the hour. Just be back in plenty of time."

They turned their horses around and walked over to the starting line where the jockeys were already walking their horses onto the track area.

"You okay, Deana?"

"Huh?"

"What's the matter with you, are you hurt?"

Deana looked down at Chip and said, "No, I just don't remember what happened after the gun went off. I think I froze. I don't remember giving Chance any cues. He just took off when the gun went off. At first, I was being pelted with mud balls and then there was nothing until the yelling at the finish."

"You pulled out in front half-way through the race. Chance didn't even look like he was doing anything more than keeping pace until the last length of the track. Then he just stretched out those long legs of his and left the others behind."

Deana kicked her feet out of the stirrups and let her legs dangle down Chance's sides. "Wow, after awhile that hurts the knees."

"We still have a long day a head of us."

"Tell me how this works. I sit out a race, then race again?"

"This is a progressive race. You win, you race again. You lose, you're done."

"Who am I racing?"

"The winners from the previous races and any newcomers."

"My horse will be at a disadvantage. He's going to get tired."

"He'll have an hour to rest and after that it's your problem. If a horse is in good shape, he'll be fine. Each race is only minutes long. Chance is in prime condition. We don't have to worry about him."

By the time they reached the trailer, the clouds had covered the sun. Chip helped Deana from the saddle. She stretched her back muscles. "I'm going to wash up. Do you mind if I use the bathroom inside?"

"Go ahead, I'll take care of Chance." Chip paused to look her over. He grinned, "You don't look as bad as I thought you would. And remember, mud packs are supposed to be good for your complexion."

Deana shot him a suspicious look. Then saw the bootjack by the step, "hey, where did this come from?"

"I had it inside the trailer. I figured you'd need some help getting those boots off once your feet started to swell."

Deana stuck the heel of her boot into the jack and gave a tug. The boot slid free. "This is great." She looked down at her silk jersey and saw the mud plastered to her, "I can guess by your look that my face is worse than this jersey."

Chip shrugged, "Who am I to say." He handed her a small brush with stiff bristles. "This should get the mud off your clothes. It's kind of funny that your boots are the cleanest thing that you're wearing."

In stocking feet, Deana jumped from the metal stairs to the trailer stoop. She glanced back at Chip, "I only have an hour. I'd better start now."

"Think you can handle another race?"

"Second Chance did all the work. I was just along for the ride."

"Not if he takes a header out there. You have to be prepared to hold him up or bail off."

"Are you tactfully telling me I shouldn't ride in the second race? Did I do something wrong or did you find another rider?"

"No, I just want you to remember you have an important job up there and you're not just along for the ride. That track is only going to get more dangerous after each race. I want you to stay prepared and not get lazy. Laziness leads to accidents and I don't want to take any chances with your safety."

Deana sobered up and said seriously, "I do understand how dangerous it is ,Chip. I'm sorry. I was teasing you."

"Go clean up," he said gruffly before he turned away.

53

Deana knew what to expect with the second race. She sat poised and ready for the signal. In a constant drizzle, the four riders waited anxiously for the starting gun to go off. The rain-covered goggles blinded her. She reached up with her fingertips and wiped them off. Deana grabbed the leather but her hands weren't set on the rein when the shot sounded.

Chance surged forward. Deana's fingers slipped over the wet leather. The running horses on either side of her slapped her legs, crushing her between them. Chance took the bit in his teeth and with a loose rein, stretched out, galloping toward the first turn. To keep her seat, Deana gripped the saddle with her legs. The goggles, streaked with mud and rain, were useless. Around the first turn the other horses crowded in front of them. Chance threw his weight right into the middle of them and then slipped. His four legs worked frantically. Mud flew in every direction. Deana, her breathing shallow with fright, grabbed a handful of mane, leaned over his shoulder and tightened her hands on the reins and shifted her weight to give him time to catch his balance. The other horses had already rounded the corner when Chance regained his footing and leaned his weight into the bit. The powerfully muscled chestnut surged forward, bearing down on the horses in front of him. He moved right through the pounding bodies. Suddenly, the mud stopped battering her as they flew over the finish line. Deana gave a wild shout as they cantered toward the gate. Whipping the helmet off, she waved it frantically at Chip.

Chip was running toward her. The same two officials cut him off as they rode in front of her. Instead of the impressive red coats, they wore clear rain ponchos, "Congratulations, again."

"Thanks. Thanks a lot." Deana cried. The adrenaline flowing fast through her system made her dizzy. She could feel the mud sliding down her cheeks, toward her mouth and down her chin. With her sleeve, she wiped it away.

Chip walked up when the officials left. Deana still wiping at the mud, kicked her feet out of the stirrups. "I can't believe we won again."

"Congratulations, but what happened at the starting gate?"

Deana remembered the fear and helplessness she felt that instant when she lost the reins. "I did what you warned me not to do. I lost the rein. Then Chance slipped. I thought we were going down and I knew I couldn't bail off so I did what I could to help him."

"What ever you did worked. Last year's winner was in this race. He was the first one out in front, but after the last turn when you passed them, he never caught you."

Deanna reached down to stroke Chance's muddy neck. "He didn't wait for me that time either, Chip. When he slipped, I thought it was over."

"There's still four more races and you have to ride in two of them. I'll have to get you a pair of gloves, or would you rather not ride?"

"Of course I'll ride. We have a champion horse here. I'm not going to let my mistakes stop us from winning."

"That's my girl. I knew Ajai was right about you."

Deana wanted to pry Chip for details of any conversation he had with Ajai where she was mentioned, but bit her tongue to stop herself. Ajai caused her concentration to wander and Chip was right, she needed to concentrate on Chance and the next race.

The rain held off for the race that Chance didn't run in but when they stood waiting on the track, the drizzle covered the unprotected skin of her face. This time she left the goggles off. She couldn't keep them clean and she couldn't race blind, so she had to take a chance with the flying mud. Chance was well aware what all of this meant and he pawed at the mud, chewing constantly on the metal bit. The gun went off and he was a stride ahead of the others. He ran alone out in front the entire time. In spite of the rain, there were no mishaps during this race. Deana wore gloves and remained in control. Chance kept his footing and pulled ahead, racing alone right down to the last furlong.

When Deana rode off the track, she was drenched. She couldn't wait to leave the arena. Chip grabbed the bridle and led them out of the gate. Deana, with shaking hands removed her helmet and pushed her wet hair out of her face. Barely able to stop her teeth from chattering, she asked, "Where did the cold wind come from?"

"I don't know. You'll have to change out of those clothes and get warm before the next race."

"It'll be miserable putting wet clothes back on, but I guess you're right," Deana complained. When they arrived at the trailer she was freezing.

Chip slipped the bridle off Chance and clipped his lead to the trailer. "Sit in front of the heater and use the blow dryer on your clothes. It'll dry some of the wet."

Still in the saddle, she waited for Chip to help her down. She didn't think she could do it alone. To keep Chip from noticing how much she was shivering, Deana didn't speak, knowing that her chattering teeth would give her away.

"I put out dry towels and a blanket. Wrap yourself up in all of them then drink some hot coffee. Your teeth are chattering."

"I know," Deana said. She clenched her teeth together but couldn't stop the shaking in her jaw. Her legs aching with every move, she slowly leaned forward to swing her leg across Chance's wet muddy butt when strong hands dragged her out of the saddle and set her on the step.

A sharp voice said curtly, "Sit. I'll get your boots off."

Deana pushed her unruly hair out of her eyes. She looked

up and saw, not Chip, but a curly-haired man leaning over her. Chip stood behind him next to Chance. When he saw Deana staring at him, Chip shrugged and disappeared behind the horse. Speechless at the sight of Ajai, who seemed to appear again out of thin air, Deana pulled her foot away from the boot and then the next.

"Get inside the trailer, Deana, and get out of those clothes as fast as you can. I'll be right back." When he saw the expression on her face his eyes lit up and he slowly grinned, "That's not what I mean. You'll warm up faster if you put something dry on. I have a few things to say to Chip." The grin faded into a stern line. Ajai took another look at her and angrily walked away to find Chip.

Deana, without a word, hurried up the metal steps and opened the door. Warmth touched her cheeks and enveloped her shivering body. Chip must have turned the heater on full blast. It felt heavenly. She twisted the plastic rod to shut the curtains and locked the trailer door then wasted no time in peeling the wet pants and shirt off her clammy skin. One towel she piled around her wet hair, and then rubbed her skin with another until it tingled in protest. She pulled on her sweatshirt, and it hung below her hips. Standing in front of the heater, she wrapped the oversized Indian blanket around her shoulders and tucked the ends around her bare feet.

After a few minutes she stopped shivering. The interior of the trailer smelled like heated wool, leather, and horse manure. Deana gave a sigh and felt better already. She grabbed a heavy ceramic mug off a hook hanging under the counter and poured coffee, adding a lot of cream. A narrow chair shoved under a small table was close enough to the heater so she sat down. Sipping the coffee, Deana absently rubbed her hair with the towel wondering what was going to happen now that Ajai had arrived.

She knew he was going to ride in the last race. Annoyance at his overbearing attitude rose inside of her until she saw the pile of muddy, sodden clothes lying in a heap on the floor. A feeling of relief replaced her irritation. She leaned over to pick them up, and cautiously shook the material. Dirt scattered around the room. Deana set the cup down and began pressing the shirt flat against the table. Just in case I'm wrong and Ajai's not prepared to ride, I will be, she thought.

She grabbed the hair dryer and plugged it into the outlet next to the table. When the heat hit the material the smell of horse and earth overpowered the other smells. Deana turned the blower off and pushed them back on the floor thinking, Ajai's riding whether he's ready or not. There's no way I'm putting these back on.

Holding the ends of the blanket around her waist she stretched out her aching legs. It wasn't just her legs, her whole body ached. She closed her eyes. In forty minutes she'd either be back on the track racing for the championship, or on the sidelines. Chance was still going strong but she wasn't.

There was a bang at the door. Deana's eyes flew open and she sat up. "Who is it?"

"It's me. Are you decent?"

Deana wrapped the blanket tightly around her waist as she leaned over and unlocked the door.

Ajai flung it open and his eyes swept briefly over her. His laugh sounded rough, "I can't believe Chip allowed you to ride under these conditions. You look awful. No race is worth this, Deana. Why did you agree to do it?"

Deana refused to be intimidated. She stuck her nose in the air and said in a haughty tone, "Glad to see you too and you're welcome. I'm so glad I helped you out."

"Helping somebody out and killing yourself doing it isn't the same thing. Did you want to continue riding when it started to rain?"

"Do you think Chip forced me? You know Chip better than that. I've ridden polo in worse conditions than this."

"It looks like you ran the races instead of the horse."

Deana attempted to jump to her feet ready to protest but quickly sank back into the chair clutching the blanket around her. "Please get out. I have to get dressed for the next race."

"No, you're not. I'm riding the next race."

Deana glared at him and said huffily, "So you get to have all the fun and run the final race. I don't think that's fair at all."

"Your clothes are soaking wet. Your face is covered with mud. You look white as death and you think I'm going to allow you to ride again. You are the most stubborn woman. Don't you realize the reason these horses are in the finals is because they are either mean enough to butt the competition out of the way or fast and bulky enough to beat off the competition, like Second Chance. The final race is a test of strength and endurance, not just racing. I can't believe I'm actually arguing with you because I want to keep you out of danger." He turned and bellowed out the door, "Chip, you've lost your mind. Deana looks ready to drop."

Deana jumped to her feet with a secure hand on the blanket and yelled out the door, "I am not, Chip. Don't listen to him. You better not take this out on Chip. He was just following orders."

"Bull he was. Chip has never followed any orders from me so why should he start now. He just hates to give up and as long as you were willing to keep fighting, he was ready to send you out there."

Deana heard Chip's voice from outside. "Quit fretting about her, Ajai. She's the one who got us into the finals."

Deana shot him a smug look.

"You stay put. I'm riding the next race." Ajai said, before he stomped out of the trailer and slammed the door shut. Deana remained standing and listened to the angry voices outside. Never before had she heard Chip argue with anyone and it was all because of her.

The door opened again. Standing outside, Ajai shouted,

"Chip, what did you do with my riding clothes?" He looked inside and saw Deana in the same spot. "Aren't you dressed yet? How am I supposed to get ready in time?" He yelled to no one in particular.

Ajai kicked off his shoes and stomped up the steps into the trailer. He walked to a cupboard and removed a green and white silk outfit that matched the one Deana had worn.

"I'll change in the truck," he said tersely. Then he left slamming the door behind him.

Deana stared open-mouthed at the closed door. It swung open again. Ajai stuck only his head inside, "Thank you for riding Chance. You, young lady, have more courage than sense. I never thought I'd be saying that to you. I sound like my father." He fell silent then grinned at her, his expression softening, "You're the best, Deana."

Deana had not moved, did not want to move. With a sigh, she remembered that afternoon when Ajai kissed her in the parking ramp. Tears burned her eyes and she buried her face in her hands.

54

After Ajai rode off on Chance with Chip leading the horse, Deana realized she only had ten minutes to get over to the racetrack. She dropped the blanket and scrambled to grab her jeans. There was no way she wasn't going to watch the final race. Bundled in her raincoat and boots, she hurried down the path to the track. The crowd of people surrounded the fences and the entrance of the race-track. She slipped through the people until she found where Chip was standing.

Panting, Deana ran up beside him just as the gun cracked into the air. Deana spotted Chance on the far outside. The horse burst forward ahead of the group but this time the rest of the pack stayed with him.

Deana watched, holding her breath as the scene played out in front of her, her gaze glued to the big chestnut's legs as he fought through the mud. The horses crowded into a cluster as they raced toward the first turn. Mud flew in every direction. The group remained tightly together as they raced toward the second turn and then down the backstretch. The horse surged through the group. First they were neck and neck and then Chance's legs were out in front. He had passed the black horse crowding him. Chance nosed steadily out into the front and put the black a full length behind as he crossed the finish line.

Deana grabbed Chip's shoulder jumping up and down screaming at the top of her lungs.

Laughing, Chip grabbed her as she threw her arms around his neck and hugged him.

"Let's go and congratulate him. I'm glad you didn't ride that race. If you were going to get hurt it was with that last bunch. They were rough on each other."

"Okay, I'll admit Ajai was right, but why does he have to move in and take over, pushing both of us around. We don't deserve that. We worked so hard today."

Chip grinned at her, a knowing look in his dark eyes, "You like him, don't you?" He said laughing at her.

"What? I do not. Why would I like that bossy, arrogant man? He makes me crazy. Okay, I do like him, but only as a friend."

"I remember a thirteen-year-old describing her favorite horse in the same way and that thirteen-year-old liked her horse very much and still does."

"Quit being so irritating, Chip," Deana quipped and turned her back on him, walking away.

Ajai rode to the grandstand where the officials waited to present the prizes to the riders. The third place winner was given a trophy and a ribbon. Ajai arrived just in time to see the jockey of the black horse receive a second place trophy and ribbon. The official placed a narrow collar of woven flowers around Chance's muddy neck and handed Ajai the largest of the three silver cups. Ajai leaned forward to say something to the official and he nodded, motioning to the announcer. A few moments later the loudspeaker went off and she heard her name and Chip's announced to go to the grandstand for the final ceremony.

Deana groaned out loud, "What's Ajai thinking? Why do we have to go up there?"

Chip took her arm, "Come on, it only makes it harder if you drag your feet. Everybody wants to go home and get dry, including me."

With Chip's firm hold on her hand, Deana hurried across the mud torn ground until they reached the grandstand. Ajai had removed the helmet and his face was covered with mud except for the raccoon circles left from the goggles around his eyes. Seeing Ajai's face, Deana's hand flew to her cheek. She suddenly remembered that she had forgotten to wash her face before coming over here. She probably looked worse than Ajai with dried mud all over her face. She turned to Chip and demanded, "I forgot to wash. Is there mud all over me?"

Chip looked at her and said, "No, it must've flaked off."

Deana made a face and said, "Unfortunately I'll have to accept that, but I'm sure I'm a mess."

Ajai leaned down and handed Deana the trophy saying, "This really belongs to you."

Deana, smiling, held the cup with a racing horse and jockey on the lid, and turned to Chip, "Actually it belongs to the Jacoubi Stables. So Chip, it's yours."

Ajai slid off Chance's back and moved to stand between them. "She has a point, Chip. I think it will be a nice addition to the stable trophy case."

Chip smiled at the officials and shook their hands while he said his thanks.

"Wait, there's also a check for the winner. The judge has it at the grandstand."

Ajai looked at Deana, then Chip and both of them declined the money with a negative shake of their head.

Ajai stepped back, holding Chance's bridle while Chip walked to the judge. He said, "The Jacoubi stable would like to donate this check back to the city of Barnum. We heard you're raising money for a children's center to be built, so the money can be used for that."

The judge made the announcement over the loudspeaker and the crowd cheered. The judge held onto the check and shook Chip's hand again.

Deana waited next to the grandstand for Chip to return. She watched while the muddy horses were led out of the gate along the fence toward the winner's circle. The crowd, lined up along the fence, kept up a continuous cheer as the horses passed by. Deana was surprised by their continued enthusiasm, despite it being the end of an exhausting, wet day.

A man standing with the big bay horse that had finished in

third place called to Ajai. On his head he wore a baseball cap. He had a barrel chest and a thick brown cigar hanging out of one corner of his mouth and a toothpick hanging out of the other. He stepped away from the group around him. "Hey, Ajai! What are you doing riding in the race? I thought you were done with horses when you gave up on polo? Didn't you decide to take it easy sitting behind a desk?"

Ajai laughed and handed Chance's reins to Chip. He walked across the muddy track to where Tom Kellerhuis stood with a wide grin on his sun-roughened face, chewing on the unlit cigar.

"Don't give me that line of bull, Tom. You're just sore you didn't get this gelding at the auction when you had the chance."

"What would I do with another winner? My stables already full of 'em."

The rain started to fall again. Tom pulled the brim of his baseball cap down to shelter his face, "You ever want to get back into polo on the Duluth Team, just let me know. I might be able to pull a few strings, maybe get you in as a replacement rider."

Ajai grinned while shaking the man's hand, "If anybody could talk me back into playing polo, it'd be you. My dad always said you could sell sand to an Arab, and sweet-talk anybody. Thanks for the offer, but I'm happy the way things are going."

"Heard your dad is on the mend. I'm real glad about that," Tom's gruff tone quickly changed to one of concern

"So am I," Ajai agreed quickly. "I'll let him know. Why don't you stop by the house and tell him yourself and don't forget to stay out of trouble."

"I always do," Tom said with a deep-chested laugh. His blue eyes twinkled with mischief as he touched the brim of his hat to Deana and then, leading the bay horse, walked off in the opposite direction.

Ajai turned to Chip, as they walked toward the trailer, "I didn't know Tom Kellerhuis ran his horses here. I'm surprised Deana did as well as she did."

Chip shrugged, "Tom rarely misses the local events. I talked to him for a while last night. He took second and third place with those two geldings, he should be pleased."

"Not Tom. I'm sure he wanted all three. He's a tough competitor. He's had that bay gelding forever. I always wanted to buy him. The one horse Tom could never be convinced to sell."

The drizzle turned into a steady rainfall. Chip had tied Chance under the tree next to Deana's car while the three of them hurriedly cleaned up the tack and loaded it into the trailer. Chip handed Deana the saddle and bridle to be wiped down and then Ajai bundled them into the cloth bags to protect them. Soon all the gear was packed away and Chance was loaded into the trailer. Chip climbed into the cab of the truck and waved goodbye through the closed window.

Ajai stood next to Deana as they watched him pull away. The trailer rocked from side to side as the tires sank in the mud.

Deana was grateful to have her long raincoat and her boots on. Even with her hood pulled over her head, the rain dripped into her face. Ajai had changed into his jeans and rain gear before Chip left. The two looked at each other. It was time to say goodbye. Ajai's truck was parked next to Deana's little red car and there was no reason to stay in the rain any longer. Even under the protection of the leafy overhang the rain began to pelt them.

A beat-up light blue pickup truck slowed as it pulled up next to them. Sitting in the passenger side sat Tom Kellerhuis. The driver gave a blast on the horn. Deana looked inside to see a young man with blond hair holding onto the wheel, "My grandson." Tom explained.

There were more than a dozen people sitting in the open

back of the truck.

Tom took the thick cigar out of his mouth and asked through the open window, "Why are you standing out in the rain? They're serving dinner in the community center. Hop in the back and join us."

Ajai looked at Deana. "What do you think?"

Deana smiled, "I'm game if you are. I'm not sure what they'll be serving, but I bet it's hot."

"Hold on just a minute, Tom." Ajai yelled. He took Deana's hand and they ran to the back of the truck. Ajai climbed onto the truck bed and pulled Deana's resisting body into his lap.

Laughing, Deana struggled to move away, "Will you let me sit next to you?"

The truck started to move and Ajai clamped his hands around her shoulders to keep her from bouncing to the ground. He said in her ear, "If you knew how much water has soaked through the seat of my pants you'd be thanking me instead of fighting. Now hold still or we'll both end up in the mud."

Deana had no choice but to relax into the steelly arms that were holding her.

55

As the truck rolled to a stop in front of the silver rectangular building, the boisterous group of young people were already climbing over the sides and jumping off, leaving Deana and Ajai the only two sitting in the back. Deana jumped down and walked around to thank Tom as he climbed out of the cab. He walked toward the double doors chewing on the toothpick and holding the cigar in his fingers. Tom said to Deana in a booming voice, "Now don't be shy about coming in, there's plenty for everybody, always is."

The group disappeared inside and Deana looked for Ajai. He was scraping the mud off his cowboy boots onto a rock. "Can't dance with muddy boots," He said walking to the door. A hand painted sign above it read Barnum Community Building.

"What do you mean dance?"

"There's always a dance after supper. Haven't you ever been to the Barnum races before?"

"No," Deana said as she slipped her raincoat off and walked into the coat closet to find a hanger.

After the cold and wet weather, the room was steaming with heat from the mass of damp people. The smell of stewed chicken overwhelmed Deana at first and then became secondary to a myriad of other smells, the most overpowering being wet horse.

Deana followed Ajai as they moved single file through the crowd to a serving table covered with a plastic tablecloth. The table held plastic tubs filled with ice and cans of pop. A huge coffee pot and a large plastic bowl brimming with red punch stood guard at each end. Smiling women and men stood behind the tables to offer glasses and napkins and take orders for roast beef or chicken dinner.

Holding their cans of pop, Ajai led the way to the serving window where they waited for their meals. Shortly, two plates emerged from the window like magic. Deana took her plate that was heaped with chicken, dumplings and a roll, and then she was handed a piece of corn on the cob. Ajai's beef was layered with bread stuffing and mashed potatoes. Walking to the back of the room, Deana laughed at the amount of food crammed onto the plates, "I'll never eat all of this. Do you think they offer to-go containers? My father loves this kind of food."

Ajai, moving slowly through the crowd, said over his shoulder, "That's because it's comfort food. My mom always cooks like this whenever it's cold outside. Nothing tastes better. It warms you up and makes you think whoever made it thinks you're pretty special."

"My dad does the same thing and always has. I'll have to thank him when I get home. I haven't appreciated him as much as you appreciate your mom."

Ajai set his plate down at a table that was littered with used napkins and empty pop cans. He set his white cowboy hat in the middle of the table, scooped the garbage into a pile, and carried it to a trashcan. Returning, he pulled a chair out and said, "Milady, your seat."

Deana sank into the cafeteria-style chair, "Thank you, kind sir. This is like being in high school again."

Ajai sat across from her and studied her glowing face. "You look young enough to still be in high school and I'm happy you look completely recovered from your ordeal this morning. If you'd gotten sick because of Chip's idiocy..."

"Don't you dare say a word against Chip. He's been a true friend to me, and whenever I ask, he always helps me out. I was happy to help him."

Ajai narrowed his eyes. "Here I've been worried that David was the competition. Don't tell me it's been Chip all along?"

Deana laughed outright, "Chip? My…"She sputtered. She wiped her mouth with the huge napkin. "Chip is not someone I'm in love with. He's just my friend."

Ajai picked up his fork and stared at his roast beef. He said softly, "I wonder if Chip realizes how lucky he is."

Even though Ajai had mumbled, she heard what he said. In confusion she stared down at her plate. Why did he insist on making comments like that?

They spoke little as they ate and contented themselves with watching the people and racket going on around them.

A band began to play and men and women began to clear the empty tables to make room for a dance floor.

Deana watched in awe as a group of polo groupies surrounded Ajai. He acted like each one was a friend. In a crowd, his charm seemed infallible. Deana hoped he didn't have political aspirations.

When Ajai asked her to join the dancers, Deana never hesitated. He stood and pulled out her chair and then took her by the hand to lead her onto the dance floor. He put his arm around her waist and they moved slowly among the dancers on the crowded floor.

The look on Ajai's face when he smiled at her made her forget that her hair was a mess and her clothes were far from clean. She followed his lead and enjoyed being with the best looking cowboy on the dance floor.

The slow song ended and the band started a two-step. Deana felt completely lost. Ajai said, "Just follow my lead."

Deana tried to relax and let him lead while she stumbled along. When she caught on enough to keep up with him, she enjoyed the gentle twirling. Deana laughed every time she tromped on Ajai's cowboy boots. Looking down, she tried to watch where he put his feet.

Ajai placed his fingers under her chin lifting it until she looked him directly in the eyes. He pointed at his eyes, "Here, this is where you look. Watching your feet only makes you trip. Just relax and follow my lead." He twirled her around in a series of quick turns that left her breathless as they completely circled the floor.

Deana's senses rushed with heady pleasure. Her betraying heart sang its song, "Have no pride. Tonight I'm in his arms. Tonight, I'm at the center of that sparkling golden look. Tomorrow he might be a million miles away, but tonight, it's me with him."

When the dance ended, and they walked off the floor to find two empty chairs, Deana blurted out, "I'm having a great time."

"I still can't believe you've never been to a country dance. Did you go to any school dances?"

Deana watched the dancers, "No, I was always busy at home."

Ajai covered her hand with his and gave a gentle squeeze. "Then I'm happy you were able to make this one. It's a lot better than any high school dance I ever went to."

"Even the one when you were nominated for Spring King?"

"Way better than that one. I lost, you know.'

"Of course I know, but your girlfriend at the time was queen, so you were the king anyway."

"Why do you remember things like that?"

There was no answer that Deana could give. She had no idea why she clearly remembered a high school dance she hadn't attended and had no desire to attend.

"Deana, I want to tell you where I went this week." Ajai said. "But it must be kept totally secret."

Deana nodded silently.

"I went to investigate a business that wants to move a branch of their computer company to Duluth. My father's been working to bring new businesses to the area. He has been for two years."

"That's why he's been hiring consulting firms outside of the Jacoubi groups?"

"When did you find out?"

"Just last week, I found it in the personnel files. Edward had retained the same number of employees while paying outside firms. It didn't make sense, but now I can see why. You know he's paying thousands of dollars for the same services? If you cut the number of employees then payroll will drop and the company can recoup some of the losses. It amounts to thousands and thousands of dollars."

"I pointed all of that out to Dad and he said it's only a temporary loss. The company is making enough to compensate, so there's no reason to downsize employees."

"It's incredible that, with a company of this size, your father still worries about the individual employee. I can't believe his compassion. Tell me, what kind of father was Edward?"

"What do you mean?"

"Was he the kind who was never home? The kind that showed up for holidays and the occasional sports games and never knew the right thing to say so ended up saying something rude. Or did he know you so well that he could say exactly the right thing to make you completely furious with him. Then when you were ready to blow up, he apologizes and gives you a kiss and a hug so what he said didn't matter."

Ajai was silent for a minute, "I don't know about the kiss and hug, but I guess he was all of those things. When I was young, he was gone a lot. But as soon as I became a teen-ager and started getting into trouble, suddenly he changed. He was home all the time, and it was my dad who held me accountable whenever I broke the rules. How about Frank? What was he like?"

"My dad, never thought I did anything wrong. I wasn't the rebel type, but I still made plenty of mistakes. He just never noticed, or if he did, he never did anything about it."

"I've seen plenty of the rebel in you. How did Frank miss it?"

Stifling a yawn, she said, "I've noticed that whenever I'm around you I do have a tendency to say whatever's on my mind," Deana said, as she felt her shoulders droop toward the table.

"We better get going. We still have an hour's drive a head of us." Ajai pushed his chair back.

The band began to play the soft melody of familiar love song… a love song that had been popular when they were in high school. He reached across the table to take her small hand in his. He said softly, "Do you think we have enough energy for one last dance?"

As she slipped into the warm comfort of his arms, Deana felt her strength desert her. He held her close and she fit nicely into the curves of his body. He pressed his arms across her back. His face rested on the mass of hair that framed her head.

Deana curled her arms under his and placed her palms across the smooth cotton of his shirt. She danced with her eyes closed. Her cheek pressed against his chest, submersed in the tide of emotions that coursed through her. The strains of music circled them, until it suddenly stopped. Deana peeled herself out of his arms and, with the words from the song floating in her head, 'you were always on my mind' she walked toward the exit.

56

Deana ignored the aches and pains in every soft muscle of her body as she glided down the steps. The lyrics of the song she had danced to with Ajai last night kept circling her mind.

Frank stood at the kitchen sink washing out his coffee cup. He had his back to her when she walked into the sunshine-filled room, humming softly. "Good morning, Dad," she said cheerfully.

Deana walked to the refrigerator, opened the door and took out the container of orange juice. Moving to the sink she said, "Excuse me, can you grab me a juice glass, please?"

Frank opened the cupboard and handed it to her, "Late night?"

"Not really, it was only ten-thirty."

"There's a write up about the Barnum Derby in the morning paper. And there's another column you should probably read before we go to church." Frank said.

Deana set the juice glass down on the counter and snatched up the newspaper. There in living color was a large picture of Ajai and Chip, with her in the middle. Chip was holding the cup.

"I look awful!" She grimaced.

Frank, looking out the window, asked, "What exactly went on yesterday?"

"Ajai was out of town and Chip called and asked me to ride Chance. Then Ajai returned in time to ride in the final race and they won. The weather was terrible. That's why I look like a mess."

Frank walked up behind her to look over her shoulder, "Nice picture, now read this." He held out the local society column.

"From the look on your face, I'm not sure I want to."

"I think you should."

Deana's heart sank. She closed her eyes, "I don't..."

Rattling the paper, Frank said, "You have to."

With a heavy sigh of resignation, Deana took the paper. "Where?"

"The Maddie Flowers column," Frank said.

Under the headline, JACOUBI WINS, the article said, "Ajai Jacoubi was kicking up his heels last night after the Barnum races with his stand-in jockey of the day, Deana Michaels. I received an anonymous tip that Ajai had proposed to the same Deana Michaels the week before. I can't tell in the sports picture whether Ms. Michaels is wearing an engagement ring. Can you imagine the whopper that Ajai must have presented to her? Those sports photographers don't know what's important when they take photographs of people. Let's hope I can pin the elusive ex-bachelor, Ajai Jacoubi, down for a personal interview and confirm the announcement soon. Watch for it in my column tomorrow."

When she saw her father's expression, Deana's face flushed with embarrassment, "It's all a misunderstanding, Dad. You know that. Say something."

Frank looked at the picture of the three of them, "Nice picture." He said and turned away. "I'm leaving for Mass in fifteen." He walked out of the kitchen.

Deana read the article again and rubbed her forehead. She busied herself fixing Colleen's bouquet and while carefully tying the ribbon, thought, Ajai must have forgotten to tell his family. Now what are we going to do?

She reached for the telephone receiver but never picked it up. She didn't have any idea what to say to Ajai and what if his mother answered the telephone? Deana hurried out of the kitchen to finish getting ready for Mass.

57

At the side altar of the Saint Joseph Church stood a six-foot statue of Saint Joseph lovingly holding the infant Jesus. The two looked down on the parishioners sitting in the front pews of the early Sunday morning Mass. In the second row directly in scrutiny of the blessed father and son, sat Frank and Deana Michaels. Colleen had loved the spot and the family had always sat there and neither Frank nor Deana cared to sit anywhere else.

Deana could hear the people moving into the church from outside. She also could hear the many whispers and more than once her name was spoken loud enough to clearly hear it. Her thoughts were far from filled with preparation for the coming Mass.

Doggone you, Ajai. How could you have let this engagement story get this far? Deana thought, trying to ignore the whispering. Deana remained kneeling and kept her head deliberately low so that she didn't have to see the curious looks of the congregation. I just know Ajai won't show up for Mass today, she thought angrily, and what am I supposed to say to these people? After yesterday everybody including the media will be having a complete field day with the story.

The service started exactly on time. Deana was so apprehensive she felt even the priest on the altar might be looking in her direction more than usual. As the organ began playing the final hymn, Deana concentrated on the hymnbook as she sang. When the last chords from the organ died, Deana took her time replacing the book and remained in her seat until the other parishioners filed out.

Frank stood in the aisle and said to her, "You have to go out there sometime. Might as well face it and get it over with right now instead of hiding in here."

"That's easy for you to say," she whispered fiercely. "I don't know what to say."

"Tell them the truth. It's all a misunderstanding."

"They'll think I'm the one who tipped Maddie Flowers."

"Tell them you didn't."

"I don't want to tell anybody anything. It's none of their business."

Just bring your flowers to Mom and nobody will bother you. Where are your flowers?"

"I left them by the gate," Deana said as she turned around to look at the back of the church. It was empty except for the narthex in the back, which was filled with people talking. Through the open window, happy shouts and lively conversation echoed.

Frank was right, she had to go out there, and right now. With her head held high and her back ramrod stiff, she marched down the aisle. When she reached the back she smiled at the familiar faces but kept walking even when someone attempted to start a conversation. Then she saw Mr. and Mrs. Jacoubi standing just outside the church doors. Right behind them stood Ajai. Deana had the advantage of seeing them first. Her rapid flight faltered, but only for an instant as she abruptly changed course. She turned away from the main door and walked out the side door that faced the cemetery. She walked down the path toward the gate and saw that Ajai was waiting for her. In his hands he held her bouquet for her mother's grave.

Deana didn't slow her steps. She shot him a glare and snatched the flowers from his hand. She hissed at him, "What are you doing? Everyone is watching us." Deana lifted her hand to return a wave to Mrs. Jacoubi. Frank was now standing with the Jacoubi's. They walked toward the parking lot with a group of people. Deana knew exactly what they were discussing, "My father the traitor. Do you think he's explaining what's really going on to all those people?"

Ajai glanced over his shoulder and smiled, "Do you blame him? I wouldn't want to be the voice of doom when everybody seems so happy about the whole engagement."

"How can you say that? I'm certainly not happy. I'm a complete wreck."

"I know and I'm sorry."

Deana spun on her heel and walked along the uneven path to the graves. She shot over her shoulder, "I suppose my father has gone to your parent's house again to bum another meal from your poor mother. What is this turning out to be? A Sunday ritual?"

"I kind of hope so. Wouldn't it be a nice way to spend our Sundays?"

Deana stopped short and turned to look at him, placing her hands on her hips. "What is wrong with you? You act like there's nothing wrong. I don't think I should have to remind you that even though we've gotten the press involved, this engagement doesn't exist."

"You're talking about the gossip column?"

Deana couldn't control her shriek of frustration, "Of course I'm talking about the gossip column! How could you have not done what you promised? How could you forget something so important?"

Ajai reached down to scoop up a daisy with two layers of delicate white blossoms. "I did tell my mother."

Deana stopped and stared at him, stunned. "Then what happened? Who told Maddie Flowers?"

Ajai began pulling the petals from the daisy, chanting low, "she loves me, she loves me not, she loves me,"

"Ajai! Who do you think told Maddie? Certainly not my father. He would never do something like that. Edward?" She glanced at Ajai and shook her head, "Your father wouldn't have, especially when he knew it was a mistake. Will you help me try to figure this out and stop playing that child's game?"

Ajai grinned and said, "I've decided neither you nor I enjoyed our childhood enough and I'm beginning to relive it and enjoy it now. What do you think?"

"I think you're a fool and you've been working too hard."

"I agree with you," Ajai said, and, putting his hand through her arm he led her along the path toward her mother's grave, "Why don't you ask your mother what she thinks about the newspaper article? She might know who sent that tip to Maddie."

Deana let him lead her, but gave him a suspicious look, "Are you making fun of me? I don't expect my mother to answer me from the grave. I've always found it easier to face my problems after I've admitted them out loud."

Ajai nodded, "I agree, and I won't stand here and listen. Instead I'll go back to the gate and wait for you there. Take your time. There's no hurry. Maybe I'll duck back inside and say my confession to Father Jim."

Deana laughed at him, "I don't know if Father Jim can handle your confession. You'll have to see the Bishop."

"At least I made you laugh," Ajai said smugly when he walked away.

Deana stood, watching him leave. She glanced down at the gravestone. A new bundle of bright sunflowers filled her father's vase. Deana sank to her knees ignoring the fact that Ajai might still be watching. "Mama, you know what that article said is everything I've ever wanted, but it isn't real. I just hope I have enough strength to hold my head up after the truth comes out."

Unable to think of another thing to say, she set the roses in her own small vase and stood to leave.

58

Ajai, as he promised, had his back to her until he heard her behind him. Only then did he turn to open the gate for her.

Deana hurried past him and into the parking lot. "I just can't even imagine what the people at work are going to say tomorrow. Genie's going to kill me. She'll think I've kept all of this a secret from her. You don't think Genie suspected something and decided to tell Maddie Flowers." Deana answered her own question. "No, that's lying and I don't think Genie would outright lie."

"Deana, can we talk for a minute." Ajai interrupted.

Deana glanced around the deserted church lot and gave him an odd look, "Why?"

"Well, I have some confessions to make to you, not the priest, and this seems a pretty appropriate place to do it."

Deana felt her throat constrict with fear, "What else can you possibly have to confess to me?"

"You've never been very quiet about your opinion of me."

She started to speak, but he held up his hand to stop her interruption. "Don't say a word just let me get this out."

Deana nervously clasped her hands together to keep them still.

"I know you think I'm the kind of guy who likes to play the field and I admit at one time that was true, but I was never as much of a playboy as you implied.

"In high school you got any girl you even blinked at. I'd dare say tomorrow, if you tried, you could get any girl in the exact same way."

"The thing is, I don't want to try. And by the way, I've been shot down just as many times as any other guy, so I know how that feels too."

"Poor thing," Deana muttered sarcastically.

"I'm not complaining. I'm just explaining."

"You don't have to explain to me. It doesn't matter."

Ajai leaned against his car. Deana watched him, wondering where this was leading.

"Well, actually it does matter. You see I'm the one who tipped Maddie Flowers."

Deana laughed outright. Her laughter pealed musically through the quiet churchyard.

"No, really... Deana, I sent her a note."

Deana wiped her eyes, "Why? Why would you?"

"Because I truly am a devious soul at heart, and I planned all of this."

Deana stepped away from him. Her suspicions rising, she demanded, "Planned what?"

"Planned the tip-off, planned the dancing last night. I was hoping there would be reporters at the social after the races to take pictures of us and once all of it hit the paper and was printed in black and white you might feel... obligated to agree to really get engaged."

Deana stared at him, "I'm either drunk or dreaming."

"I have to warn you, besides the gossip column, I stared adoringly in your direction through the entire Mass. I think Father Jim was going to publicly reprimand me. Last night in Barnum, I told anybody who would listen that you were soon to be my fiancée. They ate it up."

"This is crazy why are you doing this to me?"

"I know you don't want to marry me. You barely want to have anything to do with me. But from the way you kissed me in the parking ramp, you can't really dislike me completely. Maybe somewhere you really do have feelings that we should explore before we call the whole thing off. Last week, I couldn't get you out of my mind. All this time, the girl of my dreams is the girl next door."

Deana looked into those eyes and felt her heart thumping

erratically. She rubbed her arms, feeling a chill run through her. "Are you teasing me again? Because this isn't funny."

"I want to be honest about this devious plan of mine so at least you'll know I'm an honest deviant. I know I'm not the man you pictured yourself with, but if you give me a chance, you'll see that I've changed. I'm ready for the rest of my life to start and I want it to be with you. I'm not asking you to make a commitment to marriage but let's give ourselves some time together, and who knows what will happen? Marriage might not be impossible."

The blood drained from Deana's face leaving her pale and shaken. She stared at him with large, watery eyes. Her mouth was dry when she whispered, "I had no idea you felt this way. I can't..." She reached for his arm and held onto it. She had to be certain this was really happening. "I have no easy way to say this." She said, "I can't marry you, Ajai. All of your life you've had everything easy. Do you even understand what marriage really is? You might think forever love is the fireworks, and yes, I admit there are fireworks, but it's not enough for a relationship. There has to be the basis of trust that you'd be there... even on the ugly days. It's the, 'til death do us part' and then being willing to help that person meet God with dignity. But that only comes after you have spent however many months and years caring for them until death finally does take them away from you. Once I marry, I'll never *not* be married to that person. The first time is for keeps, and I'll never get a second chance. Please try to understand why I have to say no. I'm afraid we can't be partners for a lifetime, and, if we aren't, then our marriage can't last. What happens when you get restless again and want to take off looking for adventure? What happens to me if you decide to never come back?" Tears streamed unchecked down Deana's pale cheeks. She brushed them away, "I'm so sorry, Ajai."

59

"Flight 576 non-stop from Madrid has just landed. Passengers will be deplaning in fifteen minutes." The announcement subdued the idle chatter of the people in the waiting area of the Northwest terminal in the Minneapolis airport.

The big silver bird slowly wheeled the last few feet before coming to a stop outside of the observation window. The red-eye flight had arrived in Minneapolis, Minnesota. The sky was cloudy and the temperature was a brisk 34 degrees Fahrenheit. When the plane left Madrid, the temperature in Spain had been 72 degrees.

The disembarking passengers slowly filed one by one up the gangway. One of the last to make his way off of the plane and up the gangway was a man darkly tanned with sun-bleached hair that curled in an untidy mop on his head. In his hand he held a carry-on bag. He paused to sling the nylon duffle bag over his shoulder before he walked to the bank of monitors nearby. The stubble of a gold beard covered his cheeks. Deep lines around the corners of his eyes and deep grooves in his cheeks made him look older than his years. He stared with sleep-deprived eyes at the dark monitor and the bright green print for a moment, then winced as he shifted the handle of his carry-on. The palm of his hand was covered with a wide white bandage. Ajai walked down the long crowded corridor to the baggage claim area. He looked at the store display windows that lined the walkway. Already they advertised Christmas in October. He reached the baggage claim and stood on the fringe of the passengers he had just spent eight hours with and had not spoken a single word to anyone of them.

He heard a woman nearby comment excitedly, "Look, dear, the first snow of the year."

Her husband did not look, he grumbled, "Snow already? It's only October."

Ajai glanced out the window and saw the flakes floating through the air. It was the kind of snow that showed itself but made no mark on the ground. While he waited, he allowed his mind to wander over the last few weeks. With the sound of Deana's refusal ringing in his ears, Ajai had run away to Spain.

Edward had returned to work the first part of September, and Ajai took off for Spain the very next day. Alberto helped Ajai sign on as a deckhand on a charter fishing boat. Ajai thought it would help him forget Deana. His hope had been wrong. He quit blaming her and began to understand her. It was his bad reputation, his lack of responsibility throughout his life that made Deana doubt him. Deana's reaction to his marriage proposal was a shocking reminder of how selfish his actions had been.

The initial blazing fury he felt when she said no was actually because he was so stunned. He never expected her to refuse. She certainly told him enough times how she felt, but neither could he forget her reaction when he kissed her. It wasn't a fake kiss. She'd kissed him back. She might demand he be honest but she wasn't being honest with herself.

Deep inside he knew Deana was right about the settling down part, but he also knew that the fireworks are important and that strong relationships needed passion too. But Deana was right about one thing—there has to be trust.

Ajai knew what he had to do. Now that he had gotten over being rejected, he wanted to prove to her that he had changed. He planned to start the moment he got to Duluth... to home.

60

Deana walked briskly down the corridor toward her office. She knew Julius Bascomb was right on her heels ready to deliver her paycheck, and she wanted to be waiting for him. She had sent a request in an e-mail to personnel last week and hoped that a reply of some kind would be sent from that office in her pay envelope.

Genie stuck her head out of her office and smiled, "I knew you weren't Julius. You walk way too fast."

"How are you doing, Genie? Over the engagement jitters yet? Or still fainting every time you stand up too fast?" Deana teased her.

"I did not faint. I only got dizzy. I'm so giddy, I'd forgotten to eat for two days."

"Don't do that at the wedding or you'll pass out, fall off your high heels, and ruin your gown."

Genie leaped toward Deana to grab her arm. She let out an ear-shattering squeal of excitement, "I can't believe it. I'm getting married. A man actually asked me to marry him and not just share the bills for his apartment." Genie stopped to give Deana a stern look, "You had better make it back here for all the wedding parties. Matt's parents are throwing an engagement party the first weekend in December and then there'll be wedding showers and you're the maid of honor so you have to do everything with me and tell me what I'm doing wrong... no, tell me what to do first, and then I won't do anything wrong. We're going to have so much fun. I just can't believe that right when I need you most you're moving out of town. I can't believe you decided to transfer to the accounting department down in Minneapolis. You're not hoping to run into David, are you? I can tell you he isn't worth it."

Deana laughed, "Don't be silly. David's ancient history.

I'll be coming home every weekend. My father is still here and Journey too."

"That's what everybody says. I'll be back every weekend and pretty soon they have new friends, new boyfriends and they don't want to come back except for the holidays which are way too few and too far between."

"I've lived in Duluth all my life and I don't agree with you. Everything I need is here."

"Then why transfer?"

"I already explained that. Mr. Jacoubi approached me about the position. It's Julius' job in Minneapolis with a much larger department and more employees and I'll be the supervisor. It's a chance of a lifetime, and I'm shocked he thinks I'm capable of doing it. This is the kind of promotion most people only dream about."

"Its funny how life works. I always thought you would be the one getting married and I'd be the one leaving town to move to a larger city. What a switch."

"I don't know why you'd think that. I've never set my sights on getting married."

"Maybe not, but you'd look great with a whole crew of babies and a big house all messy with toys and cookie crumbs."

"Now you'll have to do it instead of me. I'll even come over and clean your house for you if you name one of your babies after me."

"Just because it didn't work out with David and that whole big mess with Ajai, I don't think you need to talk like you've given up on guys."

"I'm not giving up. I'm just moving on. And speaking of moving on, I've got to get going. I want to head home right after I get my paycheck. I'll talk to you on Monday," Deana said as she walked away, waving goodbye over her shoulder.

Genie is totally wrong, Deana thought as she walked into her office. She wasn't giving up on marriage. She was running away from Duluth and her job at Jacoubi Enterprises. The aftershocks caused by the newspaper articles were much worse than Deana had believed were possible. Deana had been at a loss about how to deal with the circus her life at Jacoubi had become. Out of the blue, Edward Jacoubi approached her, not at the office, but at the house. He offered her a transfer and a promotion. Whether he did it because he knew how hard it was for Deana at work or not, she didn't know or care. This was a way out and she was taking it.

Julius Bascomb gave two sharp raps with his knuckles on her open office door. He stepped inside the room and with a nervous air and looked around.

"Anything the matter, Julius?"

He shook his head, "No, I've got something to say to you that I would rather say in private."

Deana was surprised. "Really," she said, and waited for him to continue.

"I was wondering," Julius began, then cleared his throat. "What prompted you to request a transfer? I realized after watching the mandatory discrimination videos issued from the main office, that my attitude toward you and Miss Caldwell might be misconstrued. I have always considered you my equal, Miss Michaels. You do excellent work, and I will have a difficult time replacing you. Are you certain you wish to leave?"

"I've been offered a promotion, Julius. I'd be a fool to turn it down."

He gave a sigh, "Very well." He handed her the envelope and shifted his feet.

"Is there anything else?"

Julius shook his head, "No, I believe I must speak to Miss Caldwell personally. She will be the only woman on this floor and I wondered if she'll be comfortable with that."

Deana walked toward the coat tree and said, "You're right, that's something you'll have to discuss with her."

Reluctantly, Julius turned and walked out of the office.

Deana did not bother to watch him leave. The little snake, he wanted to cover his own tracks of bigotry and then turn around and get rid of Genie. Deana slipped her arms into the stylish navy coat made of wool. The coat was a new purchase for her life down in the Twin Cities. She did not plan on bringing many of her old clothes. Instead, she planned to replace all of them. The raise in pay was going to help enormously with her personal life. She could splurge a little. Not too much, with the holidays coming so quickly, but just enough to make a presentable supervisor in the big city accounting department.

61

The old house was winterized and had a fresh coat of white paint. It was ready for the onslaught of cold weather. When Deana got out of her car she smelled wood smoke in the brisk October air. Her father must have started a fire in the fireplace. Early October was too soon to start the furnace and begin burning fuel. The only way to keep some heat in the old house was to keep a fire in the living room fireplace. Deana sometimes started a fire in her small fireplace in her bedroom. Tonight might be just the night to do that; there was supposed to be a frost. The house looked cozy as she stood outside looking at the bright lights through the windows. Autumn was her favorite season, with honey crisp apples in abundance in the stores, and pumpkin and spice smells in the kitchen. Harvest vegetables of bright orange, gold and red, along with cool nights and warm Indian summer days made Deana nostalgic for her childhood. Deana shivered with anticipation, avoiding the thought that she was not going to be home for the remainder of October. Soon she was off to start her new life in Minneapolis.

Deana hurried up the walk and inside. The kitchen was dark, but the lights throughout the lower level were on. The table was not set nor was the oven on. Deana hoped her father hadn't forgotten it was his turn to cook dinner.

She rushed into the living room. She was right about the fire. The crackle and smell of smoke greeted her even before she walked fully into the room. She heard the sound of metal gates closing and looked to see her father, hunched over, stirring the fire.

"What's the big idea of not putting the casserole I made in the oven? I'm starving," she scolded Frank. She shook her coat out and draped it over the back of the couch.

"I didn't know you wanted me to." A deep voice that didn't belong to her father announced.

Deana gasped.

Ajai stood next to the fire grate, the iron poker still in his hands. "Hello Deana, I haven't seen you for awhile."

"I... You've been out of town."

Ajai's voice was cold, "Yes, I proved you right. You turned me down and I turned tail and ran. Only you weren't completely right, Deana, I came back. And now I find out that *you're* leaving town. I got news of your transfer today. Is it because of David?"

Deana gave a short laugh. She felt angry and betrayed that Ajai was here waiting for her. After telling her father everything and trusting him to back her up, Frank had allowed him into their home.

"Your father wasn't here when I arrived. I thought I should start a fire. Everything was laid out ready to be lit, so I did."

Deana regained her composure and walked toward the couch keeping her back to him. It took immense effort for her not to turn and run from the room. If they just talked about work then she could handle him.

"Are you going to answer my question? I think I at least deserve a straight answer."

"It certainly is not because of David. I was offered a promotion at the Minneapolis office. Something I could never have if I stayed here."

"Who offered you the promotion?"

"Your father."

Ajai shook his head, "I suspected it, but why? Why all of a sudden is there a supervising position in accounting so conveniently available, Deana? You don't have to take it. The same opportunity will happen here."

"Not for years. Bascomb won't move on for at least ten more years."

"So you're completely resolved to leave? You're leaving

your father, your horse, and your freedom, to become buried in a job in a strange town. Think about it, Deana. I know you're afraid. You're afraid to take on the challenge of really living. I think I know partly why. It's because you watched your mother suffer for three long years before she died. Not only did she suffer, but also the people who loved her suffered and continue to suffer without her. Life is something we have to learn as we live. There's no book that teaches us how not to be hurt by living, but to sit back and just let it pass you by is wrong too. I don't blame you for not accepting me. But don't give up on life and lock yourself away in a job. Money is no compensation and neither is power. When you're tired of it and alone, you have nothing. I know there's a part of you that's been hidden away. If it's not me that's going to make you happy and unafraid, find someone else that you can love."

Deana shuddered as she fought for control of her emotions. She wiped the tears from her face and sniffled.

The clock ticked and the fire crackled when the outside door slammed. Deana turned when Frank walked in the room and said, "You two look like a pair of prize fighters waiting for the bell."

"Dad, where have you been?"

"I got stuck in town later than usual. Nice fire. When did you get back, Ajai?"

"Yesterday. The first thing I heard about was your daughter's transfer. I've come over to tell her I'm refusing to accept it."

In outrage Deana stepped forward, "You have to accept it. Your father gave the okay."

Ajai shrugged indifferently. "I'm denying it and so far as I know my father said my decisions will not be contested. Did you know about this?" Ajai demanded turning to Frank.

Frank stood silently in the hallway watching the two of them with a poker face. "The girl has put enough of her life on hold for me. I told her I am only a conscientious objector. I think I'll let you two argue this one while I go put dinner in the oven."

The silence held until Frank disappeared, and Deana heard the door of the kitchen click shut. Pointedly, she turned her back on Ajai, "You have no right to meddle in my life. You can't know how horrible it's been at work since all of that publicity about our engagement came out. I've been approached, propositioned, and even pinched by so many of the male employees at Jac. E that I've got no peace. Not even in the basement."

"Really? That's not what I heard. You keep pushing people away, Deana. You'll end up old and alone."

"I am not afraid. Why do you keep telling me that I'm afraid and I don't want companionship?"

Ajai stepped close to her. His body emanated heat. Her body felt cold and she wanted to feel the warmth. "It's okay to be afraid, but it isn't okay to let fear control you."

Deana sighed folding her hands together, "Fine, you've completely convinced me I was afraid to make this move. And you're right, I need to face this fear and overcome it. I'm even more determined than ever to do this, Ajai. It's all been arranged."

"Why are you doing this?" he demanded. "I know it isn't money, because money doesn't matter to you, nor does the promotion. If it's because of what happened between us, I'll make certain you don't ever have to look at my ugly face again. Don't do this, Deana. Don't leave everything you love because of what happened. It'll blow over. I'll take out a full-page ad in the paper and explain how everything was my fault and just a series of misunderstandings.

For you to leave this house, your horse, and your father… all of this is a part of you and it's a huge mistake to walk away. You have no idea how leaving it will tear you apart. I do know. I've been there. It's a hole, an ache that constantly nags at you, giving you no peace. I'll leave. I can return to my internship in Minneapolis. I'm already settled there, Deana. I know the people in the company. I have an apartment. The cost of living down there is triple what it is in Duluth. I guarantee as soon as something more exciting happens to someone with more crowd appeal, the gossip about us will die. If you're worried about me bothering you, then don't. I'll stay out of your way."

Deana stared at him and choked out, "Th... that's very generous of you, Ajai. Thank you but... I'll have to think about it."

Ajai reached for his coat and walked toward the hallway. "Of course you will. I'm really sorry about everything. I hope you reconsider." He cupped his hand to his mouth and called, "See you later, Frank," He nodded to Deana and then walked out, slamming the glass door behind him.

62

"If I do accept this promotion and move to the Twin Cities, Ajai's going to believe it was him that chased me out of my job and my home. I couldn't bear to give him that kind of satisfaction, Mother. He's already so self-righteous. He thought I'd accept his marriage proposal without question. The nerve of him. He didn't care whether we were right for each other or not. He thought I should have accepted his proposal of marriage just because he's Ajai Jacoubi. I pray he never learns how difficult it was for me to turn him down. I know now the difference between a crush and true love. True love feels like I've been kicked by a horse right in the stomach. Nothing is enjoyable for me anymore. I dread work. I dread after work because I don't even enjoy riding anymore. I feel like a spoiled rotten brat who wished for a pony and when I finally got it, I was allergic to it. I don't know how to fix it, but I know leaving isn't the answer. The only thing is how do I tell everybody? And what happens when Ajai finds out? This has gotten so complicated. Much more complicated than if Ajai had asked me out in high school. Then I would've found out he was a jerk and never gotten into this mess.

I thought of letting Dad tell everyone that I changed my mind and won't be leaving. I hope Ajai finds somebody else and gets married quick. That'll shut everybody up." The thought of Ajai married made her feel physically ill. "What am I going to do?" she moaned.

A fat sleepy honeybee floated toward the white field daisies Deana had placed in the vase on her mother's grave. The unusually warm Indian summer must have confused the bee's hibernation plans, so it alone found the blossoms in the field of dying summer grass that whispered dry murmurs in the wind. The colors of the pale blue sky and the gold and orange of the leaves that covered the brown grass displayed a spectrum that Deana loved. It was not often that, in Duluth, warm days in October gave a breath of the return of summer. After a moment she stood and brushed her hand across the cold stone statue of the Sacred Heart, "This will probably be one of the last really good conversations we can have until next summer. The leaves have all fallen and soon the wind off the lake will be too cold for me to stay out here for very long. By next spring this whole thing with Ajai will have died down to idle gossip and nobody but me will remember it happened. I'll tell you the outcome in the spring because right now I'm not too sure what's going to happen."

From a discreet distance behind her, Frank's voice said, "I'd like to put a microphone on this someday and hear what it is you talk about."

"It's a deal. If you tell me what you tell Mom, you can listen in on what I say," she said with a smile.

"Deal. Most conversations were about you anyway."

Deana immediately became contrite. "Why? Are you worried about something or am I simply driving you crazy?"

"Somebody else would like to talk to you about your decision not to take that promotion." Frank motioned over his shoulder.

Deana turned and saw Ajai next to his little blue sports car in the church parking lot.

"He asked me to come out here and ask if you have a moment to talk. He thought you would prefer meeting him here rather than in the office tomorrow."

"Of course, I'll talk to him, but you'll wait for me, Dad."

"Sure honey, how will you get home if it isn't with me?"

"Don't be a smart-aleck," She retorted and followed her father along the path.

Frank nodded to Ajai as he passed, and said to Deana, "Take your time Honey, I'm going to run to the truck-stop for a paper. Wait for me, I'll be back to drive you home."

Deana stared after him in disbelief. He was deserting her once again. Can't even trust my own father anymore, she thought.

Ajai watched everything that was going on but he kept his distance. When Frank drove off, Ajai said, "I appreciate you talking to me, Deana. I know I promised not to bother you, and after this I will keep that promise. Will you hear me out?"

Deana didn't look directly at his face, concentrating somewhere around the buttons of his shirt. Suddenly she felt very shy and uncertain. What little resolve she maintained was becoming weaker every time they met again, especially when it happened in the secluded, peaceful churchyard. "I don't mind really."

"My father told me you decided against the promotion. That means you won't be leaving Duluth. I've decided not to work in Minneapolis. For me to leave here, just when I'm getting my life in order and because it is important that I work with my father, I just can't move right now. For the first time in my life, I'm going to finish what I've started. After another six months here, then I might be able to go back down to Minneapolis. I realize that I've backed out on what I said to you."

Deana felt his scrutiny and it unnerved her. "You didn't have to tell me in person, Ajai. Dad could have passed the message to me."

"We've tried that before and it didn't work. I wasn't going to take that chance again. What a crazy relationship we've had for this past summer. I don't think there have ever been so many ups and downs in my life except on a roller coaster."

"It has been crazy, but also memorable. We won the Barnum races."

"But we lost the regatta."

"I guess we can't win them all."

"I found that out the hard way. Why did you turn down the

promotion? You sounded so enthusiastic about it."

Deana gave a deep sigh. "I was enthusiastic, but I'm really just a coward."

"I don't believe you. Nothing you've done since I've known you has been cowardly."

A small frown creased Deana's brow when she looked him in the face. "There's something about you that makes me courageous."

"I also might as well tell you right now. I've decided I'm going to wait for you Deana. I'll wait until you see first hand that I'm a man you can trust. Waiting for you will be the hardest thing I've ever done, but you're not the only one who thinks marriage is an important and lasting institution. I feel the same way. I have parents that love each other. Every day they face life together. I know they have days when neither one of them wants to look at the other, let alone live in the same house together. Through the days filled with suffering and pain or days sharing all the wonder and joy life has to offer, they face them together. That's the example I've been a witness to. I'm sure that's what you want of your marriage. It's what I want of mine. I know I'll make plenty of mistakes, but I'll never break your heart, Deana. I promise you that. If you find someone else you want to marry, then I'll have to learn to live with it, but if you find out that I'm your man, then I'll be right here waiting."

Deana stared at Ajai through a blur of tears. She choked out, "What can I possibly say to that? This is what you've decided to do?"

"I have no choice. I've tried to forget you, but I don't want to forget. I want you in my life, and if I have to wait, I'll wait, and all the while I'll be praying you'll change your mind."

"I had a crush on you in high school, you know." Deana said, looking him straight in the eyes to see his reaction.

"Your Dad has hinted at it."

"I've had to be careful. I didn't want to make the mistake

of confusing my current feelings with the old crush. I've come to the conclusion that it really isn't a crush at all. It seems I've been in love with you for a long time. I knew you as the wolf, but I also know how kind and considerate you are. Now you're telling me you won't run out on me when I'm all gray-haired or when I'm round and waddling pregnant." Her voice fell to a whisper, "Believe in miracles, Ajai , because I have no doubt they happen. There's never been anyone else for me but you. I thought I'd ruined my chance for happiness. I never thought you would ask me again, and that I'd have the opportunity to say yes, but here I am doing just that. How do you feel about a New Year's Eve wedding?"

Ajai looked down at Deana and she could read the sparks of love in his eyes. "I prayed for a miracle today. I certainly never expected it to happen so quickly."

Deana stepped closer to him. "Aren't you going to kiss me or hold my hand or something? I feel like we're still fighting."

"You mean we aren't?"

Deana slipped her arms around his waist and she smiled when she lifted her face to look at him, "Not anymore. We'll probably have many misunderstandings, but this is forever, so there's plenty of time for us to learn."

"I've been waiting a long time to do this," Ajai said as he leaned closer to her. With his warm breath caressing her skin, he gently kissed each cheek, the very tip of her nose, and then his strong lips claimed a kiss on hers—a kiss that lingered until they both were breathless. His hand moved along the back of her scalp through the thick mass of silky hair until she rested in the full embrace of his arms.

To order additional copies of

Sailing Home
Northern Lights Magic
or
Summer Storm

call:
(Superior, WI/Duluth, MN area)
715-394-9513

National Voice and FAX orders
1-800-732-3867
E-mail:
mail@savpress.com

Purchase copies on-line at:

www.savpress.com

Visa/MC/Discover/American Express/
ECheck/Accepted via PayPal

All Savage Press books are available at all chain and
independent bookstores nationwide. Just ask them to
special order if the title is not in stock.